Books by Elizabeth Thornton

BLUESTOCKING BRIDE*

HIGHLAND FIRE*

CHERISHED*

VELVET IS THE NIGHT*

TENDER THE STORM*

ALMOST A PRINCESS

THE PERFECT PRINCESS

PRINCESS CHARMING

STRANGERS AT DAWN

WHISPER HIS NAME

YOU ONLY LOVE TWICE

THE BRIDE'S BODYGUARD

DANGEROUS TO HOLD

DANGEROUS TO KISS

DANGEROUS TO LOVE

*Published by Zebra Books

ELIZABETH THORNTON

BLUESTOCKING BRIDE

ZEBRA BOOKS
Kensington Publishing Corp.
http://www.kensingtonbooks.com

ZEBRA BOOKS are published by

Kensington Publishing Corp.
850 Third Avenue
New York, NY 10022

All Kensington titles, imprints and distributed lines are available at special quantity discounts for bulk purchases for sales promotion, premiums, fund-raising, educational or institutional use.

Special book excerpts or customized printings can also be created to fit specific needs. For details, write or phone the office of the Kensington Special Sales Manager: Kensington Publishing Corp., 850 Third Avenue, New York, NY 10022. Attn. Special Sales Department. Phone: 1-800-221-2647.

First Printing: December 2003
10 9 8 7 6 5 4 3 2 1

Printed in the United States of America

For Mollie

Chapter 1

Richard Fotherville, Marquis of Rutherston, flicked the ribbons of his matched grays, urging them into a brisker trot. His cousin, Charles Norton, an open-faced young man of three and twenty, looked at Rutherston with an appreciative twinkle in his eyes.

"By Jove, Richard, you are in a foul temper today. You have hardly said two words to me since we set off from the Bull & Finch. When I think of it, my dear cousin, you have been in a blue funk since we set off from town yesterday. Now what can have occurred to put you in the dismals?"

Mr. Charles Norton smiled broadly as he observed the frown deepen on Rutherston's brow. He thought that he had a fair idea of what was troubling his cousin.

"It don't have anything to do with the fact that you have just celebrated a birthday, Richard?" He paused for effect. "A thirtieth birthday," he added with a chuckle.

Lord Rutherston gave his cousin a sideways glance, and seeing the open laughter on his face, relaxed his own grim countenance. "You may well mock, you young whelp, but I see little to be amused about." A smile belied the harshness of his tone. "How the devil I had the folly to confide in you I shall never comprehend." He flicked the ribbons impatiently, urging his grays on.

A comfortable silence descended, and each man was left to his own thoughts as the soft rolling hills of Surrey flew by.

Rutherston's frown returned. He *was* in a blue funk, and Charles had unerringly fingered the cause. He allowed his thoughts to wander to that night, only a fortnight before, when there had been a small family gathering in his mother's house on Green Street to celebrate his thirtieth birthday.

The conversation at the dinner table on that cold January evening in the year of our Lord 1811 had been all of the Regency Bill that had just come before Parliament. With the sovereign, George III, reverting to one of his mad and melancholy spells and retired once more to the seclusion of Windsor, it was imperative that his heir, the Prince of Wales, be appointed to the national helm as regent. Too many matters of importance vital to the safety of the country had been left in abeyance, Rutherston reflected, and the British army in Portugal was suffering from lack of direction as a consequence.

Rutherston's brother-in-law, the Duke of Beaumain, voiced his gloomy predictions.

"Daresay the prince will oust the Tories and bring in his batch of Whig supporters. If he does, we can expect even less support for Wellesley in the Peninsula. Then who will be left to clip the wings of that damned upstart Corsican?"

"Oh, I don't know," Rutherston returned thoughtfully. "The prince, as regent, may not wish to align himself with the opposition. The Whigs have served their purpose. Now that Prinny is taking over the reins, he will not need their support against his father and his ministers. No, I think the Whigs may be counting their chickens before they are hatched if they expect the prince to bring in a new government."

He had tried to prolong the conversation as long as possible, but he had known that his mother was anxious for a private interview with him. When the covers had been removed and the port decanter and glasses set on the gleaming mahogany table for the gentlemen, she had asked Rutherston if he would escort her to her sitting room for a few minutes' private conversation.

He had squared his shoulders and set his expression resolutely, like a man about to embark on a well-matched duel. He was aware of a knowing smile exchanged between his older sister and her husband, Duke Henry, as he offered his mother his arm to lead her dutifully from the dining room.

Their interview had been brief and to the point. The marchioness had merely reminded him, as she had so often done in the last number of years, of his promise.

That deuced promise! He tried to recall the circumstances that had induced him to make it. He had been a mere five and twenty at the time. It was the sense of anxiety, he decided, that had pervaded the atmosphere when he was in the presence of his mother and sister and had intruded upon every conversation. To them, it was an intolerable thing and not to be borne that his name should die out and the entailed estates and the title revert to the crown.

They had used all their powers of persuasion to get him married, exerting all their energies to introduce him to every eligible young female of their acquaintance who would, by birth and breeding, make a suitable wife for the sixth Marquis of Rutherston. So relentless were they that Rutherston had begun to feel beleaguered. In desperation, and exasperation, he had promised them that he would marry, putting off the evil day till he should attain his thirtieth year. A five-year respite had seemed like an eon to him then, but the day of reckoning had come all too soon upon him.

He knew that he was in no worse position than any other eligible young man of his station. They might buck and rear, but in the end, so it seemed to him, they were always broken, bridled, and hobbled. It was the way of the world. His Name, his House must continue. And he had no doubt that if and when he had an heir of his own body, he would expect the same filial duty to Family as he was now preparing to offer.

His mother had settled herself more comfortably into her chair, but he had remained standing and looking out the window as a light fall of snow blanketed the city streets in white.

"Well, Richard?" his mother had begun with a touch of asperity in her voice.

"Well, Mama?" he returned, mocking her tone as he moved to take his place on an adjacent sofa.

"Richard, I rely on you to keep your promise and do your duty to your Name and your House." His mother spoke with impatience, not at all in the voice he was used to hearing from his doting parent.

"Is there to be no reprieve then, Mama?" he asked, charming her with his boyish grin.

"Fustian!" she replied, not taken in. "Marriage to the right woman will be the making of you."

"Ah, the right woman! And where am I to find this paragon, pray?"

"I said the *right* woman, you incorrigible flirt, not *paragon*. Surely among your acquaintance there must be a girl with some starch—someone who isn't afraid to give you a good tongue-lashing when you fall foul of her?"

"A good tongue lashing?" Shock registered on Rutherston's face, and his mother smiled smugly to see the effect of her words. "You must be joking, Mama, if you think I would countenance a match with a tempestuous wench! The woman I choose to be my marchioness will be sweet-tempered, docile, and biddable."

"Bah!" the dowager retorted in disgust. "Just like the mount your sister insists I ride now that I'm into my dotage, I suppose—a wishy-washy creature with no spirit. A comfortable ride, I grant you, but so predictable!"

"No! The Indomitable Belle Fotherville reduced to such a pass? Never say so, Mama!"

"Ah, you may chuckle at your mother's misfortune, you young whelp, but when I was a gel, let me tell you, I had some spunk. And your father admired me for it."

The marquis, perceiving that his mother was about to embark on her favorite reminiscence of how she had escaped from the clutches of her wicked guardian to come to his father in little more than her shift, exerted himself to head her off.

"When you come down to Fotherville House, Mama, I promise to find you a more spirited mount."

"A more spirited mount? We were talking of a suitable bride for you, I think. Now how did you contrive to turn the subject into horseflesh, you naughty boy? No matter. Let us return to the terms of your promise."

"Yes, Mama," replied Rutherston, suppressing a sigh.

"You will own, I think, Richard, that since you made that promise, your family has put little restraint on your mode of life. But now," she continued seriously, "that must change. It is time for you to marry and set up your nursery."

"Oh, I have no disinclination to set up my nursery," Rutherston joked, "if only I need not marry a wife!" He gave her a quizzical look, expecting to see her smile, but the dowager was not amused.

"It will not do, Richard, it will not do. Your mode of life is a constant worry to me and an irritation to your sister. Richard, if I have grandchildren, I would wish to be proud of them, not have them hidden from my knowledge because they are base born."

She heard her son's sharp intake of breath, then a soft laugh as he bent over to kiss her gently on the cheek. "Am I such a worry to you then, ma'am?" he asked affectionately. "I need not be. It has not come to that, I assure you. You may rest easy, for I intend to stand by my word. But you will not mind if I take more than a se'ennight to find a suitable wife?" He brought her hand to his lips. "Mama," he said, all signs of levity gone from manner and expression, "I know what I owe my Name and my Station, and I promise that before long you will be the happiest of women."

The dowager marchioness had searched her son's face intently, and what she saw there seemed to satisfy her.

Rutherston mused on that penetrating look. His mother understood him very well. Perhaps she had seen more than he had been willing to concede. Had she grasped that his gay, bachelor existence was, in fact, a crashing bore? There was only one mode of life that he could imagine more boring, and that was the state of wedlock. "It is a case of damned if I do and damned if I don't," he thought, a deeper melancholy settling upon him.

He had considered at one time abandoning his idle existence to join Wellesley in Portugal. But the reprobation of his family had stifled that ambition. Heirs to titles did not have the same freedom of choice as younger sons, but had responsibilities and duties to assume about which their younger brothers knew little. He glanced amusingly at Norton, envying him his carefree life. And now he had this drat promise hanging over his head like the sword of Damocles.

Lord Rutherston must marry, but he had no inclination to find a wife. Women were a bore, especially the empty-headed widgeons that graced the balls, halls, and drawing rooms of fashionable London when the Season was at its height.

If one found a woman of intelligence, she invariably had the face of a horse; if she were endowed with beauty and grace she was bound to be bird-witted; and if she had that certain something that he called "quality," she was almost certainly as cold-blooded as a fish.

He let his mind linger fleetingly on the warm-blooded women he had known—the fashionable impures, those Cyprians whom he had on occasion allowed to share his bed. He thought of Marguerite, whose protector he now was. She was beautiful, intelligent, and passionate. She was also grasping and ambitious and fast becoming a bore. His mind strayed to Lady Pamela, his latest conquest, and his gloom deepened.

His reverie was broken by a question his cousin had flung at him. "My dear fellow," said Charles amiably, "do strive for a little countenance. You look like a general who has just lost a battle—not at all like the man of title, fortune, and favor that you are. Now do pay attention. I asked you how far it is to your uncle Bernard's estate. Surely it can't be far now?"

Rutherston replied that they would be there directly, and once again, for the umpteenth time, explained to his cousin why his uncle's estate, unentailed as it was, had been bequeathed to him.

"Well, it don't seem quite the thing," said Norton with some vehemence. "When you think of all the younger sons of no fortune and with little prospects, that he should leave it to you just because you read classics at Oxford!"

"Not because I *read* classics, Charles. 'Twas because I *excelled* at classics," Rutherston corrected mildly. "There is a difference, you know."

"Fudge!" retorted Norton, not mincing words. "My argument still stands. He left his property to you on the merest whim when there are probably a dozen more worthy candidates to whom such an estate would be regarded as a plum. You don't need it, nor even want it, I'll be bound."

Rutherston turned away to hide his smile. Norton, as a younger son, was talking with the vehemence of personal experience. Rutherston fully intended, with the utmost discretion of course, to ease that young man's way in the world when he judged that the time was right. Meantime, his young cousin was content to idle away his days, hoping no doubt that the right girl with the right face and fortune would just happen to come his way.

With some semblance of equanimity in his voice, Rutherston wondered aloud at the eccentricity of a doddering old uncle who had bequeathed a choice estate to a relation—a connection really—whom he had hardly seen, and upon so trifling a circumstance.

The news of his inheritance had come to him on the day following his birthday, and he had grasped at the excuse of paying a visit to the neighborhood to look it over. It would be a short respite from the task his mother had set him. Two weeks later had seen Rutherston embark on his journey in company of his young cousin, Mr. Charles Norton, who was enthused at the prospect of the riding, shooting, and hunting that Rutherston had promised. The two men enjoyed each other's company, despite the difference in their ages, and the marquis felt himself to be much more in the role of elder brother than distant cousin. The prospect of male camaraderie in thoroughly masculine pursuits for the next month or so was a most pleasant diversion from the petticoat government of Green Street and the muslin company of the demimonde, and did much to relieve his lordship's black mood.

Norton eased back in the curricle, observing appreciatively his cousin's handling of the high-stepping grays. It would be going too far to say that he hero-worshipped the older man, although he held him in the greatest affection and highest esteem. But Norton was well aware of his cousin's flaws, although he owned that a man who had such a title and fortune could be excused for being a trifle high in the instep. Norton wriggled uncomfortably in his place at the thought of his mild disloyalty. Not that Richard had ever displayed that side of his character to him. Their relationship had always been marked by cordiality and informality. And then, for some reason or another, unfathomable to Norton, Richard had taken to him. In his manner to others, however, he sometimes displayed an aristocratic hauteur that kept them at a distance. It was not exactly pride, but something very close to it; not a sense of his own consequence but more a sense of his own worth, not as a marquis, but as a man. It was hard to define, and Norton soon gave up the effort.

"Well, Charles?" Rutherston broke the easy silence that had fallen between them. "Do you mind giving up a few weeks of the Season to bury yourself down here with me?"

"Not I," said Norton with a shake of his head, "but I am surprised that you should."

"I?" Rutherston asked in some surprise. "What can you mean?"

"Oh, only that I would have thought that the hunting in London was more in your line."

"Hunting?" repeated the marquis in some confusion. "In London?"

"Well, I only surmise that the kind of game you are looking for will be much bigger in town—but of course, the Season ain't underway yet." Norton suppressed a chortle.

The confusion on the marquis's face gave way to enlightenment.

Rutherston was about to return some freezing rejoinder, but seeing the shaking of his friend's shoulders, he stayed the retort on his lips.

After a moment or two, his face broke into a grin, and then his laughter joined his friend's.

Thus it was, on a fine afternoon in February, near the beginning of the London Season, the good folk of the village of Breckenridge, in the county of Surrey, beheld two fine London gentlemen almost doubled up with laughter as their curricle bowled along the High Street at a spanking pace, with a livened groom perched up behind.

Chapter 2

Catherine Harland paused atop her perch on the rough-hewn country stile and looked irately at the muddy patch of water that barred her path to Branley Park. A thick mass of bramble bushes on either side of her formed an impenetrable obstacle. The puddle had to be crossed. After only a moment's hesitation, she gathered up her skirts and threw herself bodily across the mire. She fell headlong on the soft ground, but her pelisse brushed the surface of the puddle and a dark stain spread along its hem.

"Damn!" Catherine muttered under her breath, borrowing one of her older brother's hackneyed expletives. She looked round guiltily to ascertain whether or not she had been overheard. Satisfied that no one was in the vicinity, nor like to be, she picked herself up and repeated her expletive more forcibly. "Damn! And damn again!" Her amber eyes danced merrily to hear her own audacity—a shocking want of conduct, she knew, in one of her gentle birth.

Catherine was not overly anxious about the state of her appearance, for she had donned her plainest attire that afternoon to walk the three miles from her home, Ardo House. With a cursory shake to the hem of her pelisse, she made her way through the leafless copse of willows and birch, following the well-trod path that led to Branley Park.

It was a large house, much grander than any in the neighborhood, and bordered her father's estate. She loved this house—not because of its style or furnishings, which were rather shabby and old-fashioned, but because here she had been—her mind searched for the word she wanted—not happy, but comfortable. That was it. She had been comfortable and at her ease in a way that was not possible at home. In the late Bernard Fortescue, country gentleman and scholar of some note, Catherine had found a congenial companion. It had been Mr. Fortescue who had encouraged one of the few accomplishments Catherine possessed, a love and knowledge of all things Greek. It was he who had taught her the rudiments of the language almost ten years before when a sudden downpour of rain had put an end to the annual picnic that was always held at Branley Park for the people of Breckenridge and its environs.

Catherine, a child of eleven, had wandered into his library to while away the time. He had found her, curled up in a chair, book in hand, poring over the Greek alphabet. Merely thinking to humor a disappointed child, Mr. Fortescue had answered all her questions and piqued her interest. She had proved to be an apt pupil and had been invited to return. This had been only the beginning.

At first her mother had indulged Catherine's whim to learn, but when she saw that she excelled and that this was no harmless pastime but a dangerous snare that might have her unfortunate daughter labeled "clever," she had put her foot down. Gentlemen did not like women who were clever, and women who were clever concealed this fact from men.

But Catherine had found a supporter in Uncle John, her father's brother, who was himself a teacher of classics at Oxford, and his influence with her father had given

Catherine a reprieve. Greek she could learn, but only if she applied herself to all the other accomplishments that were the mark of the true lady of quality.

It had been her habit, in the last number of years, to spend one afternoon a week with Mr. Fortescue in his library. She had long since mastered the intricacies of the language, and their time together had been mostly spent in discussing Greek life and thought in general. He had widened her scope to include other fields, and Catherine had taken to the intellectual life.

As a matter of habit, Catherine found herself making her way to Branley Park as if she still had her weekly appointment with Mr. Fortescue. But she would have no one now to share her insights, no more delightful conversations or heated arguments on the characters who peopled the masterpieces of the Greek playwrights.

The copse ended abruptly on an expanse of winter-brown lawn, and Catherine followed a cobbled path to the back of the house. She unlatched the outside door and entered a large, airy kitchen, shaking her pelisse free of grass and dust, smiling a greeting as she did so.

A spry, elderly country woman rose from a table where she had been polishing a silver tray and came forward to greet her, and she relieved Catherine of her mud-spattered cloak.

"Ah, Miss Catherine, I'm that pleased to see ye. Will ye have time to stay and have some refreshment?"

"Yes, thank you, Mrs. Bates, if it's no trouble to you," Catherine replied warmly. "I see you are putting things in order for his lordship. Do you expect him soon?"

"He sent word that he would be here within the fortnight. But he'll be sending down his own town servants afore he arrives. When his lordship comes, Mr. Bates and me will learn what's to become of us."

Catherine put her hand on the older woman's arm and said encouragingly, "I don't think you need worry, Mrs. Bates. A house of these proportions cannot lie empty. Even if his lordship chooses not to let it, he must keep it in order."

Her reward was to see the older woman smile in appreciation.

"Eh now, Miss Catherine, you'll be going to the library. I'll put the kettle on and bring you a nice dish of tea."

Catherine opened the door that led to the living quarters, making her way to a large saloon near the front entrance. She removed her bonnet, threw it on the chair, and walked to the center of the room. She turned in a circle, surveying what she considered to be her domain. How she loved this room!

Long windows opened onto a terrace, and the light streamed in on two sides. Apart from the fireplace wall, every available inch of space was covered with books. She walked to the section containing her favorites and ran her fingers along their spines, murmuring the names of the authors: Aeschylus, Euripides, Sophocles, as if their names were musical cadences.

In a moment she had found her favorite, the most perfect play ever written, with the character of the most perfect man. Settling herself in one of the wing chairs flanking the fireplace, she was soon engrossed in the beauty of the poetry and the tragedy of the plot. When Mrs. Bates entered quietly a few minutes later with the promised tea, Catherine gave no sign of awareness. Mrs. Bates placed the tray on a small side table and discreetly withdrew. Miss Catherine was a real bookworm. It would take a thunderbolt to get her attention now.

So it was that Catherine, curled up in her chair, did not hear the clip-clop of hooves as Rutherston's curricle drove up to the front door, nor was she aware of the bustle just outside the library as he gave instructions to his groom, Simpson, for the stabling of the grays and disposal of the baggage.

Some time later, a shadow fell across the page of Catherine's book. She moved it to a better light. The shadow followed, and Catherine looked up straight into the cold gray eyes of the Marquis of Rutherston.

"My dear Daisy, or Dolly, or Polly, or whatever your name happens to be," he began in frigid accents, "I approve of your devotion to literature, but I would be obliged if you would put your picture book away and attend to your duties. You will find Mrs. Bates upstairs in a bustle and short of hands."

Catherine, whose first reaction had been dismay, now found her own ire rising. She surveyed the young man more closely, and saw that he was above average height, dark hair rather long on the collar, broad shouldered, and of muscular physique. The cut of his coat proclaimed the aristocrat, but the effect was spoiled by the supercilious scowl that marred his handsome face. Catherine had no doubt that she was facing an enraged Marquis of Rutherston.

She snapped the book shut, and more slowly than she needed to, uncurled her legs from the chair and stood up. She lowered her eyes, which she knew were flashing with anger, and dropped the hint of a curtsy. She had not meant to play the role he had cast her in, but before she could stop herself she heard herself say, "If it please your lordship, I didn't mean no harm."

It was the marquis's turn now to appraise the slip of a girl standing before him.

Rutherston, who was accustomed to the finery of London ladies, supposed that Catherine's plain gray frock, which he had only glanced at in a cursory fashion, was the mark of a superior servant, distinguishing her from the kitchen domestics. He noticed her trim, well-formed figure, an abundance of russet hair hugging her oval face, and dark lashes curving along her cheek. She would be only a pretty chit of a thing, he thought, except for her glowing coloring. Her dark auburn hair cast a golden glow on her creamy complexion. Although her eyes were still downcast, Rutherston sensed that her demeanor was provocative rather than demure, but dismissed that suspicion instantly from his mind. No chit of a maid would dare to tease one of his consequence.

"Let me see which of my books has taken your fancy," he said in a more conciliatory tone as he drew the book from Catherine's grasp. Was it his imagination, or did he feel a slight resistance? He opened the book, then quickly looked down at her in astonishment. "Greek?" he demanded incredulously.

"Is that what it is, your lordship?" she asked, meeting his eyes for the first time. "I was only tracing them there squiggles with my finger. The letters are so pretty. Can you read it, sir?" she asked archly.

Amber eyes widened in mock admiration and smiled into gray. Their eyes held for a long moment and all mockery left Catherine's face as she read the expression in Rutherston's eyes. He heard Catherine's gasp as she turned for flight, but in an instant he had her in his arms.

His kiss was hard and thorough, and so shocked was Catherine that she made no move to pull away. She recognized that in some way she had been at fault and was deeply mortified to think that she had put herself into an intolerable situation.

But as his kiss lingered, and she felt his warm tongue trying to probe her lips apart, she strained back as hard as she could. Rutherston responded by pulling her close. Something stirred within her, her breath quickened, and she found herself parting her lips to receive his kisses.

When she found herself thrust roughly away from him her embarrassment was acute, and she could not bring herself to meet his eyes. He laughed shortly.

"You must excuse my ardor," he drawled, striving to steady his voice, "but the force of your charms quite overcame my scruples. You can go now, my girl, and in future I suggest that you keep out of my way." In an attempt to mask his own embarrassment and want of discretion, Rutherston's demeanor had assumed a forbidding hauteur.

Catherine felt as if she would die of shame, and wondered how she could retrieve herself from such an impossible position.

It was at that moment that Charles Norton walked into the library in search of his cousin and stopped on the threshold, one hand on the door handle.

Chapter 3

Catherine turned toward the intruder in relief.

"Miss Harland," Norton said in delight, striding toward her and taking her hand in his. "Mrs. Bates was just telling me that you were in the library, and I came at once." He glanced at the glowering marquis, suspecting that he had walked in on a confrontation. "I see you've met my cousin," he added uncertainly.

Catherine's laugh sounded forced in her own ears. "How good it is to meet you again, Mr. Norton," she managed in a normal voice, and with genuine pleasure. "I am afraid you have walked in on a scene of mistaken identity. No, I have not had the pleasure of being introduced to your cousin."

She turned to face Rutherston, chin high and eyes steady, daring him to reveal one scrap of what had taken place between them.

"Richard," said Norton, happy to oblige, "this is Miss Catherine Harland, you know, old Harly's niece. Miss Norton, may I present my cousin, Lord Rutherston?" Catherine curtsied deeply, and Rutherston gave a slight bow that just stopped short of being uncivil.

Norton was surprised to see the set of his friend's face, and rightly supposed that the case of mistaken identity of which Catherine spoke had been a cause of embarrassment to him.

"Old Harly?" asked Rutherston. "I don't recollect . . ."

He looked from one to the other in polite inquiry. He didn't care whose niece the chit was. She had behaved like a hoyden and put him in a ridiculous position. He would soon put her in her place and make her wish that she had never crossed swords with the Marquis of Rutherston.

"Don't you remember, Richard? Old Harly taught classics at Oxford. Didn't you read under him? I thought you had, somehow. That's where Miss Harland and I met, when I was up at Oxford and Miss Harland was visiting her relations. Tell me, Miss Harland, how is your brother, Tom? Haven't seen him in an age, though I don't think the fault is all his."

Catherine searched his face quickly, determining at once that Mr. Norton's inquiry was not uttered as a matter of form but from genuine interest, and in a moment or two she was animatedly describing her older brother's adventures and scrapes since he had come down from Oxford to take up the life of a country gentleman. These reflections, as a matter of course, led to an exchange of reminiscences on life at Oxford, and Rutherston, who had been observing them covertly, a fixed smile upon his lips, heard his cousin ask Catherine if she was still keeping up her Greek studies.

"Ah, that explains it," said Rutherston, determinedly breaking into the conversation. "I found Miss Harland reading this." He held up the copy of "Hippolytus." "I take it, Miss Harland, that my uncle gave you the run of his library, no doubt taking you for a kindred spirit? A veritable blue stocking, if I'm not mistaken?"

So saying, he proffered the book which Catherine took into her hands, but he did not release it immediately. "Please feel free to continue using my library whenever it suits you. I am sure that you won't be in the way. Mr. Norton and I don't intend to be much in the house."

He had hardly uttered this uncivil speech when he regretted it. No one could doubt that he was giving her a set-down, and in so doing had betrayed his own lack of composure.

"Please do, Miss Harland," Norton interjected, trying to make amends for his cousin's discourtesy. "And if you don't mind company once in a while, I'd be delighted to, er . . ." He waved his hand vaguely in the general direction of the books.

"You cannot think that I will accept your kind offer," said Catherine to Norton, her voice warm with gratitude. "I know perfectly well that your love of books is in proportion to your distance from them—or so I've heard you say on many occasions."

Norton laughed and eyed Catherine in frank admiration. "Miss Harland, I had hoped to come into a part of the world where I might pass myself off as a sage. I see that I shall have to mind how I go on, since you know me so well."

Catherine joined in his laughter, but was uncomfortably aware of Rutherston's tense stand. She turned to face him.

"My lord," she began, "I do beg your pardon for trespassing on your hospitality. You must believe that I should never have come here if I had known you were so soon to arrive. Indeed, your housekeeper assured me that you would not be here until your servants had come from town."

Rutherston waved his hand as if to signify that it was of no consequence.

Catherine continued, "I thank you for offering me the freedom of your library, but I do believe you mistake?"

"I?" said Rutherston with a lift of his brow.

"I believe that this is my library, my lord, left to me under the terms of Mr. Fortescue's will?" Her voice was light, but her intention unmistakable, and Rutherston was completely taken aback.

Catherine gave him her sweetest smile. "Pray feel free to make use of it whenever you like, my lord, until such time as I have made arrangements to have the books transported to Ardo House. I collect the terms were one year?"

In a few minutes she was gone, having taken her leave, very prettily, of the two gentlemen, but not before Norton had promised to call on her family to renew their acquaintance at his earliest convenience.

He turned back into the room, his brows knit in puzzlement, and surveyed his cousin thoughtfully. Rutherston was leaning against the mantel in an attitude of studied nonchalance.

"Well, what a piece of luck meeting Miss Harland like this," Norton began.

"Do you think so?" Rutherston drawled indifferently. "I can't say that I approve of Miss Harland's want of propriety."

"Want of propriety? Whatever can you mean? Why she's as prim and proper as any young lady of my acquaintance. You'll have to explain yourself, Richard, for I'm sure I don't know what you're talking about."

"I was referring to Miss Harland's lack of embarrassment on finding herself unchaperoned in the company of two gentlemen."

"Oh, that don't signify! Country manners are not so formal as town manners. I don't see why you're in such a taking. You've never been overfond of chaperones, as I remember. No, you'll have to do better than that. I can see that you've taken Miss Harland in dislike—no, don't hoax me. It's all the same to me. You've made up your mind that she's not in your style."

Mr. Norton, who had heard his cousin's views on women on numerous occasions, now warmed to his sport. "She's intelligent, beautiful, and has a certain wit. 'Course, we can't tell if she's as cold as a fish." On seeing Rutherston's color mount, he raised a speculative brow, but held his tongue in check.

"If Miss Harland is such a paragon, Charles, I'm surprised you haven't tried to fix your interest with her."

"Oh no, cousin!" Norton laughed, shaking his head in derision. "I may be a nudgeon, but I'm not as witless as all that. You have the freedom to marry where you will, but as you well know, my case is entirely different. Miss Harland's family and connections may be unexceptionable, but I'll wager her portion is negligible. I own that she's a taking little thing, but I hope I have some sense. Besides, neither her relations nor mine would countenance such a match."

He turned to look at Rutherston and saw that his cousin was eyeing him with a good deal of amusement.

"What's this, Charles?" he said. "I do believe you have given the matter some thought. Sits the wind in that quarter?"

"No, no, cos. It never entered my head." When he observed Rutherston's disbelieving look, he went on, "Well, not for more than a se'ennight at any rate, when her brother Tom introduced us at Oxford. But believe me, I soon put that thought behind me!"

"Yes," said Rutherston, clapping his cousin affectionately on the shoulder. "I see that you must. Younger sons, so it seems to me, invariably fix their interest where fortune outweighs favor."

"Well, it ain't as bad as all that. At least our fond

mamas are not always badgering us to get leg-shackled just so's the succession will be secured! Now that I wouldn't like above half."

A thought suddenly occurred to Mr. Norton. "I say, Richard, did you know that Miss Harland was coming into your uncle's library?"

Rutherston looked thoughtful. "I knew that a lady was to receive Uncle Bernard's books, her name had slipped my mind, but I had expected that lady to be . . . something different."

A picture of that Miss Harland, whom his uncle's lawyer had described as "a dear friend of Mr. Fortescue," flashed into his mind. He had imagined her as an elderly spinster with white hair braided high on her head.

What a fool he had made of himself! No! By God, what a fool she had made of him! She had deliberately provoked him into forgetting who he was. To kiss what he supposed was an upstairs maid was not to be thought of. Such conduct in one of his rank was reprehensible. He groaned inwardly at his folly, but his chagrin soon turned to fury when he thought of the cause of his embarrassment. She had done this to him—teasing him into forgetting himself. Well, two could play at that game. Miss Catherine Harland had proved, by her warm kisses, that she was no lady, and he was not going to let her forget it. The arrogance of the chit—to invite him to browse in his own library.

She had found him an object of sport, and his wounded pride would not tolerate it. Miss Catherine Harland would be taught a lesson she would not forget.

Chapter 4

True to his word, Mr. Norton arrived the next morning to call on Catherine's family. He was received in Mr. Harland's downstairs study, the ladies of the house being engaged in the ladylike occupation of sewing and mending in Mrs. Harland's upstairs private back sitting room. They could hear the delighted shouts of the young gentlemen as they greeted each other jovially and clapped each other on the back, and the sounds of their warm reunion brought smiles of appreciation to the ladies' lips.

"This is a signal honor that Tom's friend is paying us," said Mrs. Harland, looking up from her needlework and surveying her two daughters, "for I am persuaded that he is here only by Lord Rutherston's consent, and if he has consented, you may be sure that he approves of the relationship."

"Why shouldn't he approve, Mama?" The question came from the younger Miss Harland, a girl of about eighteen years whose resemblance to her elder sister was quite marked.

"Well, of course, there's no reason why he shouldn't approve, Lucy, but one never knows with the nobility. Some are so full of their own consequence that they are a law unto themselves."

"But Mama," interrupted Catherine who had been listening in some impatience, "Mr. Norton said yesterday that he would be calling on Tom. As a gentleman, he could not go back on his word, whatever his proud cousin might say." Catherine laid aside her embroidery, thankful for any excuse not to have to continue with so dreary a task.

"That may be, my dear," said her mother with infuriating complacency, "but you will allow that I have more experience in such matters than you. You may be sure of it, if Lord Rutherston had not wished the young man to renew Tom's acquaintance, he would not."

Catherine bent to her work again to conceal her irritation, and was consumed with an unreasonable resentment against the Marquis of Rutherston, who had it in his power to influence so malleable a young gentleman as Mr. Norton. She felt herself in some agitation, wondering if Rutherston had accompanied Norton on his call, since the ladies had no way of knowing, but when her brother opened the door to admit Norton, she could see that Rutherston had not graced them with his presence. Catherine could not make up her mind whether she was relieved or disappointed.

When the introductions were made and a few pleasantries exchanged, Mrs. Harland asked the young man if he would be staying in the district for long.

"That depends on my cousin, ma'am. I am quite at his disposal. You know, of course, that Lord Rutherston is here to oversee Mr. Fortescue's estate. We could be here for a fortnight or a month. My cousin is quite a capricious fellow, and I have no way of knowing what he will take into his head to do next."

Mrs. Harland caught Catherine's eye with a speaking look, and the conversation turned to general topics, Norton regaling Tom with stories of mutual acquaintances from Oxford days. The conversation moved from Oxford to London, and he learned that Catherine and Lucy were to be in town for the start of the Season to make their come-out under the auspices of their father's sister-in-law, Lady Margaret Henderly.

"And do you look forward to your first Season, Miss Harland?" he asked the younger girl, who colored prettily at this signal attention from a young gentleman. She managed to reply in the affirmative with some composure, and when it looked to Tom that his young sister and friend were about to embark on a conversation that held nothing of interest for him, he impatiently recalled his friend's attention, reminding him that his father would be waiting with horses saddled and bridled for an exploratory ride round the neighborhood.

Norton rose and took his leave of the ladies, bowing over their hands. "Lord Rutherston sends his regrets, ma'am," he said, addressing Mrs. Harland. "He would have accompanied me here this morning, but there was much to attend to. He begs your indulgence and hopes to make your family's acquaintance once we are more settled in Branley Park."

The door had hardly closed upon the two gentlemen when Mrs. Harland exclaimed, "Such civility is most unexpected! Why his lordship should favor us in this way is beyond understanding! I had not expected it!" She looked at her daughter questioningly, but when she saw that Catherine was thoroughly absorbed in her needlework, an object that was more prone to evoke feelings of disgust than enthusiasm in that young lady's breast, she thought it the better part of discretion to say nothing more on the subject of Lord Rutherston. A marquis would be such a catch, Mrs. Harland thought inwardly, and gentlemen were known to be capricious when choosing a mate. For a few moments she allowed her fancy to take flight, then brought herself back to reality. No, it was highly improbable, and she would not allow herself to become one of those vulgar mamas who outraged every feeling of delicacy by encouraging their daughters to set their caps at every eligible male.

Mr. Norton was agreed to be a very personable gentleman, with easy manners, and Tom a most fortunate young man in engaging such a charming companion for his friend. It was at the dinner table that evening that Catherine was surprised to hear Lord Rutherston described in much the same terms by her father, for Mr. Norton had insisted, as they returned to Ardo House, that they break their ride at Branley Park in order for them to meet Rutherston in person.

The two gentlemen from Ardo House had been very gratified by their reception, finding Rutherston not at all stiff or lacking in attention.

"I took it upon myself to engage the young gentlemen for dinner next Thursday evening." Mr. Harland smiled at his wife, sure of the warm reception of his words. He was to be disappointed.

"Mr. Harland, surely you did not! You cannot have invited his lordship when I have nothing to put before him! I do not know how you could be so unfeeling. Cook will never manage, on two days' notice, to prepare as many courses as Lord Rutherston is accustomed to." Her voice rose in agitation, and Mr. Harland's face grew stern.

"Mama," Catherine hastily interjected, trying to relieve the situation, "it is quite nonsensical of you to think that Lord Rutherston would expect such attention. He must know that we keep a much simpler table than townfolk do."

"Catherine's right, Mother," said the younger Mr. Harland, helping himself to another portion of sirloin of beef.

"He don't expect it, and he don't want it. Said he was looking forward to some good country fare, since his French chef covers everything in hideous sauces. I told him nobody hereabouts keeps a better table than you."

These words, spoken with all the confidence of the country gentleman in the superiority of country ways and manners, somewhat mollified Mrs. Harland, but on one thing she insisted—that there be other company to help entertain their guests, for she knew that however much the London gentlemen might protest that they merely wanted to take pot luck, they would expect more in the way of conversation and entertainments than could be reasonably provided by her own small family. Thus it was that on the very next morning, Master Tom was dispatched to invite their very good friends and neighbors, Sir James and Lady Kelvin and the elder members of their offspring, to a quiet evening of dining, conversation and cards at Ardo House for the following evening.

Mrs. Harland rose, intimating that the ladies would leave the gentlemen to their port, and followed by the other ladies, withdrew to the large drawing room upstairs which was reserved for company occasions. Dinner had been a most decided success, Cook having excelled herself on the number and variety of her dishes, and the London gentlemen having highly gratified their hostess by partaking of a hearty repast.

Catherine settled herself into a chair as her friend, Mary Kelvin, sat down at the piano with Lucy to while away the next half hour until the gentlemen should join them. There was no need for these ladies to make the least effort to entertain each other. They had so much occasion to be in each other's company that their manners with each other were very free and easy. Lady Margaret and Mrs. Harland were engaged in a quiet tête à tête on the sofa, and Catherine could well imagine the subject of their conversation.

Meeting Lord Rutherston had been much less of an ordeal than Catherine had imagined it would be. He had scarcely said two words to her, but everything in his manner had conveyed that the circumstances of their first encounter were to be forgotten.

She had been greatly relieved at dinner to find herself seated between Mr. Norton and Master James Kelvin, and had exerted herself to pay attention to their conversation. On more than one occasion, she had caught herself glancing in Rutherston's direction. That gentleman, however, seemed to be unaware of her presence, and Catherine felt herself regaining something of her confidence. He was a true gentleman, after all, and she need fear no embarrassment from that quarter.

It was herself that she blamed for the stolen kiss in Mr. Fortescue's library. She had been teasing Rutherston, she knew, but it had not occurred to her that a gentleman would conduct himself in such a forward manner, whatever the provocation. But then, she knew so little about gentlemen. Kisses had been stolen from her before, but those kisses had not been like Rutherston's kiss. She cringed inwardly as she remembered how she had responded, and prayed that he had not noticed. In an attempt to put all thoughts of that encounter out of her mind, she picked up a book and set her mind to concentrate.

A shadow fell across her book, and Catherine looked up to see Rutherston looking down at her in some amusement.

"Miss Harland," he said softly, taking the book out of her hands and sitting down beside her in an adjacent chair, "this seems to be a habit with you. Do you always forget your surroundings when you pick up a book?"

Catherine's eyes flew to her mother in consternation.

"You must excuse my daughter, Lord Rutherston, but like all young women of today, she wastes her time on rubbishy novels." Mrs. Harland frowned at Catherine, conveying all the displeasure she felt that a daughter of hers should be caught out in such a solecism, and at such a time. She hoped fervently that the book that was now in Rutherston's hands was just as she had described and not one of Catherine's bluestocking books.

"Oh no, Mrs. Harland, please do not blame Miss Harland, for I see that she and I have much the same taste in books. I am eager to hear Miss Harland's opinion on this, er, novel."

He turned back to Catherine, effectively shutting out the rest of the company, and Mrs. Harland, quite reassured by Lord Rutherston's gallantry, turned her attention once more to Lady Margaret, animatedly discussing the details of the young ladies' wardrobes as they prepared for their first Season in town.

"Well, Miss Harland?" queried Rutherston quizzically. "I am waiting to hear your opinion of the book."

Catherine gave it to him. "I consider it to be the most perfect of all the Greek tragedies; indeed the finest of any play ever written, surpassing even those of Shakespeare."

"Then we are in agreement, Miss Harland. Now tell me, what think you of Hippolytus?"

Catherine looked at him uncertainly. The quizzical tone was still in his voice, but she could not see how a discussion of Euripides's Hippolytus could be a matter of sport, unless the marquis thought that she did not know her subject.

"Hippolytus is a romantic figure, of course, but so

tragic, so high-minded, so far above the common run of young man. His high ideals, his principles . . ."

"Come now, Miss Harland," said Rutherston, rudely breaking into her eulogy, "Hippolytus is a prig, and so taken with his own high-mindedness that he spares not a thought for the feelings of a woman of passion who is pining away for love of him."

"But she is his stepmother." Catherine's voice rose in indignation. "Her passion outrages every feeling of decency."

"Ah, my dear Miss Harland," he said smoothly, "I had not thought that one of your warm temperament would show so little understanding, so little empathy for one of the weaker members of your sex."

He smiled at her in a knowing way, leaving her speechless. There was no mistaking that the Marquis of Rutherston was deliberately trying to provoke her, and was relishing her confusion. So that's the way of it, Catherine thought, looking balefully into his lordship's eyes. She was just about to put this outrageous member of the nobility firmly in his place, when they were joined by Norton, and Catherine bit her lip in frustration.

"Ah, Charles, I have just persuaded Miss Harland to allow me to borrow her book," said Rutherston affably, lying in his teeth and slipping the slim volume into his coat pocket. "We cannot agree on the merits of the various characters, and I hope to refresh my memory before joining battle with Miss Harland again."

Charles Norton smiled, but he was not deceived. He had no idea what was going on between his cousin and Miss Harland, but he knew his cousin well enough to know that it was not for his sake or for the desire of rustic company that he had consented to dine at Ardo House. No, Catherine had either discomfited Richard or piqued his interest, and, either way, Norton felt it incumbent upon himself to protect his friend's sister from Rutherston's unwelcome attentions.

"My lord," said Catherine in her most engaging manner, "how ungentlemanly of you to reveal that a mere female would demur in your opinions. Pray do read the play again, and when your memory is refreshed and you have come to know the subject more thoroughly, I am sure that you and I shall be of one mind." She hoped that that had put the insolent lord in his place.

Rutherston was delighted and wondered if the little chit was aware of how enticing she was. He would have been more than pleased to continue their conversation in such vein, but Charles's presence forbade any further sallies that might lead Miss Harland into dangerous waters, and he reluctantly turned the conversation into channels more suitable for polite society, excusing himself after a time to join Miss Kelvin at the piano.

Catherine determined not to be in Rutherston's company for the rest of the evening, but she need not have exerted herself. He paid her no more attention, and divided his time equally among every person present. It was only as he was taking his leave and bowing over her hand that he whispered in her ear, "Ah, Miss Harland, I do hope we may resume our conversation soon. So instructive, I do assure you. Perhaps I may hope to find you in my library sometime soon? In the meantime, may I suggest that you employ your time in reading 'Andromache'? Now there is a woman worthy of your emulation, though the task might prove somewhat beyond your capabilities."

Catherine eyed him in astonishment. "Emulate Andromache? You must be funning! That spineless pattern card of obedience and passivity? I would not waste my energies on such a poor-spirited drab. Do you say that you admire her? Well, I am not surprised."

Rutherston noted the curl of Catherine's lip. "But of course," he returned smoothly, "what man wouldn't? She is the perfection of womanhood." And with a wicked grin, he was gone.

After the last of the guests had departed, the evening was declared to be a resounding success, and Lord Rutherston truly the well-bred gentleman. Catherine outwardly concurred in all that was said, for she could not reveal to her family that Rutherston's manner to her had been anything but gentlemanly. She surmised that he had tried to engage her interest out of a feeling of boredom, and she was not well pleased with that thought. He had thrown down the gauntlet, daring her to pick it up. Well, she would not. He was ten years her senior and a man of the world, whilst she was just a green girl. Catherine was not at all sure what a man of the world was, but she recognized one when she saw one, and he was a dangerous breed. Her manner would be polite, but distant, she determined, when next they met. She would behave with all the insipidity and propriety that she could command. And on these resolute thoughts, Catherine went to bed, but not to dreamless sleep.

Chapter 5

Catherine wheeled the glossy chestnut out of the Ardo House stable, and the echo of clattering hooves on the rough cobblestones hung on the still air of daybreak. She set her mount at a brisk canter to follow the well-trod path that led to Branley Park, and her spirits soared as she felt the motion of the mare beneath her. She savored the pleasure of her solitary ramble, inhaling the pungent scent of the ground softened with dew after an evening of gentle February rain.

Gypsy needed little guiding, knowing the path well, and the mare turned toward the expanse of woods that marked the boundary of the adjoining estate. Catherine guided her mount along a narrow track that led upward to wide-open meadowland, and as they approached the gap in the trees, she urged Gypsy to a faster pace.

She was now on Rutherston's land, but Catherine never gave that a thought. She thumbed her nose at the town-bred ways of the higher ranks of the nobility who, so it seemed to her, spent the better part of their days abed. In the week that the gentlemen had been in residence, she had continued her daily practice of exercising Gypsy before breakfast and had never once so much as caught a glimpse of Rutherston or Norton.

Catherine gave Gypsy her head, and with ears flattened, the mare moved at breakneck speed across the rain-softened earth. For the space of half an hour or more they moved as one, wheeling, cantering, and galloping toward higher ground, until they came to an outcrop of rock and Catherine reined in. She turned her mount, patting it affectionately on the neck.

"Good girl, Gypsy," she murmured in the mare's ear. "And now, a sedate trot home, I think."

Catherine sensed his presence before she saw him. She wheeled to her right and in the distance espied a lone rider on a low ridge. He had halted his steed and was surveying the horizon. Shielding her eyes with one hand against the rising sun, she gazed curiously at the figure, and as she watched, he dug his heels into his mount's flanks and shot forward.

She remained immobile, unalarmed, since the rider was not moving in her direction, but in a moment she had guessed his purpose. She brought her crop smartly against Gypsy's rump and spurred the mare forward, hoping to reach the gap before Rutherston cut off her retreat.

Horse and rider dashed toward the trees, Catherine leaning low in the saddle, but out of the corner of her eye she saw Rutherston on a magnificent black stallion come plunging toward her. He reached the gap well ahead of her and wheeled his steed around to bar her way, almost unseating himself in the process as his stallion reared and stamped its displeasure. Catherine slackened her pace and reined in a few yards in front of him, watching warily from beneath lowered brows.

Rutherston grinned from ear to ear as he brought his stallion alongside of the chestnut.

"Trespassing again, Miss Harland?" he reproved mildly.

Catherine gave him a look of cold dislike and urged

her mare forward. "You are barring my way, sir. I wish to pass, if you please!" Rutherston swung his mount round to block her way once more.

"Why so angry, Miss Harland? Can it be that the intrepid Miss Harland is a poor loser?"

"A poor loser!" Catherine expostulated in outrage. "When you are mounted on that black fury? If my mount were half a match for yours, my lord, and I were not compelled to ride sidesaddle, I would have beaten you easily, and you know it!"

Rutherston's grin widened. "Do you hear that, Diabolos?" he asked silkily, stroking the snorting stallion's smooth neck. "The lady pays you a compliment, but for your master she displays only contempt."

Catherine sat mute, casting Rutherston a black look, but he took no pains to disguise his admiration. The wind had whipped her cheeks to a warm glow, and her russet curls peeped out saucily from a bonnet that was slightly askew. In the bright sunshine, her eyes, glinting like gold, seemed lighter than he had remembered them, and the plain dark green riding habit molded her figure in the most becoming way. He saw that she was watching him with a guarded expression and he put an end to his idle musings.

"Why such a placid nag, Miss Harland? Does your father not trust you with a more spirited mount?"

Catherine grinned in spite of herself. "It is not Papa who makes these decisions, my lord, but Mama. Cannot you tell that Gypsy's gentle temperament is the ideal for a lady of breeding and gentility?"

"With your obvious equestrian accomplishments, I would have thought you rated higher than this docile beast," he returned gallantly.

It was a prettily turned compliment, Catherine owned silently, but if the marquis expected her to be dazzled by such flattery, he was much mistaken. She had been well schooled by her mother in preparation for her first Season to discount the polished flatteries of dandies and men-about-town, and Catherine knew how insincere such blatant gallantry was on the lips of a man of Rutherston's stamp.

Catherine's tone was mocking. "Oh, to be sure I *do* deserve a more spirited mount. But if ladies had the mounts they deserved, think how galling it would be for the gentlemen to be bested in what they consider is a masculine preserve. It would not do. A man's pride must be protected at all costs. If I had beaten you to the gap," she went on more hotly, "do you think that you would be in such high humor? I think not!"

A wicked light gleamed in Rutherston's eyes. "Do I detect a note of pique, Miss Harland? Never say that you are one of those females who believes that woman is the equal of man?"

"That would depend on the man," replied Catherine, dimpling prettily. "In general, men are as vain as peacocks and with as much intelligence. Women are trained from childhood to flatter them into thinking that they are the superior sex. Come now! Admit it! No one of any intelligence truly believes it!"

"Oho! Is that a challenge, Miss Harland? If so, I accept—any contest, any terms you choose to name."

Catherine gazed at him doubtfully, a feeling of unease beginning to creep over her. Rutherston saw it and pushed his advantage.

"So craven, Miss Harland?"

Nettled beyond endurance, Catherine retorted rudely, "If your display of ignorance respecting Euripides is anything to go by, my lord, I wonder if the contest will be worth the effort?"

Rutherston's laughter pealed out. "So be it, Miss Harland. Combatants we shall be, in every sphere, and no holds barred. But I give you fair warning, I am an unscrupulous opponent and I give no quarter." He gave her an appraising look, then stood up in his stirrups and leaned over to take the reins from Catherine's grasp. She saw her chance and dug in her heels. The frightened mare sprang past a startled Rutherston and was instantly through the gap. Catherine heard Rutherston's furious oath as he turned his stallion to give chase.

In a matter of minutes they were hurtling down the track and into the open, the black stallion thundering hard at the chestnut's heels. As Rutherston drew level, he reached out his hand to grasp the reins and pulled hard on them.

The chestnut reared at the sudden pressure on her mouth, dislodging a surprised Catherine from the saddle. She was thrown to the ground, the wind completely knocked out of her. In a moment, Rutherston was by her side, his face grim. Catherine rolled over and leaned back on her elbows, her gown halfway up her thighs. She looked up at his frightened face. "You stupid, impetuous man!" she sputtered when she had regained her breath.

"Thank God you're all right," Rutherston said fervently, and at the unexpected prayer on his lips, Catherine's laughter rang out, and he found himself smiling back at her.

"Oh give me your hand, you unscrupulous man!" said Catherine brusquely, but still smiling. He helped her to rise, brushing the mud and dirt from her gown.

"Miss Harland, that was unforgivable! I apologize . . . I had not meant . . ." He saw the laughter dancing in her eyes and he was nonplussed.

"Perhaps I deserved it," she said generously, moving to

retrieve the reins of her mare. "I baited you outrageously. But you are an impossible man, you know. I have never met anyone like you! You bring out the worst in me." She went on in candid good humor, "I am quite afraid to be alone in your company."

He cupped his gloved hands and threw her into the saddle, then stood looking up at her, one hand on the reins. "In my circles, ma'am," he replied provocatively, "a young lady who flaunts convention by appearing unchaperoned is inviting attention."

"Really?" retorted Catherine, refusing to be discomfited by his veiled insult. "Then I beg to inform you, Lord Rutherston, that in this neck of the woods we generally accept at face value those who appear to be gentlemen until we learn better." She moved off and flung him her parting shot. "And I have learned better!" And with a saucy flounce of her head, she took off, leaving a disconcerted, amused, and admiring Rutherston in her wake.

"Oho, Miss Harland, you impertinent wench!" he flung at her retreating back. "So you think that I am no gentleman? Then so be it, for you are decidedly no lady! What you need, my proud beauty, is a lesson in humility, and I am just the man to teach you!"

Chapter 6

The natural outcome of Rutherston's dining at Ardo House was that a host of gentlemen came to call at Branley Park and a proliferation of invitations arrived to various outings and soirées throughout the neighborhood of Breckenridge. It soon became known in the district, however, that Lord Rutherston, although of the most genial disposition, went into company only to oblige his cousin, Mr. Charles Norton, and that Mr. Norton went only to oblige his friend Mr. Thomas Harland, so that if the eager hostesses of Breckenridge wished to secure Lord Rutherston's presence, the Harland family had to be included in their invitations.

Thus, whether she would or not, Catherine found herself constantly in Rutherston's company, and although she took pains never to be in his presence alone, and he did nothing obvious to arouse the suspicions of jealous mamas, she discovered that a gentleman, if he had a mind to, could always contrive a few moments' private conversation with a lady, even if the rest of the world looked on. His manner always appeared proper to anyone who should happen to glance their way, but his remarks to Catherine were either blatantly improper or cast in such a way that she could read two meanings into what was said, the one a deliberate attempt to outrage her feminine sensibilities, the other wholly innocuous.

Catherine, although at first taken aback by such ungentlemanly behavior, soon came to recognize that she looked forward to Rutherston's sallies and found herself responding in kind. She wondered if he behaved in this manner with all the young ladies, but when applying to her sister and friend in a most circumspect manner for their opinions on the handsome and debonair marquis, she discovered, by dint of careful questioning, that he treated them as if they had been duchesses. This information left her more in doubt about the propriety of his conduct toward her, but as he always seemed to take pleasure in her company, she reassured herself with the thought that their sport was such as might exist between friends rather than acquaintances. In two weeks she would be leaving for London, and it would be highly unlikely that their paths would cross again, for his circles in town were sure to be far more exalted than hers, and any of the balls at which they both might be in attendance would be such large affairs that he could quite properly ignore the rustic Miss Harland without having it said that he had cut her.

Rutherston, for his part, did little to analyze his feelings for Catherine, but she had roused his hunting instincts, and he felt himself to be in hot pursuit. He admired her adroitness in avoiding his maneuvers to be alone with her and had taken steps to end that situation. This was one maneuver that the elusive Miss Catherine Harland was not going to sidestep!

A small select company of gentlemen from Breckenridge had been invited by Rutherston to shoot on his estate. The plan had been to set out after an early breakfast and return to Branley Park for dinner. It was a regretful Lord Rutherston who met his guests to inform them that he was unable, due to unforeseen circumstances, to accompany them, but that his cousin Charles would act as host in his stead. Charles looked perplexed, but no one would have deemed it civil to inquire into the unforeseen circumstances of which his lordship spoke. Rutherston's manners might be easy, but it would have been presumptuous to assume an overfamiliarity with one of his consequence.

The gentlemen departed, and Rutherston returned to the house to bide his time. He did not think that Miss Catherine Harland would miss this opportunity when she was so secure in the knowledge that his lordship would not be at home for many hours. It was nearly an hour later, as he watched from an upstairs window, that he saw her wend her way to the back of the house. She had removed her bonnet, and the pale February sun cast golden glints in her hair. Rutherston watched her intently, a smile spreading across his handsome face, and he was struck once again by the arresting beauty of her glowing coloring. He waited till he thought she would be thoroughly absorbed, then made his way cautiously downstairs.

She was ensconced in a library chair, in her usual position, feet curled under her, a small frown of concentration on her brow. He approached soundlessly, and stood by her chair absorbing everything about her—the cluster of russet curls at the nape of her neck, the delicate glow of her flawless complexion, and the rounded swell of her breasts beneath her modest gray frock. He waited, then deliberately cast the shadow that he knew would rouse her from her reverie. She looked up with a start, an expression of consternation on her face.

"My lord," she gasped, trying to rise, "I do beg your pardon, but . . ."

"No, no, Miss Harland, stay just as you are," replied

Rutherston, pushing her shoulders gently against the back of the chair. "I invited you to browse, and indeed I am glad that you have taken me up on the offer."

His pleasant, unaffected manner persuaded Catherine that she had not offended him, and had nothing to fear. She forced herself to control her confusion and to assume an easy pose.

"What is it this time?" he asked with a smile. "Ah, today it is 'Antigone.' Miss Harland, the scope of your reading astonishes me." He took the book from her hands, flicking through the pages until he found what he wanted.

"These choruses!" he said, shaking his head. "Wouldn't you say, Miss Harland, that Greek women of old had a healthy respect for 'eros'?"

Catherine nodded her agreement, not sure of where the conversation was leading or whether Rutherston was quizzing her or really interested in a serious discussion.

"How do you translate *eros,* Miss Harland?" He remained standing over her, making Catherine, she knew not why, feel very uncomfortable.

"Love," she replied briefly.

"And *philia?*" he went on. "How do you translate that?"

"Love," she said again.

"You translate both words as love? Then what is the difference?"

She tried to read his eyes, but the light was behind him and she gave up the attempt.

"I suppose," she began seriously, *"eros* is closer to passion and *philia* is closer to affection, but love is as good a translation as any for both words."

He put the book down and leaned toward her, placing his hands, one on each arm of her chair. Catherine was by this time thoroughly frightened and cursing herself as all kinds of a fool for having been inveigled into playing his game.

His face was only inches from her now.

"And which of these two words, passion or affection, describes most accurately the feeling that we share for each other, Catherine? Shall we put it to the test?"

He bent to kiss her, but Catherine quickly ducked under his arm to make her escape. He caught her wrist in a viselike grip and pulled her slowly into his arms. He held her head firmly with one hand and tilted it back so that she was forced to look into his eyes.

"Catherine," he drawled, "you have only yourself to blame for what happens next."

He bent his face close to hers, and Catherine lashed out with all her might, but he was prepared for her resistance and tightened his arms around her with such violence that the breath was knocked out of her. She was overcome by a feeling of helplessness and sagged against him for support.

With unhurried deliberation, he brushed her eyes and mouth with his lips, and when she felt his hot breath on her breast through the thin fabric of her gown, Catherine protested weakly. One hand slid down her back to pull her thighs hard against his loins.

"No!" moaned Catherine against his mouth. "Let me go," but his answer was to close his mouth over hers until she could scarcely breathe. A tide of emotion that she had never before experienced surged through her and she felt her will yield to his. His tongue probed insistently against her lips, demanding entry to the softness of her mouth. She could deny him nothing, and opened her lips to receive him, and she trembled in anticipation. She was dimly aware that she was surrendering to the sheer power of him, and she felt her body melt against his.

Rutherston lifted his head and Catherine looked up to see him regarding her intently. She heard his breath quicken, and a groan broke from his lips.

Suddenly Catherine felt herself crushed savagely to him in a bruising embrace. His hands slid to her back, and she felt the urgency in his fingers as he deftly undid the buttons of her gown. Then his warm hands were caressing her naked breasts and moving under her gown to explore her body. She gasped in fright and would have pulled back, but he held her firmly and soothed her fears, his soft voice murmuring unintelligibly against her ear. She felt the heat of his passion penetrate her every pore, arousing her to a fervor to match his own, and her hands slid under his coat to return his caresses.

"Catherine," he said thickly against her hair, "let me take you to my room." One arm slipped around her shoulders and he made to pull her toward the door, but something inside her resisted. She froze, her eyes dilating in fear. She looked up to see him watching her, the desire naked in his darkening eyes.

It came to her then that Rutherston had planned from the beginning to seduce her. She felt dizzy with nausea, knowing that he had done this to her deliberately. Gathering her reeling senses together, she wrenched violently away with all her strength and stood, shoulders heaving, trying to control her breath.

"Catherine." He reached for her, his voice thick with emotion.

She took a step backwards, and what he saw in her face halted him.

"You plotted this," she hissed between clenched teeth. "Didn't you?" She could not stop the catch in her throat. "You knew I would come thinking you were not here!"

Her voice broke, and Rutherston reached for her again.

"Don't touch me!" Her voice betrayed all the desperation she felt, and Rutherston's hands dropped to his sides.

"Catherine, listen to me, I beg you."

"I see it all now!" She was livid with anger, and hardly paused for breath.

"I should thank you for teaching me a salutary lesson. In my ignorance, my blindness, I had supposed that you and I were becoming friends. I see now that the easiness with which I allowed you to converse with me was, in your eyes, a mark of my impropriety, or worse—depravity." She despised herself for the quaver in her voice and the obvious trembling in her limbs.

"Catherine, you don't understand. If you would only calm yourself and give me time to explain! It is not as you think!" He longed to take her into his arms again, to soothe her, but her whole demeanor warned him not to make the attempt.

Catherine went on as if he had not spoken.

"I should thank you, my lord, for teaching me something about myself." At this point she hesitated, but gathered herself as if to take a fence. "I have discovered a new side to my nature of which I have been in ignorance till now! That I have it in me to conduct myself like a . . ." she cast around in her mind for the worst word that she could think of, "a whore, is more than I can comprehend. It is an unpalatable truth which fills me with shame! But you wanted me to discover that truth, didn't you, my lord? Didn't you?" Her voice rose in her agitation.

"Catherine, please don't say these things. You must know they are not true." He saw that there was no placating her.

"Love!" She almost choked on the word. "How well you led me on, my lord! Passion! The glory of men and a stumbling block to every woman of delicacy!" Her voice shook with scorn. "I should have paid more attention to my Greek lessons, then *eros* might never have taken me by storm!"

It was all he could do not to smile, and with a great effort of will he managed to keep his face grave.

"Catherine!" He put out his hand in an appeal. "Let us forget what has happened here and begin again."

"You wanted to punish me, to disgrace me in my own eyes! Well, you have succeeded, my lord, better than you know!" Her voice broke on a sob and she turned to run, but at the door she looked back at him, her eyes brimming with tears.

"I hope that I shall never see you again," and she wrenched the door open and was gone.

But she returned almost immediately, clutching the bodice of her gown. She advanced upon him, her eyes downcast and her cheeks flaming furiously.

"Mrs. Bates . . . I cannot . . . the buttons," she finished lamely as she turned to present her back to him.

Rutherston's eyes gleamed with laughter, but his lips remained firmly pressed together as he now lightly did up the gaping gown and Catherine adjusted her bodice.

"Thank you," she said at last without turning, and with her head held high, she stalked out of the room. When she had again closed the door upon him, Rutherston was moved to speak.

"Not at all, Miss Harland. But I do not believe that the pleasure was all mine." And he remained for a few minutes longer looking thoughtfully at the closed door. It was the first tongue-lashing that Lord Rutherston had ever received from a woman in his life, and the experience had not been in the least objectionable. Quite the reverse.

Chapter 7

In the following week, Rutherston discovered that he could not put Catherine out of his thoughts. She was an innocent, and he had all but seduced her.

What had been begun in a spirit of revenge had soon become, for him, a sport, a mere flirtation. He had not meant it to go so far. He had meant only to pierce her bravado and impress upon her that she could not fence with him and come off unscathed. But when he had felt her surrender so readily to his advances, her warm body clinging to his, passion had flared to a red-hot heat, and his one thought had been to possess her and damn the consequences.

When he had soothed her in his arms as she had resisted his lovemaking, he had murmured that he would marry her on the morrow if she wished it, and he had meant it. Did she know that she could have held him to it, or hadn't she heard, or cared, or what? He was forced to conclude that Catherine had discounted every word that he'd uttered. She had taken his measure as a gentleman and had found him wanting. The thought was not palatable to one who held himself in such high esteem.

He considered just what it was that drew him to her. He enjoyed her lively discourse, although they never seemed to agree on a single subject. She spoke her mind forthrightly and never gave the least sign that she was overawed by his superior rank, or knowledge, or prowess in any field. Nor did she go out of her way to court his favor—quite the reverse. If he had shown half as much attention to any of the debs at Almack's as he had shown to Catherine, they would be setting their caps at him, he knew. But Catherine seemed to be ignorant of the honor he had done her in singling her out.

He determined that when next he saw her he would begin by apologizing for his ungentlemanly behavior. What he would say after that would depend on Catherine's response. Somehow he must find the words to soothe her ruffled feathers, but he did not think she would be in humor to hear what he intended for their future. That declaration required a calmer, more receptive Catherine.

But for the rest of that week, Catherine proved to be elusive. She was not to be found in any of the places where Rutherston might have expected, in the normal course of events, to have met her, and he was annoyed to find himself expending so much time in useless occupations that now held no pleasure for him, and consuming so many bland dinners, when his own French chef was ensconced at Branley Park eager to tempt his appetite.

It was with studied nonchalance that he remarked to his cousin, Mr. Norton, over breakfast one morning that he hoped all went well with Miss Harland, since she had not graced any of the Breckenridge assemblies for a full se'ennight. Mr. Norton gave Rutherston his full attention.

"Which Miss Harland?" he demanded.

"Miss Catherine Harland, of course," snapped Rutherston impatiently, thinking his cousin a fool.

"Ah, I see," said Norton knowingly. "Then I have found you out, cos, since you failed to notice that *neither* of the Misses Harland has been in company of late."

Rutherston was nonplussed, and instinctively assumed his most aloof manner.

"You can come down out of your high ropes," Norton went on, not in the least put out, "and take that devilish look off your face. I am quite willing to tell you why Catherine and Lucy are keeping to Ardo House. Tom tells me they have company, the eldest girl, Lady Mary, and since the girls are leaving next week for town, they want to spend as much time with their sister as possible."

"Then why didn't you say so in the first place?" asked Rutherston with asperity.

"Because I don't believe that that's the real reason Catherine is absenting herself."

"Oh? Pray continue. What do you think, cousin?" There was a forbidding note in Rutherston's voice.

Mr. Norton now became a trifle uneasy, but decided, in all conscience, that he could not keep silent on a matter of such importance.

"I think that Catherine is grasping at this excuse so's her mama won't get wind of the fact that she's trying to keep out of your way."

"And what makes you think that Catherine—Miss Harland—is keeping out of my way?"

At any other time, Norton would have kept his own counsel. His cousin could be a devil when his temper was roused, and he had often seen him freeze into oblivion lesser mortals who had the audacity to tread on his private domain.

"May I speak freely?" The set of Norton's shoulders, the tilt of his chin, and his penetrating gaze reminded Rutherston so much of a protagonist facing him in a duel that he put his hand up to smother a smile.

"Charles, you always do!"

"Richard, what game are you playing with Catherine?

From the day we have arrived, I have been aware of something going on between you two. You're so much more experienced than she is; it would be unfair to take advantage of her—to flirt with her and then discard her. She's a green girl and not up to snuff. I wish you would let her be. Just what are your intentions toward Catherine, anyway?"

Far from being angered by this speech, Rutherston was rather touched that this young cub, whom he held in so much affection, should take it upon himself to be Catherine's protector and beard the lion in his den.

"You may rest easy about my intentions, Charles," he replied, all haughtiness gone. "Any intentions I may have in that direction will be entirely honorable. I give you my word."

All strain left Norton's face.

"Well then, cos, if that's the case, I can tell you now that we have been invited to dine at Ardo House tomorrow." He smiled broadly.

"Invited to dine? And when did we receive this invitation?

"Only last night, from Tom. I told him that, of course, I should be delighted, but due to unforeseen circumstances you were unable to accept. Naturally, Tom is too much the gentleman to question the goings on of so high and mighty a lord as a marquis."

In mock anger, Rutherston picked up his napkin and threw it at his cousin.

"I was only funning, cos." Norton ducked, his face alight with merriment. "I took it upon myself to accept for both of us. I thought this was one invitation you wouldn't refuse."

And with amicable relations entirely restored between the cousins, Rutherston set his mind to rehearsing what he should say to Catherine on the morrow.

* * *

It was in such a frame of mind that Rutherston arrived at Ardo House on the Friday afternoon, three days before Catherine was due to leave for town. He caught a glimpse of her in the garden as he dismounted and threw his reins to a waiting groom.

"You go in, Charles," he said and nodded to Norton. "There is something I must do."

Norton glanced in the direction of Rutherston's gaze, and jumping down from his mount, made as if to go with him.

"No, go in, Charles, I won't be long." The note of authority in Rutherston's voice halted Norton who remained undecided for a moment before moving toward the house.

When Rutherston came upon Catherine, he saw that she was not alone. She was walking with a lady who was quite obviously pregnant. An infant clung to Catherine's skirts, and in her arms was a robust baby, pulling at her hair and tugging at her chin. As he approached, he heard her mellow laughter, and saw the lady, whom he presumed to be Catherine's sister, bend to say something in her ear, and Catherine turned to face him.

He looked at her as if seeing her for the first time. She had never seemed more beautiful or desirable to him as she did at that moment and a wave of tenderness swept over him. He wanted to see her with children in her arms—but the children of his body. He wanted her to be like her sister, with belly swollen with child, but with his seed. He thought of the women who had tried to entrap him with their feminine allures and wondered at so simple a snare as a girl inclining her head to disengage her hair from the clutches of an infant.

His mistresses he had always flaunted as if they had been prime cattle, but Catherine he wanted to cherish as his own private possession. He would never allow her now to belong to anyone but him.

The embarrassment that Catherine evinced on seeing Rutherston was plain for anyone to see. She could only stammer disjointed introductions to Lady Mary before turning away in confusion. Lady Mary was at a loss to see her sister so obviously distressed, and looked with wonder at Rutherston.

"Lady Mary, may I beg your indulgence? I should like a few words in private with Cath . . . Miss Harland." His note of appeal was unmistakable.

"No! Pray do not . . ." Catherine looked in dismay from one to the other.

"Please, Catherine. I shall only keep you a few minutes."

Lady Mary held out her hand to the child. "Come, Jeremy. We shall go in and see Grandmama." In a few moments she had disengaged the children from Catherine's clasp, smiled encouragingly at her sister, and moved off in the direction of the house.

"Catherine, walk with me." He held out his arm, but she would not touch him. He turned to lead her to a nearby bench and, indicating that she should sit, settled himself beside her on the farthest reach of the seat.

"You must hear me out, Catherine. I promise I shall try not to distress you." He waited for some response, but Catherine was gazing at the ground as if her life depended on it.

"I cannot let you think that your conduct was at fault. I blame myself for losing control of the situation. You have my word that I never intended to insult you."

Rutherston waited, hopeful of some sign from Catherine that his words were having a conciliatory effect, but since she continued to gaze steadfastly away and maintained her stony silence, he began again.

"I beg your pardon, Catherine. My intention was not, as you think, to harm you. If anything had happened, you must see that I would be honor bound to offer for you?"

Catherine remained mute.

"The prospect is not unwelcome to me." He paused, watching her guardedly, but the set of her brows and chin deterred him from pursuing his suit.

"I beg your forgiveness! I should never have contrived to place a lady in such a compromising position. I was completely at fault. Catherine, please believe me when I say that I truly admire you."

Catherine was in no position to know that the apology that she had just received from the Marquis of Rutherston was, by his standards, a handsome one. His last few words brought an angry sparkle to her eyes and a quick retort to her tongue. She looked at him now in outrage.

"You admire me, my lord? Yes, I am sure of it! You say you are sorry to have placed a lady in such a compromising position—but you never mistook me for a lady, did you, my lord? No! The things you most truly admire about me are those things which convince you that I am, in truth, no lady."

In spite of himself, Rutherston laughed aloud, and Catherine, stung to the quick, leaped to her feet.

In a moment, he had grasped her by the wrist and held her.

"Catherine," he said in exasperation. "You must calm yourself. You cannot go on like this whenever you find yourself in my company. Do you want to have the suspicions of the whole world roused against us? I have tried to make amends. What more can I say?"

"There is nothing you can say, my lord, which is of the

least interest to me. I have only to be in your company this one last time, then I need never set eyes on you again."

Rutherston rose and stood facing her, his grip tightening on her wrist.

"You are mistaken, ma'am. You will find yourself often in my company. Let me advise you, if you do not wish to become the latest on-dit of the gossipmongers, that when you find yourself with me, you conduct yourself with propriety and civility."

His tone was so stern, so haughty, so much that of the aristocrat, that Catherine quailed.

He released her wrist and held out his arm. "Take my arm, Catherine, and allow me to escort you to your sister."

It was impossible to refuse without creating a scene, and Catherine had no wish to provoke the marquis to further anger. She wondered what he had meant when he said that she would find herself often in his company, but could not bring herself to ask him.

She was quick to see that he was right when he said that she would rouse the suspicions of the whole world against them, for she was conscious of the watching eyes of Mr. Norton and Lady Mary whenever Rutherston was in the least proximity to her, and she forced herself to smile at him and converse easily on any topic of conversation he introduced. He made no effort to say anything to her of a private nature, and on taking his leave observed that he looked forward to meeting both the Misses Harland when he should return to town.

Chapter 8

Catherine and Lucy arrived in London in the middle of March when the Season was just underway. Their aunt, Lady Margaret Henderly, had her dwelling in Mount Street, an imposing terrace of townhouses built in the popular neoclassical style and situated in that small select area where most of the leading families of Society resided when in town. The Harlands, although country born and bred, were no strangers to the big city, since Ardo House was within seventy miles—a matter of an overnight stop when traveling sedately by private coach. The Misses Harland therefore, had had occasion to be in London from time to time and to have a nodding acquaintance with town manners and ways. But the family outings and small select gatherings that they had attended as schoolroom misses were not to be compared to the succession of balls, parties, and entertainments that they would soon enjoy and that were the means of launching all hopeful debutantes into High Society.

Lady Margaret was related to Catherine's father through her first marriage, and had been a widow for a number of years until her present marriage to Sir John. That gentleman was not expected in London for some time, for he was engaged in negotiations on behalf of his country of a most delicate nature, and Lady Margaret supposed him to be in Lisbon, although she vowed she could never be sure of his whereabouts, for a diplomat's life was erratic and entirely at the disposal of His Majesty's government.

In point of fact, Lady Margaret was a connection rather than a relative, and the title of "aunt" was merely a courtesy. It had been a matter of deep regret to Lady Margaret that she had been childless, but not one to pine for the impossible, she had taken an interest in the various offspring of her many relations and in particular in the Harland family, since she saw that she was in a position to be of use to a branch of the family that was fast finding itself on the periphery of society life.

Catherine's father, as a younger son of a younger son, although comfortably situated, was not by inclination or fortune in the position to keep a house in town or spend the time necessary in cultivating those acquaintances who were so placed as to open the doors of Polite Society to his daughters. Lady Margaret, however, was so placed, and pleased to be of service. Moreover, she was looking forward to the prospect of the Harland girls' company and the new diversion they would bring in shopping expeditions and an increase in entertainments.

But it would be wrong to suppose that Lady Margaret was motivated primarily by her own inclination or a desire for her own pleasure. She was very sensible of her duty to her late husband's family and wished to see the Harland girls creditably established in prudent matches. Her circle of friends and acquaintances was such that she saw no reason why this should not be accomplished in short order—as indeed had been done with the eldest Miss Harland some four years before—and she set about planning her strategy as might any general overseeing a campaign.

So it was, in the first weeks of their stay, that Catherine

and Lucy found themselves, chaperoned by their aunt, making calls on various homes in adjoining streets to make themselves known to the young ladies and their mamas who had it in their power to ease their way into Society.

"For you may depend on it," said Lady Margaret with worldly wisdom, "that it is the ladies who decide who will be received and who will be cut. A young gentleman, be he ever so eager, cannot invite a female into his mama's drawing room if that young lady has given offense, and many a girl," continued Lady Margaret, relishing her role as tutor, "has ruined her chances by flirting with the young men while ignoring the civilities due their female relations."

Catherine and Lucy had no wish to offend the young ladies or their mamas and they exerted themselves to be as charming as they could, and found that they were enjoying themselves enormously. Their circle of friends increased rapidly, and before many days had passed, they could not drive in the park, or enter a shop, or walk down Bond Street, but they were certain to run into one of the young ladies whose acquaintances they had so recently made. And if, as it sometimes happened, a brother or gentleman were introduced to the Misses Harland and they conversed somewhat shyly, not pushing themselves forward in any way, to the eyes of the watching mamas it only proved that the Harland girls knew how to behave and that they need have no fears in promoting their society to their daughters and sons.

Lady Margaret, so it seemed to Catherine, knew everything about everyone. She kept up a running commentary on all their acquaintances. They learned that one might be only a plain Mr. or Miss, yet be related to half the great houses of England and be better endowed financially, and that the holding of a title, in itself, was not considered enough inducement to open the doors to more discriminating homes if there was anything lacking in propriety.

Catherine and Lucy absorbed it all as if learning their lessons in the schoolroom, for there was much that they needed to know before being fully launched. How much more improper did Catherine's conduct with Lord Rutherston now seem to her than it had before, and she wondered what these sedate mamas would think if they knew that she had almost succumbed to his seduction. She became aware that the qualities that Rutherston so much admired in her were the ones that she must now take the greatest pains to conceal from the watching world.

A few weeks in London had made a remarkable difference to Catherine and Lucy. They no longer felt so countrified as they had at first, since they were now in possession of the extensive wardrobes for which they had been fitted a month before. They had come up to town, accompanied by their mama, for the sole purpose of choosing the silks, muslins, and fine cambrics that were to be fashioned into the numerous gowns that every young lady of quality required to be successfully launched into her first Season. The expenses were prodigious, but not unexpected, and the funds for the occasion had been carefully set aside for many years.

In the normal course of events, Catherine would have had her come-out before her younger sister, but Lady Mary's pregnancies, always resulting in confinement at an inopportune moment, had delayed it for two years. At the same time, Catherine and Lucy were more than pleased that they should have each other for company in town, since they found Lady Margaret's manner rather daunting, much as they appreciated all her endeavors on their behalf.

* * *

Catherine was sitting by a window, idly reading a morning paper, impatiently waiting for Lucy to dress so that they might walk to Hookam's Circulating Library in Bond Street, when her ladyship's butler announced Mr. Charles Norton.

"Charles!" She greeted him as if he had been a long-lost friend, then, aware that she had inadvertently used his first name, colored, and began again. "I do beg your pardon, Mr. Norton. How glad I am to see you."

"No, no, Catherine, I believe that we are better friends than that! I am glad to think that the formalities can be dispensed with between us two. Let it be Catherine and Charles!" He looked at her with admiration. "I can hardly believe that the young lady of fashion before me now is the Catherine that I knew three weeks ago in Breckenridge."

"Oh, Charles, you will not know me at all, for besides the fine clothes, I must warn you that I am become a lady of great propriety and decorum."

He feigned dismay. "Do not say so, Catherine! I will not believe that the irrepressible Miss Harland has been persuaded to adopt the ways of the ton!"

"Charles, you must be careful not to tease me in your usual fashion when others are present, for if you do, my character will be ruined!"

"Then you must return to Ardo House before all is discovered!"

This easy address and playful manner were exactly suited to Catherine's mood. She realized with a pang how much she missed the raillery and teasing that were so much a part of a brother's converse with a sister and that had drawn in his friend.

"I must inform my aunt and Lucy that you are here for I know that they will both wish to see you. But do strive for a little propriety!"

She returned in a moment with Lucy in tow and rang for refreshments, since Norton seemed in no hurry to take his leave of them.

"Do you plan to stay long in town?"

"Oh, I think for most of the Season. My cousin has some unfinished business that needs his attention before we drive down to Fotherville House." Catherine looked at him keenly, but his gaze was so bland that her mind was soon put to rest.

"Are you always so obliging, Charles?"

"Obliging?" He looked baffled.

"I was merely observing that your cousin is uncommonly fortunate in having a friend who is so willing to subordinate his own wishes to fall in with whatever he desires!"

"Oh, it's nothing like that, Catherine. Rutherston is a good fellow—and capital company. He'd as soon fall in with my wishes, if it came to the push." She looked doubtful, and he protested, "He would!"

"I'm sure that you are right, Mr. Norton," said Lucy, giving her sister a forbidding look. "Lord Rutherston has always shown himself most obliging to all his acquaintances." She looked at her sister for confirmation.

"Oh, quite." But the disbelieving tone in Catherine's voice did not deceive Norton.

"He will be glad to hear you say so, Miss Lucy." Then, with a gleam of mischief in his eyes, "Not all his, er, acquaintances would agree with you, but he can be devilish agreeable to anyone he wants to charm."

Catherine was stunned. She wondered if Mr. Norton were giving her a warning.

"Shall we see anything of Lord Rutherston? Perhaps his business will occupy most of his attention when he's in town?" Lucy's question was uttered out of politeness, but Catherine's ears pricked to hear the answer, and she despised herself for it.

"Not see the Misses Harland? Miss Lucy, what a poor opinion you have of my cousin! However pressing his business, I'm sure that he will always find time to renew the acquaintance of those who made his stay in Breckenridge so agreeable." He was looking at Lucy, but Catherine was sure that the message was for her and she felt puzzled and confused.

The door opened and Lady Margaret entered. She noted with approval that her nieces were both in attendance to receive a gentleman caller, for country-bred girls sometimes forgot the stricter etiquette of the ton. That austere lady was soon won over by Mr. Norton's engaging manners and in a little time had discovered that he was residing at his cousin's house in Berkeley Square. Her astonishment on learning that Lord Rutherston was also acquainted with her nieces knew no bounds, and she visibly warmed toward Mr. Norton.

"I had hoped, ma'am," he said, "that I might take the Misses Harland in my cousin's curricle for a spin in the park this afternoon, if you have no objections."

What her ladyship's answer might have been if Mr. Norton had not disclosed his relationship to the Marquis of Rutherston, Catherine was not to know. Lady Margaret answered graciously that she had neither objections nor fears, since she was sure that if the marquis trusted his horses to him then she was certain he knew how to handle so unsteady a means of transportation as a curricle, and Catherine and Lucy were engaged to go riding in the park with Mr. Norton at the fashionable hour of five o'clock that afternoon.

* * *

It was a warm spring day, and it seemed to Catherine that half of fashionable London had joined them in Hyde Park. Carriages of every description crowded the drives, and so congested was the traffic that Norton held the grays to a slow trot. The Misses Harland were having a grand time nodding to all their acquaintances, occasionally stopping to exchange a word or two, and from time to time Catherine surreptitiously peeped from behind her open parasol to glance at certain ladies whose loud behavior and gaudy costumes proclaimed them to be the Fashionable Impures.

As one of the carriages going in the opposite direction pulled up beside them, Catherine had the pleasure of introducing Mr. Norton to Mr. John Ranstoke and his sister Emily, whom she considered a particular friend. They were engaged in only a few moments' conversation when Miss Ranstoke, looking past them, exclaimed, "Isn't that your cousin, Mr. Norton, in the phaeton with the splendid bays?"

Mr. Norton turned in his seat to look back in the direction of her gaze and his face froze. Catherine looked quickly over her shoulder to see what had caused the stunned alarm on Norton's face. Seated in the phaeton was Rutherston, with the most dazzling woman that Catherine had ever seen. She was laughing into Rutherston's face, one gloved hand resting lightly on his sleeve, and her mode of dress was such that Catherine, in her new bonnet and pelisse, felt like a dowd. As the phaeton came abreast of the curricle, Catherine was sure that Rutherston had recognized them, but he turned his back toward them, shielding his companion from their interested gaze. She turned back to her friends and was struck by their utter confusion. Mr. Ranstoke was intent on removing a speck from his lapel, Miss Ranstoke and Lucy were covered in blushes, and when she looked into Mr. Norton's face she found him gazing at her with the oddest expression which she could not read.

"I was mistaken," Miss Ranstoke managed at last, not daring to look anyone in the eye. Catherine opened her mouth to contradict her friend, but felt herself pinched by Lucy and fell silent. She was at a loss to know what it might all mean.

It was Mr. Ranstoke who finally retrieved the situation by asking the Misses Harland if they planned to attend Lady Castlereagh's ball the next night. This welcome change of subject helped ease the embarrassment that everyone, except Catherine, seemed to be feeling and after some desultory conversation on the coming entertainments of the Season, they parted company. Before long Catherine and Lucy returned to Mount Street.

It was the practice of the two sisters, before retiring to bed each night, to closet themselves in their adjoining dressing room to talk over the day's events, and tonight Catherine found herself particularly impatient to be rid of their maid so that she could talk privately to Lucy.

"Lucy," she began when Becky had taken herself off, "I know that was Rutherston we saw in the park today. Why did Miss Ranstoke deny it, and why was Charles so put out? Surely there is nothing uncommon in a gentleman riding in the park with a lady? Can you explain why everyone looked as if Emily had committed some dreadful solecism, or are you as ignorant as I?"

Lucy, who had wished to avoid this topic, but without much hope, now began with some hesitation.

"You remember, Catherine, what Mama told us the

night before we left Ardo House, when we sat with her in her dressing room?"

Catherine cast her mind back to the night in question, but had only a vague recollection of admonitions and threats of the doom that might befall a girl who was so unwary as to forget that she had been raised a lady.

"I miss your meaning, Lucy. What has that to do with anything?"

Lucy sighed. Catherine was her elder by two years, so much more confident and more intelligent, but in many ways, less worldly.

"Dearest," she said, knowing that thc blow could not be softened, "I believe the lady in Lord Rutherston's carriage was what Mama would call 'a fallen woman.'"

Catherine digested this piece of information for a long moment.

"Are you saying that she is his mistress? But that can't be right! She was beautiful, so elegant, so . . . ladylike!" Catherine's voice rose in astonished incredulity. She waited for Lucy's denial, but it did not come.

"His mistress!" She spat the words out. "And he had the effrontery to bring her to a public place for the whole world to see? The man is a scoundrel, worse than a scoundrel, a knave, a shameless debaucher of women— a devil." She was helpless to stop the tears brimming over and wiped them angrily away with the back of her hand. Lucy took Catherine's hands in hers, having a fair idea of how things stood with her sister.

"Catherine, it is the way of the world. Mama told us so. Men and women are not the same in this respect. The love and affection that a man feels for his wife is different from the love that he feels for . . . these other women," she finished lamely.

"Fustian!" The word was out of Catherine's mouth before she had time to think.

"Oh Lucy, I didn't mean to scold. Forgive me. But I don't accept what Mama says or what the world thinks. Women have been taught to believe that nonsense. It isn't so! Oh Lucy," she went on despairingly, "I think that I shall never marry, for I yearn to give more than mere affection, and I fear that a man's affection will never be enough for me."

Lucy's face showed all the alarm that she felt at her sister's confession, and Catherine hastened to reassure her. She forced her voice to a lightness that she did not feel.

"I daresay I shall get over it. A woman always has her home and her children, and these pleasures must surely make up for any want in a husband's regard. I know that our sister Mary believes herself to be the luckiest woman alive, and if I am half as happy I shall count myself very fortunate indeed."

She rose and kissed Lucy affectionately. "Don't worry about me, little sister. Perhaps I shall meet my knight in shining armor at tomorrow's ball. And if I behave myself and mind my tongue, perhaps he will carry me off and we shall live happily ever after."

Chapter 9

The following evening saw Catherine in her room preparing for Lady Castlereagh's ball. Acting as lady's maid was Becky, who had accompanied them from Ardo House. Becky was a maid of all trades, being accustomed at home to turn her hand to many occupations. She could adequately fulfill the duties of cook's help, children's nurse, and now, to her great delight, lady's abigail in a grand house in town. The Harlands, like most country gentry of comfortable means, put their money for servants' wages where it was most needed—the stables. Mrs. Harland might often have thought that the comforts of Ardo House could be improved with an extra maid or two, but it would never have occurred to her that Mr. Harland should deprive himself of one stablehand or groom to ease her household responsibilities. Her maids were versatile to a degree. His retainers were specialists to a man.

Becky was a robust, no-nonsense woman of three and thirty who had been in the Harlands' employ since she was a chit of fourteen years. When the Harland girls were merely children, it appeared that their mother would lose "her treasure," for Becky became betrothed to a young footman on the Branley estate. But tragedy had struck when her young man, impatient for fortune and adventure, had sailed with Nelson to drive the French from Britannia's shores.

He had never returned, and word was brought to Becky that her James had lost his life at some faraway place named Aboukir Bay. From that time on, she had devoted herself to the Harlands and had gently but firmly depressed the romantic attentions of any swain who thought to see himself in the role of suitor.

On the afternoon of the ball in question, Becky had taken the greatest pains in preparing a soothing concoction that was to be used to smooth the ladies' complexions so that they might appear at their radiant best. She would have preferred to have used fresh strawberries as a base, but since these were not in season, had substituted a cup of fine-rolled oatmeal that she had taken from a stone crock conveyed all the way from Ardo House. She added milk, honey, and a drop of oil of roses to make a thick consistency. Her ladyship's personal abigail, Agnes, watched in growing wonder, for it was evident to her that Becky's store of country remedies placed her far above the common run of domestic servants. Becky shyly disclosed that most of her recipes had been handed down from her grandmother, a lady who had lived in the wilds of Scotland.

Until that moment, Becky had found herself relegated to the lowest rung on the domestic ladder, at the beck and call of every other maid and manservant in her ladyship's household. Henceforth she climbed rapidly to a respectable position, since she was found to possess an unrivaled knowledge of those herbs and substances which, when applied externally or taken internally, could gratify the most demanding wishes of fashionable ladies for an improvement in beauty.

The Misses Harland were persuaded on the afternoon of the ball to submit to Becky's ministrations as an in-

terested Agnes looked on. Their faces were smeared with
porridge to soften the complexion; they were induced to
sip spiced tea to sweeten the breath; they were made to
dash herbal water in their eyes to cool and refresh; they
were bathed, scrubbed, pummeled and anointed until they
were finally permitted to take their rest. In the early
evening they were wakened and allowed to take a mild
beef tea. It was Agnes who now took charge, instructing
Becky in the fine art of dressing a lady's hair. She
wielded scissors and tongs with precision till the hair
curled just as she willed it. With fine-toothed comb, she
teased diminutive ringlets to lie demurely upon the brow,
and for the finishing touches, she adorned her creations
with silk ribbons and fresh flowers. Both mistresses and
maids owned that the results were highly rewarding.

Catherine had a particular reason for wishing to look
her best that evening, for Norton had intimated that
Rutherston would be at the ball, and she intended that
he should recognize how much he had lost by his insulting behavior.

But as she surveyed herself in the looking glass before
the carriage arrived to convey them to St. James Square,
she realized that her wish was bound to be in vain. Her
new gown of ivory silk over pale peach chemise, fastened
under the bosom with matching peach ribbons, made her
appear as pretty as she was ever likely to be, but all the
ministrations of Becky and Agnes could not make her a
diamond of the first water. Nor was the fine ivory lace
that modestly covered the depression between her breasts
at all in the style of the lovely creature who had hung on
Rutherston's arm. What Catherine did not realize, since
familiarity had dulled her appreciation, was that the mellow autumn tints of her hair and complexion gave her that
distinction that turns a pretty woman into a Beauty.

She drew on her long white gloves and picked up her reticule, determined to put Rutherston out of her mind. This was her first London ball and there was many a young gentleman who would be pleased to have the pretty and charming Catherine Harland hang on his sleeve.

As they entered the ballroom to the sounds of the orchestra, Lady Margaret settled herself comfortably beside the other dowagers and waved her nieces away telling them that they should make themselves known to their many acquaintances and find their own entertainment. On this advice, Catherine and Lucy turned back to survey the room. The music had stopped, and Catherine looked with open-mouthed appreciation at the splendor before her. It was the gentlemen who held her attention. Beautiful women she had expected to see, but not the fops and dandies who strutted like peacocks from group to group, wearing their fine plumage as if they had been birds of paradise, with more jewels at their throats than the ladies they escorted. She became aware that one of the dandies, whom she had been gazing at unabashed, had raised his quizzing glass to return her stare. She inclined her head gravely in a polite bow and turned away lest her mirth be detected. Her eyes, sparkling with merriment, sought her sister, who had moved slightly apart to converse with two gentlemen, and as one of them broke away, Catherine found herself looking into the appraising gaze of the Marquis of Rutherston. He came to her side instantly and raised her gloved hand to his lips.

Catherine had tried to prepare herself to meet this moment with equanimity, but when she looked into Rutherston's eyes, her heart turned over. It irritated her beyond measure to think that she had fallen in love with a man of his low morals, but she composed herself to speak and behave with a modicum of courtesy.

"Catherine!" His voice was vibrant with pleasure. "How pleased I am to see you. I would talk with you away from this crush. Will you walk with me?"

Catherine laid her hand upon the proffered arm and allowed herself to be led through the doors to the spacious corridor where several couples were promenading.

"How beautiful you are." His gaze lingered on every part of her person. "I have never seen you look so lovely." The smile he gave her was the one he reserved to melt the hardest of female hearts. Catherine returned a wintry smile.

"Naturally, my lord," she responded dryly. "How could it be otherwise. But it is Madame Celeste who deserves your compliment. It is one of her creations I am wearing." She would make him see that she was impervious to his charm.

"So modest, Miss Harland?"

"So insincere, Lord Rutherston?"

Rutherston was charmed. "Are we embarking on another contest?" he asked quizzically.

"No! We are mismatched, my lord," she snapped shrewishly, then, conscious of her momentary slip and the interested gaze of a number of spectators nearby, she softened her words with her best disarming smile. "We play by different rules. There is no sport in that."

"Indeed? I think that we make a perfect matching." He gave her a speaking look. "And I am prepared to play by your rules." He bowed to some passing acquaintances, then turned to survey her, a small smile of complacency flickering at the corner of his mouth. Catherine noted it sourly and had the strongest desire to wipe the smirk from his face.

"The only contest I am prepared to enter with you, my lord, is with dueling pistols at ten paces." She noted with satisfaction that the smile had vanished from Rutherston's face, to be replaced by a glowering frown.

"And would your honor be satisfied then, Catherine? In any event, you must know, I could never harm you."

"Such chivalry, my lord? I can scarcely believe it in you. But I should not be as obliging as you."

"And am I never to be forgiven?" he demanded testily, stopping in his tracks to face her.

"Do you want to rouse the suspicions of the whole world against us?" she hissed at him, routing him with his own words. "Let us walk on, my lord."

"Catherine, my name is Richard."

"And my name, my lord, is Miss Harland."

"I see! Then I am not forgiven?"

"My memory is at fault. You must tell me what it is I have to forgive."

Rutherston saw his chance of disabusing the overconfident young woman at his side of the notion that she could outmatch him in a game of wits.

"It would give me the greatest pleasure, Miss Harland, to recall every moment of that encounter. Are you sure you wish me to continue? Say the word, and I shall oblige you."

Catherine's false smile masked a snarl. "I know that your chivalry would not be long-lived, sir."

"Richard!" trilled a voice close to Catherine's ear. She felt Rutherston's arm tense imperceptibly beneath her hand, and Catherine looked curiously at the owner of the voice that had caused a ripple in Rutherston's cool exterior. She recognized Lady Harriet, the deb acclaimed as the Incomparable, a nonpareil in beauty who was highly conscious of everything that was owed to her. She had been out for a couple of Seasons and had all the young blades, and not a few of those who should have known better, scurrying for her favors. It was rumored that Lady

Harriet had set her sights high—on nothing less than an earl. A marquis, of course, would be even better.

A pair of hostile eyes raked Catherine from head to toe, and she instantly withdrew her hand from Rutherston's arm as if it had suddenly scalded her. The martial glint in the lady's eyes was not lost on Catherine, nor the proprietary air as Lady Harriet dismissed her with a slight nod of the head before devoting her full attention to Rutherston.

Catherine moved apart to converse with Lady Harriet's escort. She could hear Rutherston's glib tongue begin his extravagant flatteries, and Lady Harriet accepted them as her due. Catherine was disgusted.

It did not take Catherine long to engage the young man's interest, although his lover-like glance was frequently cast in the direction of the golden-haired goddess. Sisterly knowledge of a brother of aspiring Corinthian tastes gave Catherine an advantage, and she soon coaxed Mr. Sinclair to wax eloquently on the merits of Tattersall's, the neckties he favored, and the various sporting vehicles that were all the crack.

It was with something of a start that she heard Rutherston address her and invite her to join in a conversation that the Incomparable had but a few minutes before insinuated was to be a private tête-à-tête.

"Miss Harland, I beg you, rescue me from Lady Harriet's undeserved encomium. She exaggerates my equestrian ability. I have admitted to being fair, and only fair in the saddle. As one who has a more intimate knowledge of my prowess in the field, what say you?"

"Oh la, sir, you dissemble," tittered the beauty hanging on his arm, not at all pleased to have Catherine addressed in such familiar terms. "You are quite without equal, isn't that so, Mr. Sinclair?" she appealed to her erstwhile escort, pointedly excluding Catherine.

Mr. Sinclair was compelled to honesty and declared that it was universally acknowledged that his lordship was a Nonsuch without equal, drove to an inch, and had the honor of being a member of the Four Horse Club—an indisputable distinction.

"Well, Miss Harland? What say you?" demanded Rutherston, the smirk of complacency twitching his lips.

Catherine was conscious that he was enjoying himself hugely at her expense, and a look of devilment fleetingly lit up her face. She turned to Lady Harriet, her eyes rounded in disbelief.

"You wish me to contradict the noble Lord Rutherston? That, Lady Harriet, I cannot do. No, no, you will not dissuade me. It would be beyond my power, beyond my understanding, beyond anything. Besides," she went on sarcastically, "I would never wish to lay the charge of false modesty at Lord Rutherston's door."

Catherine was immensely pleased with herself, thinking that she had delivered a leveler to floor the marquis, but when she looked triumphantly into his face she was chagrined to see that he was grinning at her in the most appreciative way.

"Of course, one would not wish to contradict Lord Rutherston," began the Beauty in some doubt, "but in this case . . ."

"No, no!" intoned Catherine seriously. "It would be an impertinence. We must respect the assessment of so noble a lord."

Rutherston thought it politic to intervene at that moment and he whisked Catherine away with the excuse that he had solicited her hand for the next dance, which was just about to begin.

As he led her to their place in the set he inclined his head and murmured, "May I hold you to that, Miss Harland? It would please me excessively if you would show me even a little respect."

"You are mistaken, my lord," she returned sweetly. "I have the greatest respect for you. Only a fool underestimates an enemy."

Their eyes held, and Catherine could not look away. She thought she had angered him.

"You are wrong, Catherine." His voice was gentle, caressing, coaxing. "I would be your friend, if you will let me, and much more to you than a friend."

Catherine, for once, was speechless.

At the end of the dance, he requested that she introduce him to Lady Margaret and she had no option but to obey. Her aunt was highly gratified, and when Rutherston asked permission to lead Catherine in to supper, Lady Henderly could refuse him nothing.

Catherine was affronted at his confidence that she would so easily fall in with his wishes. Her wishes were never to be consulted!

As she danced away the evening waiting till he should claim her, she observed that he danced every dance, and she never once caught him looking in her direction. She set herself resolutely to forget him and to give her full attention to her partners, but although they were all pleasant young men, she found their conversation flat and predictable.

Then he was standing before her, resplendent in dark coat and beige breeches, the restraint in his dress proclaiming, in Catherine's eyes, the man of good taste.

As he held out his arm to escort her in to supper, Catherine was uncomfortably aware of the intensity of his scrutiny, and she could not bring herself to look into his eyes. She recalled the circumstances in the grounds of Ardo House when she had summarily refused the offer of his arm, and she was deeply embarrassed. She could feel the warmth of his arm under the fabric of his coat, and her hand trembled.

"Do you think I shall take advantage of you in the middle of a crowded ballroom?" he intoned sotto voce in her ear.

"But you have, my lord. You have taken advantage of me at every turn. You and my aunt have, between you, contrived this situation. It was not to me that you applied for this privilege. My wishes are never consulted." She smiled at him archly to sweeten the astringent words.

"And do you mind, Catherine?" His lips were smiling, but Catherine was conscious that the mockery had left his eyes.

"Why should I mind?" she asked playfully. "No doubt my being with one of your consequence has added to my own consequence."

She knew that her answer had not pleased him, for his manner became aloof, and when she tried to retrieve herself by remarking on various inconsequential subjects, he would not be drawn. Catherine wondered how such a mild piece of frivolity as she had uttered should give him so much offense, when her earlier blatant reproofs had formerly afforded him amusement.

His manner and conversation during supper could not be faulted, but she knew that he had set her at a distance, and she was disappointed.

Chapter 10

In the following weeks, Norton became a frequent visitor at Mount Street, and on occasion, he was accompanied by his cousin, Lord Rutherston. Lady Margaret observed them all guardedly, but closely, since she suspected that Norton was developing a tendre for Catherine. When she saw that his manner with Catherine was always easy, however, and that in Lucy's company he became more grave, sometimes falling into a silence altogether, she put that notion out of her head and formed an accurate conclusion.

Nor did it take Lady Margaret long to take the measure of Rutherston. Her suspicions were confirmed when she saw that in company his eye might linger on any lady in the room, excepting her niece, when he felt himself to be observed. She inferred that his lordship was conducting himself with the greatest caution until he should determine Catherine's heart.

Catherine was relieved to find that Rutherston's distant manner with her was of short duration. She knew that he had forgiven her for whatever offense she had given, and she was once again admitted to his confidence and conversations, which she could not help but enjoy. She came to see that it was only with Rutherston that she could be most truly herself. The man actually encouraged her to dispute his opinions. But what Catherine treasured above all was Rutherston's interest in her passion—Greek language and thought. She came to feel that she had one friend with whom she could share what had been, since Mr. Fortescue's death, a solitary and private pastime.

His former conduct at Branley Park she put firmly out of her mind, for if she were to rely too much upon it, she would be forced to cut his acquaintance, and that possibility was not to be borne. For the sake of his friendship, she was willing to grant a man-of-the-world such as he a few lapses, and she accepted that her own want of conduct had encouraged him to gross impropriety. Having settled the matter nicely in her own mind, she nevertheless saw the sense of depressing any hope that Rutherston might entertain of repeating the experience.

It amazed her to think that she had once believed that in London he would move in more exalted circles than she, for he was invariably present at any of the events she and Lucy attended, and made himself as agreeable as she had ever seen him. She discovered that Social Life was so much more enjoyable when he was there to tease and taunt her and share her mirth at some private joke.

Lord Rutherston's displeasure was very evident to his valet, Miles. If the grim set of his lordship's visage was not enough to convince that worthy to speak softly and tread carefully, the growing pile of discarded neckcloths cast disgustedly on the floor told its own story. Miles's face assumed its blandest mask as he helped his lordship dress for the evening's entertainment. He had already taken it upon himself to warn his lordship's butler, George, that an ominous storm was brewing, and that it would be the better part of valor to keep out of his lordship's way until the storm had run its course.

George, then, had passed the word along to his lordship's groom, Simpson, who was preparing to convey his lordship and Mr. Norton to Lady Ashwell's ball. By the time that Rutherston descended the staircase to meet his cousin in the marble-floored foyer, nary a maid, footman or lackey was in evidence—an unusual occurrence—excepting the ubiquitous George. His lordship had never been known to treat that superior retainer with anything but good-humored courtesy, whatever the provocation. George had risen to this enviable position by virtue of his having seen his lordship through many a wild scrape when Rutherston was a mere lad, and shielded him from his gov'nor, the fifth marquis, well known for his short temper and the strength of his unfailing right arm.

Norton stole one quick look at his cousin's grim face and stifled a smile. It was he who had imparted the information, with the greatest tact of course, that Viscount Boxley had made an offer for Catherine and had been refused. His cousin's complacency had suffered a rude shock at the piece of news, a salutary experience for Rutherston, in Norton's opinion.

Rutherston settled himself comfortably against the squabs of his well-sprung carriage, and having exchanged a minimum of pleasantries with his cousin, he set his mind to consider what he should do about Catherine.

In the foregoing weeks, he had tolerantly watched her gather a following of admirers. It had troubled him not one whit, for he was confident that Catherine's heart was his.

He had tried to court her with knightly chivalry, in an effort to allay her maidenly suspicions that he was a predatory male. The thought brought a fleeting smile to his harsh features. It had been an impossible pose to keep up, for he could not be in her company for more than a minute but he was tempted to make her feel the attraction of all that was masculine in him. And he had done it, he knew, but he was not sure that the doing of it had served his best interests.

He had made up his mind that she would be his wife and was determined, if it should come to it, to bring to bear the influence of her family, who would be outraged if Catherine should refuse so brilliant a match. She would be his bride, willingly or unwillingly. Her happiness, no less than his, depended on it.

The problem was that she refused to take him seriously, adroitly parrying his every attempt to fix her interest. She regarded him as a flirt, a rake, or worse, and she used her quick tongue with great effect to deflect his verbal advances. In short, she was keeping him at arm's length, a state of affairs he was no longer prepared to accept.

By the time he had dismissed his coach and entered the flower-decked ballroom, he had made up his mind that Catherine would deflect his advances no longer. It was intolerable to think that someone of Boxley's ilk might snatch her from his grasp.

When he led her in to supper, he found them places in a quiet corner, but all his efforts to converse with her privately were frustrated by the many acquaintances and friends who sat down to idle the time away by talking of trivialities. Rutherston unconsciously began to adopt his most aristocratic demeanor, which had the desired effect of frightening them away. He had just begun to approach the subject of the high regard in which he held her when Norton and Lucy made as if to join them. Rutherston turned his back toward them, effectively shutting them out.

"Do you always do that?" Catherine gazed intently at her plate and selected a choice piece of fruit.

"Do what?"

"What you have just done— exclude from your company anyone whose conversation you don't wish to endure."

"I assure you, it is not a habit with me. Do you object because I want to talk to you alone for a few minutes?"

"Oh, but it is a habit with you!" She carefully examined a grape and popped it into her mouth.

"Explain yourself, Catherine!"

Catherine's hand hovered over the grapes and selected another, which she proceeded to examine as before.

"You did it once in the park. I believe you saw me with Charles and Lucy. You could hardly avoid seeing us, or we you."

The silence that ensued began to unnerve her, and she flexed her fingers to choose another piece of fruit.

"Catherine!" She gazed intently at her plate.

"Look at me!" She met his gaze steadily, and willed herself not to look away.

"I regret what happened that day. I had not meant you to witness . . . What you saw, Catherine, was in the nature of a farewell."

He was waiting for her to say something, but Catherine did not know what to say.

"You owe me no explanations, my lord. Your conduct is not my affair."

"But it is!"

"How can that be? I am not your mama, or your sister." She strove for a teasing tone.

"Will you stop fencing with me, Catherine, and take me seriously just for once? Surely you are not such a green girl that you mistake my meaning? I have told you that what you saw in the park that day was in the nature of a farewell. Does that not tell you something?"

Catherine's eyes twinkled. "That you are prodigiously

lonely, my lord? Oh dear! I beg your pardon. I should not have said that."

"No, you should not," Rutherston replied severely. "But since you seem to favor blunt speech, let me assure you that I have long since set aside my mistress."

"My lord, I wish you would not," answered Catherine, deeply embarrassed at the turn in the conversation. She looked around nervously, fearful that someone might have overheard Rutherston's remarks.

"My dear girl, you are not about to adopt missish airs with me? Not when you have always permitted me to speak to you as freely as I wished? Believe me, Catherine, it is part of your charm."

"Yes, prudence was never one of my virtues," she said musingly. "Perhaps I should have cultivated it more."

"I hope you may—but not with me."

"No, I think it is too late to pretend to you a virtue you know very well I do not possess." Catherine spoke with disarming frankness. "It vexes me greatly, but there it is." She looked into his eyes and caught the gleam of amusement that flickered behind them. Her brows instantly drew together in a frown. "But on the subject of your mistress, Lord Rutherston, I have no wish to be your confidante."

"But what else are friends for?"

"Friends?"

"Of course!"

He could see that his last remark had pierced her defenses.

"My lord . . ."

"Catherine, will you stop this ridiculous address! My name is Richard."

"I know."

"Say it!"

"My lord, I . . ."

"Catherine!" His face and voice were austere, and Catherine felt herself yielding, as she always seemed to do with him.

"Yes, Richard."

The strains of the music reached them from the ballroom. For some reason, Rutherston appeared to be vastly pleased.

"I must take you to your aunt now, but I shall be calling on you one day soon. It is impossible to say anything of a private nature here." He led her to the ballroom and stopped on the threshold, bringing her hand to his lips.

"This seems to be another habit with me. I hope you don't intend to break me of all my habits, Catherine." She felt as if she were being embraced by his smile. Then he turned on his heel and disappeared into the crowd.

She wanted to find a quiet place to set her thoughts in order and made her way to the room where the ladies had left their wraps. She found a chair half hidden by a screen and sat down to compose her mind. What did he mean by saying that his conduct was her affair? Why did he tell her that he had set aside his mistress? Why would he think that she might try to change his habits? And why was he coming to call on her soon?

Into her confused thoughts broke the murmur of low voices.

". . . Rutherston's latest flirt."

"I hear tell that his mama insists that he marry—the House of Fotherville and all that!"

"And I have heard that the fair Marguerite has been bestowing her favors elsewhere."

The laughter, to Catherine's ears, was vulgar.

"There are two positions open then, mistress and wife. Are you tempted to apply, Isabel?"

"If I did, I should choose to be his mistress. He is

known to be uncommonly generous. His poor wife's lot will be to breed every year—an unenviable fate."

The voices drifted away and Catherine saw that her knuckles were white from gripping the arms of her chair.

"Odious women!" she half cried aloud. Did he intend to offer her one of these positions?

By birth and breeding, she was destined to be a respectable wife. But many aristocratic ladies, she had discovered, openly consorted with their lovers. Surely he would not dare offer her that! But Catherine was far from sure.

The position of wife seemed marginally less odious than the position of mistress. His mother insisted that he marry, and the reason was very evident. The Marquis of Rutherston must beget an heir. Catherine made up her mind. There was nothing his lordship could offer that would ever tempt her to accept either position.

The next few days found Catherine in a fever of activity, in the dread that Rutherston might call at Mount Street and put his odious proposals before her. She left the house early every morning after breakfast, confiding to her aunt that she missed the exercise she had enjoyed in the country, and since Becky always accompanied her, Lady Margaret saw no reason to object. She spent her mornings and afternoons wandering in Green Park or in excursions to the shops in Bond Street or the ever popular circulating library, avoiding all the places where there would be the least likelihood of encountering Rutherston. But she was in an agony of suspense lest she should meet him by chance, for it was impossible in such a confined neighborhood not to fall in with some acquaintance or other. She felt her efforts rewarded when she saw his card on the tray in the vestibule table on two successive occasions, but she knew that she could not hope to avoid him altogether.

She came in late one afternoon, avoiding all the public rooms where visitors were received, and made her way to the small green saloon upstairs. There she found Lucy engaged in her embroidery—an item that Catherine had determinedly forgotten to pack when they left Ardo House—and as her sister looked up to smile a welcome, Catherine was struck by a radiance that she had never before noticed.

"Catherine, you have just missed Charles, I mean Mr. Norton, and you'll never guess who was with him!"

"Lord Rutherston."

"No, dear. I think that that gentleman has given up hope of finding you at home."

Catherine ignored this last remark. "Who, then?"

"Our brother! He arrived last night from Ardo House. Papa wants him to purchase some stock for the stables, and he is to be in London for a week or two."

"Tom arrived last night? But I didn't hear him! Where is he?" She stood up to go in search of him.

"He is staying with Lord Rutherston." Lucy picked up her embroidery and bent her head to examine her stitches. "It was arranged before the gentlemen quit Branley Park. Lord Rutherston and Charles—Mr. Norton, are to advise on what to buy. I think Papa was afraid that Tom might be cheated."

"Tom, staying with Rutherston?"

Catherine sat down to ponder this piece of information. She began to feel like a fly caught in a spider's web—a web of Rutherston's making.

"When do we see him?"

Lucy put down her needlework and looked intently at her sister. "Who, dear?"

"I was thinking of our brother!"

"Were you? Then if you mean our brother, we dine with him on Wednesday night. He is invited to the Countess of Levin's as a guest of Lord Rutherston."

"Rutherston will be there?"

"He will, and I shouldn't plead a headache if I were you, Catherine, for he is as like to come to Mount Street to fetch you himself."

Catherine looked at her sister in consternation, but the mischievous smile that she saw on Lucy's lips brought an answering smile to her own.

"Am I so obvious, then?"

"Only to me, dear. But I have been anxious about you of late. No, don't give me that forbidding look. I must speak." She patted the sofa beside her, and Catherine sat down.

"I know that you have a tendre for Lord Rutherston, no don't deny it, or I should keep my counsel to myself."

She took some time to consider what she should say next. "Catherine, do you mean never to marry, because if that is your intention, then by all means go on as you are. But I hope you will have a care for what you are about. If you marry, you will be a man's wife, sharing his bed, bearing his children." Lucy's cheeks flamed scarlet as she said these words, but she did not waver. "Is it not better that the intimate relations which a wife must share with her husband should be of such a kind as to bring her pleasure rather than . . . distaste?"

"Lucy! What do you know about such things?" Catherine was shocked.

"We were talking about you, Catherine!" Lucy's voice wavered. "I . . . have come to understand better what you once tried to tell me, about . . . love."

"You have come to understand better? How?" There was no answer, and Catherine saw that her sister was overcome with confusion. It came to her then. "Charles! It is Charles! Lucy, you are in love with Mr. Norton! How could I not have seen it? Does he return your regard?" She saw that her sister's eyes were filled with unshed tears.

"He has not mentioned the matter to me. How could he? He must marry prudently. A match with me would not find favor with his . . . family."

"Not find favor? I don't believe it. You are the sweetest, kindest, most accomplished girl in the world." Catherine embraced her warmly and had the pleasure of seeing Lucy give a tremulous smile.

"Thank you, dear Catherine, but it will not be for any lack in my character or accomplishments that I shall be passed over. It is in my dowry that the lack lies." Catherine protested, but she was enough of a realist to recognize the truth of Lucy's words. The two sisters sat thoughtfully side by side contemplating the sad vagaries of fate that could rob them of their respective happinesses. Then Lucy rallied.

"But your position is not the same as mine. Catherine, I beg you to consider what you are about. If Charles had Rutherston's fortune, how happy we would be, and I shouldn't care a fig if he had a dozen mistresses!"

These reflections brought on a fresh outburst of tears, and Catherine, soothing her sister by promising not to do anything rash, walked with her arm in arm to their dressing room. They parted with a show of great affection and resolved that whatever the private state of the hearts of the Misses Harland, the world should remain in ignorance of it.

Chapter 11

Catherine was in an agony of indecision. Rutherston's attentions to her brother Tom, the invitation that the Earl and Countess of Levin had extended to include her family, and the court that he was paying her under the interested eye of the ton convinced her that he meant to offer for her in marriage, but she could not make up her mind whether to accept or reject his offer. The thought of sharing him with other women possessed her of a fierce jealousy. The thought of relinquishing him altogether cast her into deep despair. Either way, she was like to be unhappy.

Her sister's confidences had given her pause, and she had begun to believe that it were better to accept as much of him as he was capable of giving than have nothing at all. It irked her to think that men appropriated a double standard of conduct for themselves. Nothing had changed, she thought, in the more than two thousand years since Euripides had written his plays showing the peril of such folly.

She grieved for her sister's plight. Lucy's character was such that she would never oppose her family's wishes. Catherine thought her too compliant for her own good. But if Charles had enough resolution for them both, he might persuade Lucy to marry him despite the opposition of their families. Lucy had said that he had not spoken to her about his feelings. Perhaps the emotion was all on Lucy's part, but Catherine did not think so. She resolved to observe them more carefully at the Countess of Levin's party, to determine how things stood between them.

It was the most enjoyable party that Catherine had ever attended—not the usual crush that London parties tended to be, for there were only about thirty persons present, making it more in the nature of an intimate gathering. Most of the guests were friends rather than acquaintances, and the Harlands felt themselves welcomed and accepted, as if their particular society would contribute to the overall agreeableness of the company.

The earl and his countess were a young couple whom the Harlands had met at Lady Castelreagh's ball. Catherine's aunt had been included in the invitation, but she had made her excuses, telling the girls frankly that the countess's parties were not in the style she enjoyed.

Lady Arabella was a charming hostess. She made a point of singling Catherine out from the moment of her arrival. Catherine had the impression that the countess intended that they should become friends, and she was certain that her acquaintance was being cultivated at Rutherston's request. She warmed to the young woman, who was only a little older than herself, and thought that should she marry Rutherston, she was destined to become a particular friend of Lady Arabella.

Her brother entered with Rutherston at his heels, and Catherine thought that Tom looked as handsome as she had ever seen him, appearing quite at ease in a suit of clothes that she recognized as newly acquired. He came to her and took her hand as if to kiss it—a gallantry she had never seen him display before—but at the last minute he thought better of it and planted a kiss roughly on her cheek.

As he released her Rutherston came forward, and bowing over her hand, said softly, "Miss Harland! How I envy the liberties which a brother is allowed to take with a sister," and a grin spread across his face from ear to ear. Catherine frowned him down and turned her attention to Tom. When she had satisfied herself that all was well at home and that their sister, Lady Mary, continued in the full bloom of health, she asked him how he was enjoying his stay in town.

"I've had more fun and excitement in two days with Rutherston and Norton, sis, than ever I've had in all the times I've been here before."

"How so?"

"You're surely not such a ninnyhammer as not to know the answer to that, Kate! Why, Rutherston's name opens doors that would never open for a mere country squire!"

"What doors?"

"Nothing you'd be interested in, sis. Just the pleasures of gentlemen," and with that he would say no more, but Catherine was far from satisfied.

During the course of the evening, she watched Tom covertly and saw that his short association with Rutherston was having an effect. There was none of the carelessness of address or manner that had so characterized her brother in provincial circles. In her eyes, he had already acquired a modicum of town polish, and she admitted to herself that Rutherston's influence, at least to appearances, had been for the good, but when she came to consider those "pleasures of gentlemen" that Tom had mentioned, she felt deeply uneasy. Tom was of an age with Mr. Norton, and Catherine wondered for the first time if all the young gentlemen of the ton enjoyed the pleasures of what was vulgarly called the "muslin company."

Her gaze wandered to Rutherston, and their eyes held. As if he could read her thoughts, his brows rose in inquiry, and Catherine's cheeks began to flame. She looked away, and for the rest of the evening gave herself up to the pleasures of the party, not forgetting her resolution to observe Lucy and Norton.

Perhaps it was because there were no dowagers or mamas in attendance to monitor every word and action, or perhaps it was because her host and hostess had selected their guests with care, but whatever the reason, Catherine felt herself free to speak more openly and spiritedly than she was ever used to do, and to challenge the opinions of others who happened to express themselves on any field in which she felt herself to have some competence. The evening was well underway when it came to her that this was an unusual gathering, where discussion and argument were esteemed, and that in this company a lively imagination and an informed mind were attributes in a woman that were admired. When Rutherston came to her side with a glass of champagne, she saw that he was looking at her with frank approval. She was conscious that she had made a hit with his friends and that he was proud of her. It gave her inordinate pleasure to think so.

"Tom has been telling me how much he has enjoyed the, er . . . entertainments you have been so kind as to introduce him to, my lord," she began, choosing her words carefully.

"Has he? Then I am glad that he has found some enjoyment in such simple amusements." He was waiting for her to go on, and she did not know how to go about it. When he observed that she was in some difficulty, he became alert.

"Yes, Catherine? Go on."

She took a sip of champagne.

"Tom is quite thrilled to be taken up by a man of the world. He tells me that you have opened doors to him that were closed before."

"A man of the world? Do you mean me, Catherine?"

She inclined her head to signify that she did.

"Catherine, are you worried that I may lead your brother astray?" His tone was mocking.

"Would you not, sir?" she retorted.

"Oh, Catherine, you are off the mark. There is only one that I wish to lead astray, but alas, my efforts are always frustrated in that quarter."

"Perhaps it is time to give up the attempt, sir?"

"Do you think so? I hope not. I have always enjoyed the pleasures of the hunt."

"We were talking of Tom!"

"So we were. You wish to know how he has been passing his time. Let me assure you, the doors that I open to him are quite harmless. We have been to my clubs, to Jackson's Boxing Saloon, to Manton's Shooting Gallery. Must I go on? It's a tedious list, I assure you."

"Thank you. I did not mean you to give a detailed account of my brother's movements," she replied primly.

"I could not if I wanted to, Catherine. I am not with him every hour of the day, but I do try to keep an eye on him. Now if you wish me to give you an account of *my* movements, I should be happy to oblige."

"Oh no, sir, that will not be necessary. A *sister* must always feel some concern for a *brother's* welfare."

"Catherine, you have wounded me. Have you not observed that I wish to become much closer to you than a brother?"

She had a retort already on her tongue, but they were joined by Lord Levin, and Rutherston adroitly turned the conversation. Catherine was grateful to Rutherston. He had flirted with her outrageously, but had ensured that she would not worry needlessly about Tom. When he put his mind to it, he could be the most charming gentleman.

As she and Lucy were taking their leave, he disengaged himself from a group and came toward them, and when he offered to see them to their carriage, Lucy quickly accepted before Catherine could say a word. He took Catherine's hand in his and held it firmly.

"Catherine, I have no idea how young ladies spend their time in London, but I can't continue to call on Mount Street only to find you absent. I should be obliged if you would remain at home on Friday afternoon, when I shall wait on you. Tomorrow is promised to your brother Tom!"

"I can't, my lord. I believe I have an appointment."

"What appointment?"

"To return my books to the library." He was taken aback, until he saw her impish smile.

"Catherine! You will do as you are bid."

"Yes, my lord."

"Richard!"

"Yes, my lord Richard."

"Minx!" He snapped the carriage door shut, and brought her hand to his lips.

"Till Friday, my love."

As the carriage moved away, Catherine reached for Lucy's hand and clasped it tightly.

She said in mincing accents in imitation of her sister's voice, "Mr. Norton has never mentioned the state of his heart to me! It is his cowlike expression of devotion which has informed me of what his lips cannot say."

"Catherine, hush! The coachman will hear you!"

"Dearest Lucy," Catherine whispered as softly as she could, "he is as deep in love as any man can be."

"As deep in love as Lord Rutherston?"

"Oh, yes. My suitor only admires me. Your suitor adores you."

Lucy protested, and Catherine said no more. For the rest of the drive home, she thought of Lucy and Norton and tried to think of how their attachment could be brought to a happy conclusion, but no answer came. She could not be sure that Rutherston would lend his support to Charles in so imprudent a match. With his title and fortune, Rutherston could marry where he chose. It was the first time that Catherine had any sense of the honor that was being paid to her, and she was quite overwhelmed.

Tom Harland closed the door of the library gently behind him and headed for the stairs that would take him to his welcoming bed. London parties lasted well into the early morning, and Tom, accustomed to country ways, had been impatient for sleep these many hours past. He had left the two cousins to imbibe their second brandy of the night, and it occurred to him that he had been dimly aware of a restraint between Rutherston and Norton that he had never noticed before, but as his mind was slightly befuddled by the effects of the champagne and brandy that he had consumed rather freely during the evening, he inclined to think that he was imagining things.

Mr. Norton settled himself more comfortably in his armchair, crossing one leg carelessly over the other, and assumed as indifferent a pose as he could manage. He swirled the golden liquid in its glass and brought it to his lips.

Rutherston watched him through narrowed eyes.

"So," he said at last. "Whose turn is it to be found out now, cousin?"

"I beg your pardon?" Norton was nothing if he was not cautious.

"I said that I have found you out, Charles," Rutherston replied with a touch of severity.

Norton grinned broadly. "Well, so you have. What of it?"

There was no answering smile on Rutherston's face. "It won't do!"

"And what do you mean by that?" Norton's voice had become dangerously quiet.

"I mean that it isn't fair to the girl. You must either offer for her or stop your attentions. I'm sure you know that as well as I do."

"Are you meddling, Richard? I didn't think that was quite in your style!" A note of aggrievement had crept into Norton's voice.

"In the normal way, I wouldn't." Rutherston offered the decanter to Norton who shook his head, and his lordship proceeded to refill his own glass. "But I have a particular interest in anything that affects the Harland family."

"Oh yes, I can see that you do—I and the whole ton! But don't imagine, Richard, that I shall brook any interference from you in my affairs. You are not my guardian, you know, and I shall look out for my own interests, without any reference to you."

Norton had never in his life before spoken to his esteemed cousin in such an ill-humored way, and Rutherston paused, the decanter poised over his glass.

"The devil you will! Your interests d'you say? And what of Miss Harland's interests? Have you given a thought to that? I really don't care a brass button if you make a fool of yourself, cousin, but I won't have you making a fool of Catherine's sister."

The two men sat on either side of the fireplace looking warily at each other. Rutherston spoke first.

"Charles!" he said in a friendlier tone. "I am not warning you off if you intend to offer for the girl. I am simply trying to ascertain your intentions, as, if I remember, you once did with me some months ago."

The recollection of that earlier interview between the two cousins, when their positions had been exactly reversed, did much to ease the tension between them now. Both gentlemen found themselves grinning, and Norton held out his glass for Rutherston to refill.

"Cousin Richard, I am in a damnable position. What can I offer Lucy? A thousand a year won't go far—it would mean a life of shabby gentility. She deserves better than that. To press her into making so imprudent a match right now would be taking advantage. She's hardly out of the schoolroom—not up to snuff."

"Perhaps if you apply to your father, he will make you an allowance?"

Norton shook his head energetically.

"It won't do. The gov'nor has expressed himself vigorously on this subject ever since I came out of shortcoats. Everything is entailed on Jack, except for the money my mother left me. You don't know how lucky you are, Richard, not to be a younger son!"

"Yes, I begin to see how awkward it makes things. But knowing all that, how could you allow your affections to become engaged so recklessly?"

"I didn't know I had till it was too late to draw back. Surely you, of all people, understand how it is?"

Rutherston had to own that he did. But his case was not the same as his cousin's.

"I haven't sorted everything out in my own mind as yet, Richard, but I do want to be fair to Lucy. She's so inexperienced." He sighed and fell into a reverie of thought. Rutherston waited.

"You haven't said anything to me that I haven't been telling myself for some weeks now. If she means to have me, I will have to make a push to find some occupation that will give us a reasonable living. Holy Orders don't appeal to me, politics bore me, so it looks as if I shall have to embark on a military career." The thought did not bring any sense of pleasure or relief to his troubled mind. The two men sat for some moments in gloomy thought, sipping their brandies companionably. The prospect of having to embark on a career for monetary gain rather than a disinterested high-mindedness filled them both with repugnance. Another sigh escaped Norton's lips. "But I do see that I cannot let matters drift the way they have been doing." He put down his empty glass and stood up to go.

"Thank you for your cousinly concern, Richard. I know that you will trust me to do what I think is in the best interests of both Miss Harland and myself?"

Rutherston inclined his head gravely. "Of course."

"Then I'll bid you goodnight." As Norton reached the door, Rutherston recollected himself and called after him. "Charles! You won't do anything rash without letting me know?"

"Anything rash?" Norton's back stiffened.

"I simply meant, cousin, that if you decide to embark on a military career, you'll inform me before the event, and not after it?"

"Oh, I see. Certainly. But I can't see what difference that will make."

"Can't you? Well, never mind. Just be sure to keep me informed."

* * *

Rutherston poked the embers of the dying fire, and returned to his chair in a reflective mood. He decided against another brandy, since he needed a clear head on the morrow for taking Catherine's brother round to Tattersall's to look over the horseflesh that he had come to purchase for the Ardo House stables. He thought that it had not occurred to his cousin to apply to him, as Lucy's prospective brother-in-law, to ease their financial straits. He would, of course, whether he was applied to or not. But they were both ridiculously young. Lucy was just a girl of eighteen or nineteen years, and Norton only four or five years her senior. Rutherston did not mean exactly to depress the attachment, but he could not see why such a couple of children could not wait for a year or so to ensure that this was no infatuation, especially when the match had little to recommend it on either side but strong affection. That he was not prepared to wait for his Catherine a minute more than he had to did not strike him in the same light at all.

Nor could he see what it was in the younger Miss Norton that had attached his young cousin so securely to her side. That she was a pretty little slip of a girl, not unlike Catherine in looks, he could not deny. But she lacked his beloved's spirit and wit, and he was sure that her proper manner was an exact reflection of her inherent passivity. No, she would not do for him. With that thought, his mind began to dwell on the alluring Catherine, and he became restless to think that he had promised a whole day of his time to Tom when he was in a fever of impatience to regularize his position with her and so put an end to the wagging tongues of all the tittle-tattlers of the ton.

Chapter 12

Charles Norton arrived in Mount Street shortly after luncheon and carried Lucy off, intending to drive her to Richmond Park. It was further afield than he had ever taken her, but he wanted the time to rehearse what he should say. He had forborne to take the curricle, since he was doubtful whether he could give his undivided attention to handling the ribbons of the unpredictable grays, and had, on reflection, selected Rutherston's phaeton, since it was marginally easier to control. His good-natured cousin never seemed to mind having to accept whatever conveyance Norton saw fit to leave him for his own use, saying that he could well remember his own inordinate pleasure, at Norton's age, in handling the latest rig that put his ability as a whip to the test. The phaeton had no place for a groom, so that Norton was assured that he could speak to Lucy as freely as he wished.

As they rode along at a brisk trot, it needed but a few minutes for Lucy to become aware that a more serious humor had taken possession of Mr. Norton than she had ever observed in him before. She held her tongue in check, waiting for him to begin, but her observations did nothing to relieve the weight of her own mind. Little was said by either, except of a most desultory nature, until they arrived at their destination. Here, Mr. Norton drew in, slackened the ribbons somewhat and permitted the chestnuts to graze.

"Lucy, I have been wondering, this long time past, how I am to begin." If he had said these words in a different tone, Lucy's heart would have been in a flutter, but they were said with such gravity that she felt her spirits sink even lower.

"Yes, Charles? I can see that you have something of a serious nature that you wish to say to me. Don't keep me in suspense. Tell me what it is."

"Lucy, how old are you?"

"Pray, what has that to do with anything?"

"It has everything to do with what I am trying to say to you. You are so young, hardly more than a child, and I have not done right in engaging your affections."

"Engaging my affections? What an odious thing to say! What makes you think you have engaged my affections, sir?" The sparks fairly flashed from her eyes, and so novel was the experience of seeing his demure Lucy bristle in indignation, that Norton openly smiled. This did not endear him any the more to Lucy, who thought that it was ungentlemanly of him to begin with the state of her affections before he had declared his own.

"The reason I know that I have engaged your affections, you silly goose, is because I am so much older than you. I know the signs."

"What signs?" Her ire was roused now, and still the ignoble Mr. Norton had not mentioned the state of his own heart.

Her question recalled to his mind the enchanting rise and swell of her bosom when he had partnered her in the dance, her faint blushes and downcast eyes when she had found herself alone in his company, her eyes following him whenever he strayed from her side, and a thousand other telltale signs that assured him that the lady was not impervious to his charms.

"Never mind what signs," he replied rather uncomfortably. "I know, and that's that!" The interview was not going at all as Mr. Norton had rehearsed it, since Lucy was answering in an unpredictable way and completely throwing him off his stride.

"Lucy, I can't marry you, not yet. I have to give you time to grow up a little. When you have time to consider, you may not want to marry me at all."

"Have I asked you to marry me?" she demanded.

She blinked back her angry tears, willing them to disappear. Mr. Norton now saw his mistake in having contrived so serious an interview in such a carriage and without a groom, since he longed to take Lucy's hands in his, but was obliged to hang on to the ribbons.

"Darling Lucy, will you listen to me? I am not saying that we won't marry—only that we must wait awhile. I must be quite sure that you know what you are about. You must know something of how I am fixed. I won't ask you to make so improvident a match until you have time to look around for a bit."

"Why are you telling me all this?" She was sniffing into her handkerchief now, ashamed of the telltale tears that must confirm what he said he already knew. "You need not have brought me all the way out here just to humiliate me. Why tell me at all? You could have gone away without saying anything, and my feelings would have been spared."

"Go away without a word? When I have so shamelessly attached you to myself? That I could not do. Besides, Lucy, I want us to come to an understanding. I will wait for you, but you need not feel obliged to wait. If some other offer comes along, you are free to accept it or reject it without reference to me."

"But Charles, none of this makes sense. Are you making me an offer or are you not?"

Mr. Norton could not fathom how his beloved could be so obtuse. In his own mind, everything was clear. "I am and I am not," he said decisively. "What I mean to say is, no—not for the present, but I will make you an offer when I think you are ready for it."

"And when will that be, pray? In a year, two years, ten years?"

Mr. Norton had not gone so far in his own mind as to put the limit on the time needed for his beloved to come to a mature understanding of her own mind and situation, but he had never expected it to be as long as one whole year.

"Never mind how long." His voice was gruff. "I'll know when the time is right."

"And what do you expect to happen in that time, Charles? Is there to be a change in me?"

"You'll be older," he said reasonably.

"Oh, I shall certainly be older. Do you expect me to be wiser?"

Mr. Norton began to think that the love of his life was deliberately misunderstanding him. "Lucy, you know what I mean."

"Charles, did you know that my sister, Mary, was married when she was eighteen, and that she is soon to have her third child and is just past two and twenty? She knew her mind when she was eighteen just as she does now."

Perceiving himself to be on ground that was far from steady, Mr. Norton assumed his most authoritative voice and handed down his immutable decision.

"Lucy, I have no more to say. That is how it will be."

"Does this mean that I shall not see you again?" she barely managed, in a choked voice.

"I won't come calling as often as I have, but with Tom

as my friend, and with your sister on the point of marrying my cousin, we are bound to be thrown into each other's company quite often."

"When Catherine marries your cousin? Pray tell me more. This is news to me."

"Well, I would have thought that it is obvious that he means to offer for her."

"Oh yes," said Lucy icily, "of that I am sure, but whether Catherine intends to accept him remains to be seen."

"Refuse Rutherston? Why should she? When he's been the biggest prize in the Marriage Mart for the last ten years?"

"If he's been the biggest prize in the Marriage Mart, how is it that some girl hasn't snaffled him before now?" she snapped.

"Oh, he's been too sly for them. Besides, he's thirty now, and he promised his mama that he would marry when he reached his thirtieth year." Norton realized, too late, that he had spoken in an unguarded moment, and turned to Lucy in apprehension. "Lucy, forget that I said that. Richard would never forgive me for betraying his confidence. No one must ever hear of it."

Lucy's mouth hung open. "Charles, do you mean to say that he is offering for Catherine because he promised his mother that he would marry? If Catherine were to hear of it, she would never forgive him, never marry him, not even if he were the last man in the world."

"Of course, it doesn't mean that," snapped Norton, angry at himself, but somehow blaming Lucy for making him forgetful of his tongue. "He has the highest regard for her. It is simply a coincidence. Lucy, you must see that he is not offering for Catherine because of a stupid promise?" Lucy looked disbelieving.

"Do you really think that if he were to choose a wife

rationally, with no thought of personal inclination, Catherine would be his first choice?" Personally, he thought that she would not be his second or third choice either, but he was not about to tell her sister so.

"I suppose not. But Charles, Catherine must never hear of this promise. It would mortify her to think that . . ."

"She will never hear of it from me. And you, I know, will say nothing. So don't give it another thought. Now, can we return to the understanding that I wish to have established between us before I return you to Mount Street?"

"Oh, Charles," said Lucy sweetly, "I understand you perfectly, but you are far from understanding me." Charles glanced at her uneasily, but she now looked again the demure, compliant Miss Harland whom he had come to love, and he believed he was quite satisfied, and wondered at his own vague feeling of disquiet.

In the late afternoon, Catherine was called to the downstairs reception room to be introduced to some ladies who were waiting on her aunt. Lucy had left the house an hour earlier to go riding with Mr. Norton, and Catherine had set herself to writing some letters.

"Her ladyship says you are to come at once, miss, and not linger on any account!" Becky's voice was urgent as she conveyed her ladyship's message, and Catherine set aside her task to obey the summons without delay. She was met at the door by Lady Margaret, who beamed her pleasure, and taking her by the hand led Catherine to a lady who turned upon her the friendliest smile.

"May I present my niece, Miss Catherine Harland? Catherine, this is Lady Rutherston."

Catherine started visibly, then, recovering herself quickly, curtsied her acknowledgment. "Ma'am."

"Miss Harland." The dowager marchioness bowed.

Catherine's thoughts were in a tumult, but she soon surmised that the insufferable marquis had sent his mother to look her over before his offer became irrevocable. The thought made her lift her chin in defiance.

"My daughter Jane, the Duchess of Beaumain." The marchioness indicated the lady on her left.

"Your grace." Catherine curtsied deeply.

"And I believe you know my niece, Lady Arabella."

"Catherine." The countess of Levin inclined her head and smiled. "I hope we may see you in Brook Street before long.

The marchioness extended her hand. "Come and sit by me, my dear. I should like to know you better." The words sounded ominous in Catherine's ears, and she began to wish that she had kept to her practice of fleeing the house every day. She took the chair next to the marchioness and tried not to stare. Rutherston's mother was not as she had imagined her to be. She was handsome, and in many ways . . . Her thoughts were interrupted.

"I see that you are as surprised as I." There was a touch of amusement in the marchioness's voice. "When I look at you, I am reminded of myself when I was your age. It is our coloring, I believe. I am deeply flattered to think . . . well never mind. Tell me about yourself, Catherine. Lady Margaret has told me that your home is in Breckenridge in Surrey."

It was the most difficult interview that Catherine had ever endured. Her ladyship and her grace, in the ordinary course of the conversation, drew Catherine out to talk about her home, her father's estate, her family and relations until Catherine was sure that her ladyship had calculated to a sou the extent of her father's income and had drawn an accurate picture of the family trees of her respective parents. It was not done to give offense; nevertheless, Catherine was deeply offended, and a spirit of recklessness took possession of her.

"You have nephews, I hear, Catherine? Children are such as pleasure, don't you agree?"

"I hardly know, ma'am. Naturally, I am fond of my nephews, but I'd just as soon be with my dogs."

The marchioness appeared to be taken aback by this reply, but put it down to mere nervousness on the part of the girl.

"Do you ride, Catherine? The Fothervilles are invariably accomplished equestrians."

"Oh, the Fothervilles would rather ride than anything!" interjected the duchess.

"And I would rather do anything than ride!" replied Catherine in dulcet tones.

Lady Rutherston began to wonder if Catherine were being deliberately rude, but she put the notion out of her mind. It did not seem likely that the girl would run the risk of ruining her chances with the son merely to spite the mother.

"Perhaps you play or sing?"

"Alas, no!" confessed Catherine, suppressing a feeling of guilt that was beginning to rise in her breast. She avoided the eyes of her aunt, who was perfectly aware that Catherine possessed a rich contralto. That lady sat rigidly in her chair.

"You must do something, Miss Harland?" The duchess's hearty voice grated on Catherine's ears.

Catherine appeared to give this last remark some thought. Then her face brightened.

"Papa says that I'm a dab hand at cards, and like to fritter away a husband's fortune with sheer recklessness.

But of course, at home, we don't play for high stakes."
The room froze to an arctic temperature.

The soothing voice of the countess of Levin now held
sway. "Catherine is a debater, Aunt Olivia, a fencer with
words. I have it on the best authority that no one crosses
swords with her with impunity." The merry eyes of Lady
Arabella looked warmly into Catherine's.

The marchioness considered the implications of Lady
Arabella's statement. It was a moment or two before she
spoke.

"A quick-witted girl? A scholar?"

"I read, yes, ma'am."

"What then? Romances?"

"A few . . . novels."

"And in particular?"

"In particular . . . plays." Catherine was not at all willing to betray to these ladies an interest she was sure they
would despise.

"Shakespeare?"

"Yes . . . and Greek tragedy." She rushed the last
words.

"Are you a classicist, Miss Harland?" The dowager
marchioness did not appear to find this disclosure at all
offensive, and Catherine took heart.

"Yes, ma'am."

"Extraordinary!" The marchioness smiled. "And a girl
with spunk, to boot." And with that cryptic remark, the
interview was at an end.

The marchioness rose to go. "I look forward to seeing
you again, Catherine. Lady Margaret." She bowed and
the ladies took their leave, but the countess contrived to
whisper a few words in Catherine's ear before the door
was shut upon them. She squeezed Catherine's hand.
"Good, brave girl!"

* * *

The Marquis of Rutherston came promptly on Friday afternoon to wait upon Catherine. He asked first for Lady Margaret to obtain her permission for a private interview with her niece. It was given with alacrity, and he was shown into a small parlor on the ground floor to await the girl whom all London knew had captured his heart.

She entered, bowed stiffly in his direction, and sat down as far from him as she possibly could, but as the room was small, she was in closer proximity to him than she had hoped to be.

"Lord Rutherston," was all the acknowledgment he was given, and Catherine fell silent. Rutherston sighed.

"You are angry with me, Catherine, and it's most unjust. You cannot believe that I sent my mother to you!"

"Did you not, my lord?" Her eyes glittered.

"I did not! I did not know! It was Charles who saw her carriage at your door and brought the news to me. I was incensed and went to her directly to warn her off."

Catherine said nothing, but was so much the picture of wounded pride that Rutherston forbade to smile.

"Will you not forgive her, Catherine? She was as vexed as I, believing herself to be the last person in London to be informed of my intentions. We have not been discreet, you and I. The whole world knows that there is something between us two." He got up and moved to the chair next to hers.

"Was it so bad, my love? My mother was pleased with the interview, and approves my choice."

Catherine was somewhat mollified by his words, but she had determined that he was not to be easily let off.

"It wasn't bad, my lord, it was intolerable!"

"My name is Richard," he said firmly, and taking her hand, turned it over to kiss her palm. She snatched it away.

"I felt as if I were a brood mare."

He was startled into a laugh.

"Catherine! Do you never guard your tongue when you're with me?" He retrieved her hand and nibbled on a finger. "You wouldn't turn me down now, my love, would you? I should be the laughingstock of London."

"Do you like children, my . . . Richard?"

"What?"

"It's what your mother asked me."

"She didn't! Tell me she didn't, Catherine."

"Answer the question, Richard."

"Only if they are yours, my love, and you come to them through me." He began to kiss each finger separately.

"And would you rather ride than do anything, sir?"

"Catherine, you are tempting me to put you to the blush." She tried to pull her hand away, but he held it more firmly.

"Richard, I am in earnest. Why do you want to marry me?"

"What?"

"Answer me!"

"Catherine, you know how much I admire you!"

"Go on!"

"Are you serious?"

"Yes, I am serious."

"Well, I admire the way you stand up to me."

"I? Stand up to you? One day I hope I may, but you know as well as I that I always lie down to you!"

"Then perhaps, my love, it is the thought of your lying down to me that entices me to make this rash offer!"

"You are . . . you are . . ."

"Yes, Catherine, what am I?"

"You are a passionate man, my lord."

She jumped up and walked away from him. "Perhaps one woman is not enough for a man of your warm temperament?"

"What?"

"Richard, will you stop saying 'What?' in that ridiculous way? I have asked you a question. Answer it, if you dare."

"Catherine, what are you talking about? You know that I love only you." He came to her and cradled her gently in his arms. "My passion is all for you." A thought struck him, and he pulled away. "The woman in the park. Is that what troubles you? I promise you, Catherine, since you have come into my life, I have become as celibate as a priest. I admit I am experienced, but you did not think, did you, that I was like the virgin Hippolytus?" His eyes held amusement.

"No, I knew that you were no Hippolytus. But I have a jealous nature, Richard. I could not be happy if I had to share . . . my husband."

"I am glad to hear you say so, you silly goose. I promise you, Catherine, my passion, my love will be invested in our marriage. There will be nothing left over for anyone else."

"Oh, Richard, do you truly mean it?" She looked at him with such appeal that he was tempted to make love to her in earnest.

"Oh God, Catherine, don't you know what I feel for you? Of course, I mean it. And now, my love, will you not put an end to my suspense and tell me your answer?"

"I have forgotten the question."

"Catherine!" he roared.

"Yes, Richard, my answer is yes, if you . . ."

He stopped her lips with a kiss, but when Catherine

felt his tongue pushing between her teeth, she pulled away in alarm.

"Richard, please don't! I mean it. Don't begin like that. Where will it end?"

He released her with a sigh. "Oh, Catherine, I have been waiting for you for so long. Are you going to make me wait another week?"

"Another week? We cannot marry in one week!"

"We most certainly will!"

"But Richard, I have to let my parents know. I want to be married from my home. There are so many things that must be done."

"There is nothing that needs doing, my love. I applied to your father for his permission to wed you before I left Surrey. Your parents have been expecting your return, and I have had a Special License in my pocket since the day I arrived in town. I have no intentions of waiting for you a moment longer than I must. With or without a ring, I mean to have you, Catherine."

"You've had a Special License . . . you insufferable, arrogant, odious . . ." said Miss Harland in outrage.

"Catherine, this is not the time to stand up to me. If you don't agree to our marrying within the week, I shall take you in my arms, and you are so right, my love, where will it end?" He reached for her, but she evaded his grasp.

"I agree. We marry in one week. Now leave me, and from now until the day we wed, Richard Fotherville, I promise that you will not find me unchaperoned."

"Oh, Catherine," he drawled, bowing over her hand to kiss her farewell. "You coward!"

Chapter 13

They were married quietly, one week later, in the old parish church in Breckenridge. Lucy and Norton had traveled down from London to stand up with them, but few other guests were invited. Lady Mary had returned to her home in Hampshire to await the birth of her child, and Rutherston's mother was content to receive Catherine to her bosom when they should return to town some three weeks later.

Catherine, solemnly repeating her wedding vows to love, cherish, honor and obey, cast a veiled glance at Rutherston's unsmiling face and thought that she had never seen him look so stern. And when he took her trembling hand in his to slip his ring on her finger, she looked up to meet his steady gaze, concealing nothing of what was in her heart, and all the depth of her emotion was written in her face for him to see. For a long moment he regarded her, in perfect comprehension, and when he smiled, a look of exultation suffused his face, and Catherine, seeing that look, felt her confidence waver. He leaned down to brush her lips with his, and his whispered, "My wife," evoked in her mind all the pride of possession of the primitive male, and she trembled in dread anticipation, knowing that her destiny was bound to a man whom she hardly knew.

Catherine had proposed that after the wedding they return to London with Lucy and Norton, but in this Rutherston demurred, and when she would have argued he had cut her short. They were to travel by coach to one of his smaller estates which lay a day's journey to the northwest, where, Rutherston averred, there were many matters that needed his attention, and that he had been an absentee landlord too long.

There was nothing that Catherine could say that would change his mind, and she could scarcely tell him that the real reason she wanted to return to town was that it made her uncomfortable to be too long alone in his company. He had sent the servants ahead with their baggage some days before in readiness for their arrival, and as soon as the wedding breakfast at Ardo House was consumed, Rutherston was impatient to be off.

The journey was pleasant and uneventful, Rutherston pointing out all the places of interest on the way. She had been dreading their close proximity within the closed carriage, half fearful that, now she was wearing his ring, his ardor would be unrestrained, but everything about his manner allayed her fears. He was content merely to draw her hand through his arm, and never once uttered any kind of remark that was likely to draw a blush to her cheeks, and Catherine's overstrung nerves began to unwind and the smiles came more readily to her lips. It was exactly what Rutherston had intended, for he was conscious that his unguarded look in the church had been a tactical blunder.

It was close to dusk when their carriage approached the gates to Fotherville House, and Catherine looked out with interest to catch her first glimpse of what Rutherston had told her was his favorite residence. A gatekeeper liveried in bottle-green hurried from the lodge to open the wrought iron gates set between two stone pillars, and their carriage swung into a wide graveled driveway with an avenue of lime trees that framed the main approach to the house.

"Richard, it is quite lovely," Catherine breathed, as the house came into view. The glowing hues of the setting sun were caught and reflected in the many small-paned windows of the sandstone building, casting their fiery rays back to the golden dusk.

"It is a picture of perfect symmetry." Her voice held awe as well as admiration. The house was three stories high, with long windows on the first two floors looking out on acres of broad lawns that gave way to shrubbery and trees.

"Do you like it, Catherine?" He was watching her expression and seemed to find satisfaction in what he saw. "I hope you shall, for we shall spend much of our time here. My grandfather had it built as a sort of halfway house between London and our seat in Gloucestershire, and as a retreat from life at Court. I thought that the classical lines of the place would appeal to you, a lover of all things Greek."

"Your grandfather had excellent taste!"

"Oh, he had excellent help. His friend, Lord Burlington, found the right people to design the house and the grounds. Everything is more or less as it was when it was completed sixty years ago, except that my father and I have added to the collections over the years. Tomorrow, I shall show you the interior and the rest of the estate—if I can persuade you to ride with me—but I collect, you would rather do anything than ride?"

She had been looking out of the carriage window at the house while Rutherston had been speaking, but at his bantering words she turned with an impish grin on her face.

"Your mother told you?"

"No, my sister, the duchess. I had the devil of a time persuading her that you were only funning when you implied that you detested horses. In Jane's estimation, it would never do for a Fotherville to get shackled to someone who could not ride with the best of them. But then, I have had the pleasure of seeing you in action. Jane has not." He grinned.

"And would it matter to you if I could not ride, Richard?" Catherine asked.

"Certainly not! I would teach you!"

"Ah, but what if I had no wish to learn?"

Rutherston was tempted to respond with a remark that would lure Catherine into one of the improper conversations that so delighted him, but he restrained himself. She was like an overbred filly ready to bolt at the first faint touch, and he was taking the greatest pains to catch her unawares. He ignored her question.

"Are you going to tell me what more you said to mislead my mother when she had so kindly condescended to interview the girl of my choice?"

"Enough to give the dowager a profound disgust of me, I'll be bound. Oh, Richard, was she terribly put out?"

"If she was, she didn't tell me. She was quite close about the whole affair. No, I heard the full, shocking story of your unruly conduct from Arabella. She, naturally, thought the episode highly diverting."

"Were you shocked, Richard? You shouldn't be, you know. If you knew me better, you would know that I cannot abide interference from anyone in my affairs."

His tone was light. "Anyone, Catherine? A husband, I think, might claim that privilege as his right?"

She was looking at him intently now. "Do you think so?" Her voice was cool and noncommittal. Rutherston, somewhat nettled, was about to pursue the conversation further, but thought better of it. He now began to point out features of the building in the fading light, and Catherine was soon lost in admiration of what her husband intended would be their future home.

By the time that Catherine had bathed and dressed for dinner under the critical eye of Becky who had now been attached to Rutherston's permanent staff, it was too late to see the interior of the house to the best advantage, and Catherine, although disappointed, was ready to admit that it made better sense to wait till morning. A late supper was brought to them on trays before a crackling fire in the library, and Rutherston summarily dismissed the servants, telling them that he would ring if their services should be required.

He had prepared all with the greatest forethought, attempting to make their time together for the remainder of the evening as natural as possible. Catherine's attention was engaged, as he had known it would be, by the extent of his library, but he would not entertain her examining any of the books and manuscripts until they had eaten and the remains of their meal were removed.

Catherine surveyed her surroundings with unmitigated approval. The room was large and long, with five windows against one wall, and the glow from the fireplace and the flickering candles in their sockets high on the walls cast a warmth that gave a feeling of intimacy, despite the vastness of the interior. Against the walls were green upholstered chairs and sofas, informally grouped around leather-topped tables, and in one corner, beside a window, was a desk, which she supposed was Rutherston's. High above, running along three sides of the room, was a narrow gallery lined with books to the ceiling. This was the library of a collector as much as a reader, and she foresaw the many hours of pleasure she should have with a husband who shared her interest.

Rutherston filled Catherine's glass for the second time, and when she had drunk most of it he finally consented to show her some small part of his collection, and they spent the next hour or so pulling volumes from their shelves and talking easily of random subjects that were suggested by the titles and authors of the books. He was amused to see the stack of volumes that Catherine was rapidly setting aside for her future enjoyment while they were in residence at Fotherville House. He curbed his tongue with the greatest of difficulty. Reading was not the occupation he had in mind for their mutual enjoyment now that he had the love of his life living under his roof.

It was when Catherine made an admiring comment about the interior of the room that Rutherston became most animated and drew her attention to the intricate plaster ceiling, which he said was the pride of Fotherville House.

"Catherine, come. I want to show you another delightful interior," and although she protested that she would prefer to see it by the light of day, he dragged her to her feet and propelled her through the hall and up the broad, cantilevered marble staircase to the door of a room that she recognized as her own bedchamber, and when she turned to him with a puzzled frown and would have opened her mouth to I speak, he gently pressed his fingers against her lips.

"Hush, Catherine, no more words. Your maid is waiting for you." And saying no more, he turned her around and pushed her through the open door.

Becky took infinite pains that night to prepare her mistress for her bridal, and she chattered aimlessly as Catherine allowed herself to be arrayed in an oyster gown of shimmering satin with matching wrap. It clung sensuously to the curves of her body—a circumstance that gave great satisfaction to the maid but filled the mistress with foreboding. Catherine was dismayed that her proper mama should have selected such improper attire for her nuptials and wondered what had overcome that formidable lady's delicate scruples.

When all was accomplished, Becky asked permission to leave.

"Oh, Becky, don't go," Catherine blurted out, then blushed for her gaucherie. "Of course, you must."

Becky, who thought that she had been in the employ of the Harland family long enough to take a few liberties, patted Catherine's hand, saying, "There is nothing to fear but fear itself, my lady. I am sure his lordship knows how nervous you are." She was right. Rutherston did know.

As he entered, he paused on the threshold and took in the room at a glance. Catherine had positioned herself as far from the door as possible, her hand gripping the back of a chair. He sighed inaudibly and brought the decanter and glasses that he carried in his arms to a table before the smoldering fire, and setting them down, proceeded to fill them, pretending not to notice Catherine's frozen pose. He held out a glass.

"Will you not join your husband, my lady, in drinking to our future happiness?" She could scarcely refuse, and since he made no move toward her, she was compelled to cross the distance between them, self-conscious to a degree of the rustling of her revealing robes.

"Drink it, Catherine, it will do you good." He drained his glass and watched as she raised the drink to her lips, but when she would have laid it aside unfinished, he bade her continue until she had drunk it all, then taking the empty glass from her fingers, he set it down. He said her name softly, coaxingly, and brought her hand to his lips.

"There is nothing to fear, Catherine." His mouth was warm on the pulse of her wrist. He encircled her waist, pulling her close, and she could feel the hard muscles of his arm on her back. She heard the appeal in his voice as he murmured against her hair, "Catherine, I have been patient, have I not?" His mouth barely touched her lips, and the persuasiveness of his soft entreaties lessened her resistance and she felt some of the tension go out of her as her body responded to the gentling of his tone. He kissed her then, so tenderly, demanding nothing from her that she would not freely give.

His voice became deeper, hoarser, coaxing her into surrender. "Let me touch you, Catherine. I won't take you against your will." Her senses were lulled by his languorous pleading, and a numbing lethargy took possession of her limbs. Her wrapper slid to the floor as she felt his fingers undo the buttons of her gown. "Let me touch you, Catherine," he murmured in her ear, and she stood, unresisting, as he pulled the gown from her shoulders to bare her breasts. His voice was a low murmur of repressed desire. "Let me love you, Catherine." He watched her through half-closed lids as he brought his hands down to caress her breasts, and Catherine felt her body melt with the heat of him, and a low moan escaped her lips.

"Give yourself to me, Catherine; let me love you." She twined her arms around his neck, and he bent to kiss her breasts, and he moved his hands down to stroke her thighs, her belly, and her legs. She sagged against him then, whispering his name. He tugged her free of the impeding gown and caught her in his arms, carrying her to the bed.

"Easy, darling, easy." He pushed her back against the pillows and lay beside her, propped on one arm, trailing his hand down the length of her naked body. His dressing gown fell open, and she put out a hand to caress the powerful muscles of his matted chest. He bent to cup her breast in his hands, watching her face with languid eyes, and when he heard her gasp of pleasure, he leaned down to touch her nipples with his mouth. Catherine writhed and moaned, her senses on fire and she pressed herself eagerly against him, deep sobs sending shudders through the length of her body.

"Wait love, trust me." His hand moved down her body, parting her legs, stroking her to a feverish pitch until she was in an agony of desire. He came down on her then, thrusting deep inside her with such force that Catherine cried out sharply in pain. He was instantly gentle, soothing her with soft words of love, kissing the tears from her eyes until her body began to respond with pleasure again.

"Move to meet me, Catherine. Love me!" He kissed her lips, his tongue probing her mouth with new urgency, and she felt her body, of its own volition, rise to meet him with increasing intensity as he willed her to match his passion. She sobbed aloud and clung to him as her body convulsed, and she abandoned herself to the pleasure of their mutual desire.

He was quiet then, cradling her gently in his arms. She touched his face in wonderment, cherishing the warmth of their intimacy, until she settled into the crook of his arm to sleep.

It was a wakeful night, for Rutherston reached for her again and again, rousing her from sleep with soft kisses on her breasts, murmuring her name and awakening a response in her till she gave herself up to his lovemaking once more, until the dawn came.

Chapter 14

It was late in the afternoon of the next day before Rutherston had the opportunity of showing Catherine the house. They had slept till noon, exhausted from their night of lovemaking, and were taking a leisurely repast of breakfast at two in the afternoon, a circumstance that Catherine was certain would shock the servants, but which Rutherston assured her they would heartily approve.

He was delighted at the change in Catherine that one night of love had contrived. She came to him readily whenever he touched her, and nothing he said, however indelicate, had the least effect on her happy exuberance.

"Catherine," he said at last, pouring himself another cup of coffee, "you must explain to me what it was that put you so much on edge yesterday. Surely it was more than mere bridal nerves? I swear I was afraid to come within three feet of you. Did you notice, my love, that I did not even kiss you till I came to your room?" He caught the look of mischief on her face.

"No, did you notice that I was nervous?" she asked with exaggerated innocence, laughing at the expression of mock disgust that crossed his face. "If you must know, Richard, you and my mother between you managed to give me a case of fidgets such as I have never experienced before nor ever wish to again."

"How so, Catherine?"

She buttered her second slice of toast and held her cup out to him, which he filled from a silver coffeepot sitting at his elbow.

"You must know that every bride has her mother or some female relative come to her the night before her wedding to . . . er . . . advise her about the married state."

"Go on, Catherine. How did your mother contrive to put such terror into you?"

"Oh," she continued gaily, "she mostly talked a great deal of nonsense, but then she likened you to a stallion and me to a filly. That didn't faze me overmuch, for I'm country bred. But Richard, the morning of our wedding, my father's stud-groom put our newest filly into the pasture with John Colby's stallion. Oh, Richard," she wiped the tears of laughter from her eyes, "it was awful, for the filly wanted nothing to do with him, and he would have her whether she wanted him or no! If you had heard the braying and screaming that went on in our pasture! But he cornered her—and—well you can imagine the rest. So there I was, in my wedding finery, setting off for the church to meet my groom, and . . . will you forgive me, my dear . . . I kept thinking of you as that eager stallion and me as the reluctant filly." Her shoulders shook with a fresh spasm of laughter. Rutherston grimaced at her in mock horror.

"Go on, Catherine, what next?"

"Well, my darling husband," she looked at him keenly, hesitating before she went on, "when I saw you in church looking so handsome and solemn, I was almost reassured, until . . ."

"Until? Pray continue."

"Until, my sweet, you gave me that look I think I read pretty well."

"Yes?" he asked softly, and reached out to grasp her wrist. "How did you read it?"

"It was the kind of look Colby's stallion would have cast at our filly, if he could! It said to me, my dear husband, that I had fallen into your power and I would not escape you now, try as I may. Was I wrong?"

"Not fallen into my *power,* Catherine, surely not power. That you had come under my *protection.* That was what I felt."

"If you say so, my lord. But then, in the carriage, you talked of a husband's rights, did you not?"

"Catherine!" His exasperation was real now. "You are willfully misunderstanding me. I only meant that a husband and wife have no affairs, no secrets that the other is not entitled to share."

"Ah, is that what you meant?"

"Of course!"

"And I am at liberty to ask you any question on your er . . . past affairs? Then tell me about the woman in the park, Richard."

"Catherine!"

"My darling, I am a tease, I know." She came to him and put her arms around his shoulders, kissing the nape of his neck, and he pulled her round roughly to sit on his lap. She put her fingers over his mouth as he started to speak.

"No, love, don't tell me anything! I don't want to hear. Forgive my jealousy. I could not help but know that you are an experienced lover. There now, I admit it. I am consumed with jealousy to think that you have made love to other women."

He took her hand from his mouth and rocked her in his arms. "You are a fool, you innocent girl, if you think that I am experienced in the kind of lovemaking we shared last night. I have never before in my life exerted myself to please." He held her face between his hands, looking at her intently. "A mistress, my girl, is paid to please. Catherine, one sigh of pleasure from you can bring me to heel." He brought her face down to kiss her mouth, but when she felt his hands begin to undo the buttons of her dress, she called a halt and demanded to be shown the rest of the house.

"For, Richard," she said, quizzing him, "how would it look if, of all the rooms of this grand house, I can only describe my bedchamber when we return to London?"

It soon became evident to Catherine that the house meant far more to Rutherston than a favorite residence. It was his pride and his passion, a showplace of three generations of Fotherville men of letters and taste, and his private retreat. The walls were hung with priceless paintings of famous masters, and there was nothing in Fotherville House, no piece of furniture or glass or porcelain or book, which had not been chosen with meticulous attention. It was, she thought, almost too perfect, and she doubted that the Fotherville women had ever made the slightest imprint on the faultless setting that their menfolk had created with such infinite care.

The surrounding landscaping conveyed the same impression—a natural beauty that owed nothing to nature but had been contrived by diverting a nearby stream and moving mountains of earth to form a man-made lake flanked by gentle slopes, green with a forest of trees. She learned that while she slept, an army of gardeners toiled, night through, to maintain the lawns and grounds as a picture of perfection when their master was in residence.

"Well," Rutherston asked at last, somewhat nettled by

Catherine's thoughtful manner, "what think you of my humble retreat?"

"Humble? Why you're as proud as a peacock, you odious man!"

"Do you like it, Catherine?" He leaned over to grasp the reins of her mount and brought both bays to a stand. "Tell me what you think."

"I think," she said, choosing her words carefully, "that you have misnamed your humble retreat, my lord. It should be called Fotherville's Paradise, or Fotherville Park—it's the same in Greek!"

"Don't bamboozle me with your Greek, Catherine. What I want to know is—will it become paradise for you?" He was gazing at her with such a searching look that Catherine picked her words carefully.

"It may . . . if I can make a place for myself amidst so much . . . perfection."

"Catherine, my dear, this is your setting, the place where you belong. I never knew, till now, that any woman could improve on what I admit I had regarded as my private paradise, but without you, it will always be incomplete to me." He spoke with such serious intent that Catherine was deeply touched and gratified.

"Then, my dear husband," she replied in the same serious vein, "I am content and shall do all that I can to be a fitting mistress of my husband's domain."

To become the fitting mistress of Rutherston's domain was more of a daunting task than Catherine had ever imagined it would be. At the end of the first week of their stay, Rutherston informed her casually one morning that she had better begin with the servants as she meant to go on, and that the chef, the housekeeper, and the head butler would be waiting at her convenience to have their instructions for the day. He left her then to go to his study where he said he expected to be closeted with his agent for most of the morning.

Catherine was left in a daze and greatly agitated. Her life at Ardo House had not prepared her to become mistress of such a grand establishment, and her mother's informal interviews with Cook and their head maid seemed a far cry from what lay ahead of her now. The staff at Fotherville House, in the gray liveried uniforms of the inside servants, seemed to run the place with quiet precision, and she had no desire to interfere. Before her thoughts had time to throw her into a profound panic, the butler entered and informed her unblinkingly that the chef, André, was waiting at the door.

In a great deal of trepidation, Catherine began the interviews, but it did not take her long to perceive that each member of her staff had been well primed. André had his menus selected and ready, merely wanting madame's advice on the final choices; Mrs. Baxter, the housekeeper, had lists of linens and supplies that had been purchased in the previous months, and more lists of supplies that would be required in the future; and George, the butler, gave her a running commentary on the inside staff and had been so thoughtful as to bring her a list of all their names, which, it seemed clear to Catherine, he expected her to memorize, and since she went in more awe of George than she did of Rutherston, she determined to memorize the list without delay, even if it meant taking it to bed with her at night.

"Thank you, George. I shall do my best to learn the names of all the staff, but it will be difficult to put names to faces at first. Perhaps you will help me as I go along?"

"Certainly, my lady. His lordship has given instructions that you are to meet the assembled staff when you are more settled. He thought the delay would be more to your liking. If you would be so kind as to tell me when it would be convenient, my lady, I shall arrange it."

"Delay?" said Catherine, at a loss.

"Yes, my lady. His lordship thought that you would be too tired out with the journey to meet with the staff on the evening of your arrival."

"Thank you, George. Would tomorrow morning suit?"

For the first time since Catherine had arrived at Fotherville House, George almost smiled, and Catherine recognized that she would exert herself in future to bring that half smile to her butler's face, since it conveyed the message that she was playing her part as mistress of Fotherville House with acceptable aplomb.

She felt a sense of gratitude to Rutherston who had done as much as he could to shield her from the weight of her new responsibilities, giving her time to accustom herself to them. But she laughed aloud when she thought that there were two men in her life whom she most wanted to please, and wondered what Rutherston would think if he knew that his nearest rival was his own grim-faced butler, George.

Chapter 15

Rutherston had suggested that in their last week in residence they should assemble a small house party of about twenty or so of their closest friends. He was in no hurry to share Catherine with the rest of the world, but he had it in his mind that she should gradually become accustomed to acting as his hostess by entertaining their own intimate circle, and the invitations were duly sent out. In point of fact, the assembly turned out to have more of Rutherston's friends than Catherine's, since the journey was an expensive undertaking for anyone of modest means, but a small party from Breckenridge was expected, and Catherine anticipated their arrival with pleasure.

The interviews that Catherine now conducted with the three mainstays of her extensive staff took on new significance, for two dozen people in the house to cater for needed more careful preparations than those for two, and she came to see how critical the role of a butler could be.

George arrived for the interview well prepared, with a list of the visitors and a dossier of the personal preferences in board, bed, and recreation that they had shown in the past, and he requested similar information on the likes and dislikes of those guests whom only Catherine knew. She became aware that a hostess of her consequence was expected to leave nothing to chance in providing for the comfort and entertainment of her guests.

Armed with this information, Catherine next interviewed the chef, but when she mildly suggested that some plain English fare, unembellished with sauces, be added to the more elaborate courses that his lordship preferred, the volatile André flew into a fury. It took some time to smooth his ruffled feathers, and Catherine succeeded in pacifying him only when she promised that at their first large soirée in Berkeley Square he should have a free hand in planning the menus and might be as elaborate as he wished. When she caught the half smile hovering on George's lips, she felt well satisfied.

Mrs. Baxter, the housekeeper, was a woman of soundness and sense who took her instructions with unruffled composure. Some guests' tastes ran to hard beds with soft pillows, and other guests preferred the reverse. Some preferred their rooms to have a view of the lake, and others a view of the terrace. It was all very complicated, and, Catherine thought, quite tiresome, but it seemed that the servants of the great house of Fotherville expected no less, and the air of anticipation and cheerfulness that she observed in her subordinates as they prepared for the coming house party convinced her that they looked forward to their increased responsibilities. Her one regret was when she thought of the army of gardening lads, whom she knew would be set to toil through half the night to make the gardens and grounds of Fotherville House a thing of matchless beauty. Lord Rutherston would expect no less.

It was a week of gaiety and conviviality that Catherine long remembered, and she could not be but pleased to see that the two most important men in her life, her butler and her husband, approved her acumen as chatelaine and hostess. The gathering had been cohesive enough to allow for that easy converse that comes from a commonality of interests, and diverse enough for that novelty that adds spice to the life of any group of people who must bear each other's company for longer than a few hours.

A party had been assembled to spend a pleasant afternoon riding over the park, and Rutherston's stables were a hive of activity as the horses were readied for their respective riders, and Catherine wondered, since few of the guests had brought their own mounts, if the head stud-groom came to Rutherston with a similar list of preferences for the riders as her butler had brought to her for her guests.

They set off at a brisk canter, making for the open ground beyond the lake and the trees, but before long two of the party lagged behind and were soon seen, by anyone watching from the house, to have taken a wrong turn.

Norton had decided, since he knew the estate well, that the private tête-à-tête that he so earnestly desired with Miss Harland should take place where they were unlikely to be disturbed, and he led her unresisting mount a long way around the side of the house to a private path that in a matter of minutes brought them to the other side of the lake. Here he asked her if she would like to dismount and walk, and when she nodded her assent, tethered his own bay to the branch of a tree and helped her dismount. There was not the least necessity for him to do this, but she accepted his assistance with good-humored grace.

The track they followed was wide enough for two horses abreast and, as Norton said, would take them to a shortcut where they could, if they wished, soon catch up with the rest of the party in a short space of time. Mr. Norton lost no time in apprising Miss Harland of what had been on his mind of late.

"You appear to be enjoying your first Season, Miss

Harland?" He heard the pompous note in his voice, and to cover his mistake, hurried on. "Perhaps you feel the want of your London friends here at Fotherville House?" He cursed himself inwardly for making a mull of what he really wanted to say.

"Oh no, Mr. Norton," replied Lucy with the same formality, "I have enough friends here to make my stay quite agreeable."

"Yes, but not the particular friends who engage so much of your time and attention in town." He heard the note of aggrievement in his voice and realized that he was going from bad to worse, but he did not know how to retrieve himself.

"Which friends do you mean?"

"I mean Ranstoke, as you well know. He dances attendance on you like a grinning-faced monkey—and you let him!" Having uttered his accusation in such forceful terms, Mr. Norton now threw caution to the winds as he continued. "You not only let him, you encourage him. Don't think I haven't seen you make sheep's eyes at him. And you're seen everywhere in his company."

"But never alone, Charles. I am always chaperoned," she replied ingenuously, quite delighted to see the emotions of anger and jealousy chasing themselves across Mr. Norton's face.

"Fiddle! Like we are chaperoned now, I wouldn't wonder!" His belligerent manner, far from alarming Miss Harland, cheered her immeasurably.

"But Charles, how can you object? Did you not tell me that I should look around and make a suitable match? What have I done wrong?"

"A suitable match? Is that what you call it?" he said with bitter reproach. "You've all but thrown yourself away on a fool with nothing to recommend him but a handsome face. Ranstoke hasn't a feather to fly with!"

"I'm sure you are mistaken. I believe he has an income of a thousand a year—not a fortune to be sure, but if two people are fond of each other . . ."

"Lucy!" He was devastated. "You're not in love with him, are you?"

Miss Harland, seeing the look of wounded pride on the face of her beloved, decided that it was time to relent and lead him gently into the fold.

"Charles, you know that I don't love him, can't love him, but what am I to do? If you won't offer for me, I must marry someone. Mr. Ranstoke will do just as well as anyone else."

"The devil he will!" Mr. Norton was now beside himself with rage. "D'you think I shall step aside to let a numbskull like Ranstoke step in and carry you off? You must be soft in the head, my girl, if you think that!" In his agitation, Mr. Norton had taken hold of Lucy's wrist in a fierce grasp.

"But I don't think it, Charles. I am depending on you not to step aside." She looked at him with such longing, such unabashed devotion that his anger left him instantly.

"Oh, Lucy, what a fool I've been." He cupped her chin with his free hand and kissed her soundly, but was prevented from taking her into his arms since his other hand was attached to the reins of his bay.

"Oh, Charles!" She sighed and rubbed her cheek affectionately against his shoulder.

After a few moments, Norton broke the spell.

"I shall have to apply to your father, Lucy, and whether he will countenance the match or no remains to be seen." He tilted her chin to look into her eyes. "Lucy, if he doesn't care for the connection, we shall have to wait till you come of age."

"Yes, Charles," said Miss Harland contentedly, not deceiving her beloved in the least by her docile reply.

"I mean it, my girl. You can put all thought of bolting to Gretna Green out of your mind, and don't try to fadge me with that butter-wouldn't-melt-in-my-mouth look!"

"Charles," she pouted, "I wouldn't!"

"Oh, wouldn't you? Well, it wouldn't work and that's flat. We will do it properly, or not at all. Have I made myself plain, my love?"

Miss Harland had to own that her dear Charles had made his meaning perfectly plain, and since it seemed that her heart's desire could not be achieved by working her feminine wiles on such a masterful paragon, she turned her thoughts to devising what she might say to her father to make the match palatable to him.

"And Lucy, when I next come courting you, remind me to leave the horses in the stable."

The Earl and Countess of Levin had brought with them a young artist of an age with Rutherston, and Catherine had taken to him instantly. His name was Adrian Henderson, and he was making a mark for himself as a portrait painter of some distinction amongst the ton. When the gentlemen joined the ladies after dinner, Catherine found Mr. Henderson at her elbow and was soon engaged, in her best hostess manner, in drawing him out. It transpired that Mr. Henderson's ambition was to paint real characters rather than noble profiles, and he used the profits from the lucrative sale of the one to finance his losses in the other.

"Do you mean by that, Mr. Henderson, that you don't

find the members of High Society congenial subjects for your portraits?"

"As a rule, my lady, no, for consequence and fortune cannot add one iota of sensibility to a face that is already dull."

"Then what think you of my husband's art collection, Mr. Henderson? Do you not think that there are a few dull faces hanging on these walls?"

"Your husband is a connoisseur of distinction, my lady, with an art collection that is unrivaled in all of England, but even he has ancestors whose portraits he can hardly hide away. You will observe that those portraits are carefully displayed to attract the least attention?" His eyes glittered wickedly as he laughed, showing a mouth of gleaming white teeth, and Catherine was charmed, as much by his fair, good looks as by his lively conversation.

She lowered her voice to a sinister whisper.

"Have you considered that your talents are wasted as a painter, Mr. Henderson? Your path lies in politics. Such a pretty speech—and so innocently barbed. But I shall not take offense."

"My lady, you are mistaken. No offense to you. They are not your ancestors."

This time it was Catherine who laughed in appreciation, and Rutherston, cornered by his sister, the duchess, frowned as he glanced their way.

"Mr. Henderson, a word of advice. My husband loves a laugh, but you may find him a trifle sensitive to any criticism of this house."

"I thank you for the warning, but it comes too late. He has already asked for my opinion of his collection, and I have given it to him freely."

Catherine looked impressed. "And you still have a whole skin? It is more than I would dare." She regarded him with frank interest, wondering at his boldness, and admiration was reflected in her warm amber eyes. Henderson surveyed her in amused comprehension and broke abruptly into her train of thought.

"My lady, your husband, Lord Rutherston, invited me here for a purpose. He wanted me to meet you to determine whether I would accept his commission to paint your portrait."

"He did not mention the matter to me."

"He knows that I only accept a commission if I feel that I can paint a portrait of some distinction."

"What? Another picture for a dark corner on some ignominious wall?" Catherine asked archly.

"Hardly that, my lady. This portrait will take pride of place in this house, if I have the ability to get you right, and I hope that I may."

"Ah. Then I'm to be the pride of all his possessions?" Catherine did not know why she had said it, but was immediately contrite. "I do beg your pardon, Mr. Henderson, that was thoughtless and unkind. Tell me, do I suit you as a subject?"

"If you mean, do I want to paint you—yes. From the moment I saw you, I believed that you would be wasted on any man who has no aesthetic sense. You should belong to an artist."

Catherine was taken aback and glanced nervously over her shoulder in the direction of her husband who, she saw, was regarding her keenly. She turned back to Henderson, and his smiling face told her that he had read her mind.

"You are not trying to make me believe that I am beautiful, are you, Mr. Henderson, for you won't succeed." She forced her voice to lightness, aware that Rutherston was moving toward them.

"I would not say that you are a typical beauty, but you have a glow about you, a radiance that makes you unique. That is the quality I want to capture on canvas."

"Then you accept me as a subject?"

"I do. Now it is your turn, my lady. Will you accept me as your . . . artist?"

The man was irrepressible, and Catherine felt a flush of color creeping into her cheeks.

"If it pleases my husband to engage you to paint my portrait, then naturally I agree."

"I should warn you that I am an autocrat where my pictures are concerned. I demand the right to decide what you will wear, how you sit or stand, what background I shall paint you against, down to the smallest detail."

"Do all men always talk about their rights, or just the men of my acquaintance?" She smiled at him to disarm her words. "I shall be as docile as you wish, Mr. Henderson, but you must apply to my husband about the details. He has never learned docility, and is used to expressing his opinions quite forcefully."

Rutherston joined them then and he and Henderson were soon engaged in a lively debate on whether Catherine should be dressed in velvets or satins, reds or golds, and she moved away to join another group, having ascertained one thing—the preliminary sketches were to be done once they reached London, the following week.

As they were preparing for bed that night, Rutherston asked Catherine what she thought of Henderson.

"Is he any good, Richard?"

"He is the best, otherwise my dear, I would not consider engaging him. But I have seen some of his work, and I know that he is talented. He is also particular, now that he is becoming well-known. But I knew, when he saw you, that he would accept my commission." He was lying full length on the bed, hands clasped behind his head, observing Catherine with lazy, watchful eyes as she sat at her dressing table finishing her toilette.

"You haven't answered my question, Catherine."

It flashed through her mind that it would be dangerous and useless to be evasive with Richard. He would know, and take offense, and an offended Richard was a dangerous animal. She turned, smiling at him coquettishly.

"He is very forward, my lord, and deliciously flirtatious."

Rutherston bounded from the bed and caught her in his arms, hugging her to him.

"You little vixen, I saw you flirting shamelessly with him tonight." She was relieved to see that he was smiling. "And you a bride of only three weeks."

"Are you worried, darling?" She hoped he was. "You need not be, you know. I find you infinitely more attractive than Mr. Henderson." Her arms went round his waist and she kissed his naked chest where his shirt hung open. His arms tightened around her possessively.

"Worried? No. But I am cautious. He is a gambler and a womanizer. In short, my dear—a rake."

"If that is your opinion of him, why have you chosen him to paint my portrait?" Catherine asked in some surprise.

"Did I not say that he is the best?"

"But don't you care, Richard, that he will flirt with me?" There was a suggestion of pique in her voice, and Rutherston smiled to hear it.

"My dear, I rely on your own good sense, and Mr. Henderson's knowledge of my marksmanship with a pistol to keep him at bay, besides which, you will never be in his company unchaperoned."

"Duels, my lord? You cannot be serious!"

"Let us hope, my love, that you need never find out." He bent and kissed her then, tugging impatiently at her gown to free her of it, and all thought of Henderson slipped from their minds.

Chapter 16

The great oak doors of Fotherville House were shut upon the last of the departing guests, and Catherine, in high spirits at the happy outcome of her debut as Rutherston's hostess, slipped her arm through Lucy's, and, light of heart, led the way upstairs to a small, pretty drawing room that she called her own. Rutherston had invited Lucy and Norton to return with them in his carriage to London, and Catherine, observing a new easiness in Lucy's and Norton's manner toward each other, as if they had come to an understanding, found herself looking forward to two very pleasant days of company that could only be thought of as the most congenial.

Henderson had stayed on for some obscure reason known only to himself and Rutherston, and Catherine was pleased. Throughout his stay she had detected him, on more than one occasion, appraising her with the closest kind of scrutiny, and although she was sure that his interest was entirely professional, it discomfited her to be the object of so much unwanted attention. Once, she had caught him in the act of studying her profile, and she had stared right back.

A mood of playfulness had developed between them, which Rutherston seemed not to mind, and Catherine found herself hoping that Henderson might be included in their circle of friends when they returned to town.

The gentlemen had retreated to Rutherston's study on some business that had been mentioned in vague terms, and the two sisters, finding their absence by no means unwelcome, had settled themselves to catch up on their correspondence with their sister Mary, whose confinement was due any day.

They worked in companionable silence, and after an interval, when Catherine had completed her agreeable labor, she began to hunt through the drawers of her writing table in search of a wafer to seal the letter. When none could be found, she indicated to Lucy, who was still busily engaged, that she would try for one in the big oak desk in the library downstairs.

When she spread her hands on the great leather-topped desk in the library, however, she was far from certain that she had any right to search the contents of Rutherston's desk, and she stood looking at it irresolutely for a moment or two.

He had said, she remembered, that there should be no secrets between husband and wife, and she thought it highly unlikely that anything of a private nature would be concealed in such a public place, especially as Rutherston's work desk was in his office, his sacrosanct space where no one ever dared venture in uninvited. This settled the matter in Catherine's mind, and she opened the drawers one by one, reaching her arm deep into the recesses, her fingers groping for the telltale wafers.

In one of the drawers, her hand grasped something hard, far at the back, and she gave it a tug in an effort to retrieve it, but it snapped back out of her fingers. At the same moment, she caught the sound of a faint click, and she watched mesmerized as a small, shallow drawer slid open at the side of the desk.

Catherine leaned over to gaze with heightened interest and saw in the hidden recess a slim blue velvet box emblazoned with the name of the same prestigious jeweller in Bond Street who had supplied her pearl necklace.

"Catherine?"

Stricken with guilt, she whirled around, but when she saw that it was only Henderson, she let out her breath with a shudder of relief.

"Adrian," she breathed, then, on a more urgent note, "Where is Richard?"

Henderson moved toward her, curious about her stricken look and her fearful question.

"He's with Norton still, so don't look so conscience-stricken! Your guilty secret is safe with me, my lady. Did I catch you red-handed?"

She flushed scarlet to the roots of her auburn hair. "Ho, ho! Catherine," he teased, "what have we here?"

"I came upon it by accident. It's a secret drawer in Richard's desk. No, don't touch anything!" But he had already retrieved the blue velvet box and was in the process of opening it.

"Oh, Adrian, please put it back. We have no right." She looked with agitation at the library door, as if expecting to see Rutherston framed in the doorway at any moment.

"Well, well! This must have cost his lordship a small fortune!" Her interest was caught by Henderson's words, and Catherine looked down at the open box and gazed with stupefied wonder at the most dazzling diamond necklace that she had ever beheld.

Henderson slipped the necklace out of the box with his long, thin fingers and held it up to the window to catch the light, and the cool, glittering rays of the morning sun were caught and reflected from it like drops of water hanging from a melting icicle.

"It is perfection itself," Catherine breathed in awed tones.

"If you like that sort of thing," said Henderson brusquely, replacing the diamonds in their slim box and sliding them back into the hidden recess with a click. "I did not think you cared for beads and baubles."

"Why not?" asked Catherine, diverted. "Because I don't wear them? Well, that is because, kind sir, nobody has ever given me any to wear."

"In that case, my dear Lady Rutherston," he said ruefully, "I must apologize for spoiling what I am sure was meant to be a delightful surprise for you! Pity that I am such a curious creature, but there it is. You had better forget all about them, Catherine, until Rutherston hands them over, and if you want to save my skin, I'd be much obliged if you would receive them with as much surprise and awe as you can muster."

"If those lovely gems ever fall into my hands, Mr. Henderson," she replied lightly, as she slipped her arm in his to lead him out of the library, "the task you have set me will be very easy to perform. But in the meantime, I intend to forget that I ever found them, and you may be sure that Lord Rutherston will hear nothing of this indiscretion from me. And now, kind sir, would you take pity on two abandoned ladies and have tea with us?"

But Catherine could not forget, and couldn't help wondering who was meant to have the exquisite prize, even though she was fairly confident in her own mind that Rutherston had purchased it for her. He had given her pearls for her nuptials, a necklace she knew to be matchless, but she did not think her gems were comparable to the dazzling diamonds, and since she had worn pearls since she had been in the schoolroom, she was eager for something that would proclaim to the world that she had come of age—no longer the rose in bud, but in full bloom.

Her birthday was three months away, but it hardly seemed likely that Rutherston had purchased her present so far in advance. It came to her suddenly that he meant her to wear the diamonds for her portrait, and the more she thought about it, the more reasonable the explanation appeared to be.

She resolved that Rutherston should never know that she had behaved in such a vulgar way, letting her curiosity get the better of her. Such conduct, she knew, would be inexcusable in his eyes, and the thought brought a flush to her cheeks. She could not but admit that his conduct was everything that was pleasing. He could be the most charming, thoughtful man when he wanted to be.

And if Rutherston was aware that his wife looked at him with a more softened expression than usual, he put it down to the delightful intimacy that had grown between them in the last three weeks.

Catherine's life with Rutherston in London was very different from their life in the country. She saw much less of him, even when they attended the same receptions and parties, for it was not thought good ton for a wife or husband to monopolize each other's company, and it seemed almost obligatory, at any time of the night or day, for a gentleman to spend some time in one or other of his many clubs in St. James Street in the exclusive company of other gentlemen. When Catherine would have protested that they spent so little time together, Rutherston reminded her reasonably that they were in town at her choosing and she had only to say the word and they would remove to Fotherville House. As for Henderson painting her portrait, Rutherston informed her, he could do that just as easily on their estate.

But Catherine had no wish to leave Lucy so near the end of the Season, and thought that she might tolerate the lack of Rutherston's attention for the month or so that remained. It was not town life that she held so much in dislike, but only her husband's absence from her side. And when, for some reason, Rutherston could not escort his wife and her sister to their various functions, he called on the services of his most obliging cousin, Mr. Norton, and the ladies were not deprived of any of their pleasures.

The preliminary sketches for Catherine's portrait began almost as soon as they returned to town. Henderson came every afternoon at a time when Rutherston was usually about, and Catherine was amused at first to see how the two of them treated her as if she were an inanimate object, like a dressmaker's dummy on which to peg silks, satins, and velvets, turning her this way and that to catch the light.

The one contretemps between husband and artist occurred when Rutherston expressed the desire that Catherine's throat be encircled with pearls for her portrait. Catherine felt a pang of regret at her husband's words, and heard nothing of the argument that followed. She was bitterly disappointed, since she had hoped to flaunt the bewitching gems at the last soirée in Carlton House before the prince regent retired for the summer to Brighton.

It seemed unreasonable that she should wait three months for her birthday present, but she would not dare let Rutherston know that she had the least idea of the existence of the precious necklace. Her conduct had been reprehensible—inexcusable, and she had no wish to come under the freezing glare of the proud Marquis of Rutherston.

Shortly after arriving in London, Catherine had been received in Green Street by her mother-in-law with an open display of affection and pleasure, and she was relieved to see that the dowager marchioness bore her no ill will for her former impertinence.

Since Rutherston felt himself under a moral obligation to spend much of his time at the House or at Court when in town, Catherine had fallen into the habit of waiting on her mother-in-law most afternoons, as well as on her aunt in Mount Street, where Lucy still lived. Everyone seemed to think that she and Rutherston would want to be on their own in Berkeley Square, but in point of fact, Catherine was lonely much of the time, as even Norton had vacated the house and was sharing rooms with a friend in Jermyn Street.

One afternoon, she called in at Green Street only to be informed by the butler, Styles, that her ladyship was out, but that her grace, the Duchess of Beaumain was at home to visitors, and since Catherine could think of no reasonable excuse for making her escape, she allowed herself to be announced.

Rutherston's sister, older than he by a couple of summers, was a taking woman until she opened her mouth to speak. There was no malice in her, but her conversation was a stream of inanities, which her tongue idly articulated as every stray thought happened to flit through her head. Nor had she been compelled to cultivate that sense of discretion that guards against an unruly tongue, since her place in the Social Order put her far above the touch, or censure, of those mortals of a lesser station in life who bore the brunt of her fatuity.

His grace, Duke Henry, a man addicted to all forms of sport and whom Rutherston referred to contemptuously as "that blockhead," never seemed to see anything remiss in his consort's want of delicacy, and the stringent restraints that had been imposed on the duchess in her youth by her mother, the present dowager marchioness, had long since been thrown off.

As Catherine listened with half an ear to the ramblings of her sister-in-law, who prattled with motherly pride and affection about the latest exploits of her four growing sons, she wondered how soon she could make her excuses without appearing to be impolite, when she became aware the duchess was regarding her with a look of expectancy.

"I beg your pardon, Jane, I didn't catch what you said."

"I remarked, m'dear, that you have been married to Rutherston more than a month now. I remember how pleased Beaumain was when I presented him with an heir nine months almost to the day of our marriage."

There was no mistaking the meaning of the duchess's words and Catherine flushed, more in anger than embarrassment, and returned her sister-in-law's gaze with a glare. The duchess, unabashed, patted the younger woman on the hands held tightly clasped in her lap.

"You mustn't find fault with me for my curiosity, my dear. I was a Fotherville before I was married, you know, so I am an interested party. We have all been waiting for Rutherston to set up his nursery this long age past, so another month or two don't signify." She chortled with mirth, casting an appraising look at Catherine's trim figure, and Catherine tilted her chin in that way, singular to herself, which should have warned the duchess that she was preparing to do battle.

"What a fortunate circumstance it was, then, that dear Richard decided to get married before obliging you in your dearest wish." There, thought Catherine, that ought to depress the pretensions of the silly woman.

"What? Oh, there was no fear of his not getting leg-shackled. Of course, Mama knew well enough that Rutherston had been leading a ramshackle existence since his come-out. Stands to reason he would—nothing to stop him, was there? And those high-flyers he kept!" Her grace chuckled at some amusing memory. "Beaumain said that he was getting into petticoat scrapes long before he went up to Oxford, but that I do know Mama knew nothing about."

These unsolicited reminiscences about Rutherston were beginning to give Catherine the queerest feeling, as if she had opened her husband's private correspondence and was reading it surreptitiously. She was on the point of rising to leave when the duchess's next remark riveted her to her seat.

"Once he gave Mama his solemn promise that he would marry in his thirtieth year, of course, he had a free hand. Nobody interfered after that. Beaumain said that Rutherston would weasel out of it somehow, but I knew he wouldn't. A Fotherville never reneges on a promise! But you could have knocked me down with a feather when I heard that he was chasing you all over town."

With a supreme effort to disguise her mounting outrage, Catherine repeated tersely, "Richard promised that he would marry in his thirtieth year?"

"That was Mama's doing. Told him straight what was due his Name. Didn't have to—he knew it himself." Again the duchess chortled in her peculiarly horsey way, and Catherine found the sound offensive to her ears. "He was only five and twenty when Mama got that promise out of him. I daresay five years free of his family's interference seemed like an age to him then." This last remark was accompanied by another horsey neigh.

"I daresay," Catherine managed to reply, feeling that it was incumbent on her to say something.

"Thought myself he might offer for Burland's daughter—what's her name? Lady Harriet? She certainly set her cap at him, but he cried off. Would have been a good match too—good-looking gel, plenty of blue blood, and an heiress to boot. Never can predict what Richard will do, though!"

Catherine felt the heat of her fury almost choke her, and she was ready to burst into tears. Only her bruised pride kept her in check, and she rose in earnest now and took a hasty leave of the startled duchess.

On her return to Berkeley Square, she informed George curtly that she would not be at home to visitors that afternoon, no matter who, and hurrying to her room, she threw herself down on the bed and burst into tears of mortification. She had imagined that Rutherston had married her out of love, setting aside what must have seemed to him all the disadvantages of an inferior connection, but his sister's confidences now made her see his actions in a new light.

He had married out of duty, and he had chosen her to spite his family because of that foolish promise. They had expected him to offer for Lady Harriet, but it was just like him to do the unexpected. His family might force him to do his duty, but he would do it in such a way that he was still master in his own house.

"Odious, odious man," Catherine cried into her pillow. The thought that she might be pregnant only added to her fury and sense of injustice. She remembered the husky-voiced Isabel whom she had overheard in the cloakroom at Lady Castlereagh's ball—"His wife will be expected to breed every year—an unenviable fate," and she winced as if struck. She wanted to teach her proud, aristocrat husband a lesson he would never forget, but no plan came to her mind, and she wept the harder in frustrated anger, muttering in Greek the vilest epithets she could remember, which sounded far more appropriate than the mild "odious."

Chapter 17

It was shortly after the dinner hour when Rutherston came home that evening, excusing his tardiness by saying that he had met some acquaintances at White's and could not escape them without appearing boorish. He was in a hurry to change his clothes, for he said that he had to put in an appearance at some Court function at Carlton House, and Catherine, who pretended to be engrossed in a book, managed to speak to him with tolerable composure.

"What is it now, my love?" He glanced at the slim volume in her hands, an appreciative gleam in his eyes. "'Medea'? Believe me, Catherine, I would rather stay home with you and argue the merits of the vengeful Medea, but noblesse oblige demands that I attend this dull affair."

Catherine made no comment, and Rutherston, who was becoming used to his wife's look of preoccupation when she was reading, thought little of it and went off calling for his valet to help him. He returned half an hour later to find Catherine in the same pose as before.

"Do you stay at home tonight, Catherine, or do you go out with Lucy?"

Catherine willed herself to look at him. "I'm staying home, Richard. I have been dashing around town ever since we came back; one night at home won't hurt my reputation. I shall read for a while and go to bed early." Even Catherine could hear the brittle edge to her voice, and she was sure that it would not be lost on Rutherston.

He looked at her thoughtfully for a moment or two, then came to kneel beside her chair, and, removing the book from her hands, cupped her face in his long fingers.

"What is it, darling? Shall I make my excuses and stay home with you tonight?" The gentleness in his tone was almost more than she could bear. She longed to confide her unhappy thoughts to someone, but not to him—the cause of all her misery.

She tried feebly to pull his hands away, shaking her head, afraid her voice would betray her emotion.

"Let me go, Richard." She dropped her eyes, and found to her horror that her cheeks had become wet with tears. In a moment he had his arms around her and was drying her wet cheeks with his white linen handkerchief.

"I . . . I'm not myself tonight. I have a headache. It will pass."

"My dear girl!" He gathered her in his arms and sat down in the chair cradling her.

"Tell me about it," he said at last.

"There's nothing to tell. Don't fuss over me, Richard. I don't like it." She tried desperately to pull away, but he held her fast.

"What is it, Catherine? No, don't push me away. Can't you tell me what troubles you?" He pulled her face round to look steadily into her tawny eyes, and it was as much as Catherine could do to conceal the anger that was bringing a faint flush to her cheeks. Rutherston saw the flush and misread its meaning. He stroked her hair. "I have a fair idea of what is troubling you, my love." The gentle tone held a suggestion of mockery, and Catherine bristled.

"Do you indeed, my lord?" she asked with icy hauteur.

"Oh, indeed, I do!" He was laughing openly at her now, and Catherine's ire boiled over.

"You insufferable . . . man." She pursed her lips, her eyes glinting dangerously.

"My dear, what is upsetting you so? You must have known I would know. I have been coming to your bed nigh on every night for six weeks now. How could I not know? What has happened is nothing extraordinary!"

She broke away from him at that, flouncing out of his grasp.

"Extraordinary!" she replied vehemently. "No, it is certainly not that. It is common—so common as to be laughable. Shall you post round to your mama and sister, my lord, to convey the marvelous, vulgar tidings to them?"

Rutherston removed himself gracefully from the chair and came to stand beside her, his hands resting lightly on her shoulders.

"Catherine, forget my family. Forget everything but us. Is it not what you want?" He was watching her warily, intently.

"What I want! When have you cared for what I want? This is what you married me for, isn't it, so that you could have your heir." She felt his grip tighten on her shoulder, shaking her gently.

"Catherine!" His lips brushed her hair. "What foolishness is this? I owe it to my name, my house, to beget an heir. But surely you know it is more than that. I want the woman I love to bear the children of my body."

"Do you, my lord, do you indeed? Am I to breed every year, like my sister Mary, and think myself lucky to be so ill-used?"

He dropped his hands from her shoulders, a cold mask of indifference settling on his face.

"What are you saying, ma'am?"

Catherine hardly knew what she was saying. The disclosure of his promise to his mother and the memory of Isabel's silky voice in the cloakroom were robbing her of rational thought. She was goaded into saying things she did not mean.

"I won't . . . I won't . . ." She could not say it.

"Pray continue, ma'am. You won't?" His voice had become the affected drawl he customarily assumed when he felt it necessary to depress the pretensions of underlings, and Catherine's cheeks flamed redder still.

"I won't be like my sister Mary," she managed to say with some composure. She felt the tension between them unbearable and picked up her book for something to do.

"And I was not aware that Lady Mary found the matrimonial state so little to her liking." He had moved to a side table to pour himself a shot of brandy, and stood watching her closely as he sipped it.

"Her case is not the same as mine."

"Indeed? You must instruct me, Catherine, for I find I am unable to follow your reasoning." His drawl was grating on her ears, making her nerves raw.

"You know perfectly well what I mean," she snapped at him. "I have no intentions of breeding every year to gratify the pride of the great House of Fotherville." It was the closest she could come to telling him that she knew about his promise to his family, for she could not bear him to know how much she had been wounded by it. She saw his hand flick back as he drained his glass in one gulp. He replaced it carefully on the table and moved toward her with unhurried ease, and when she looked into his glittering, cold stare, she began to tremble.

"You will have to speak plainer than that, ma'am." He waited for her to reply, but Catherine looked at him helplessly, unable to go on. She hung her head in embarrassment, and Rutherston's eyes softened to see her confusion.

"Are you denying me my conjugal rights?" His voice sounded amused and disbelieving.

"Yes . . . no . . . I don't know." She could hear the petulance in her own voice, and she squirmed.

He reached out his hand and caressed her cheek. "Wouldn't you say, Catherine, that your logic is a trifle awry? What sense is there in forbidding me your bed now?" He possessed himself of her hands and drew her into the circle of his arms. She stood unresisting, her eyes cast down, unwilling to meet his gaze. "Catherine," he coaxed, his voice husky with sudden desire, "you are carrying our child. If you are afraid . . ."

"No! Not our child, but your heir! There is a difference, my lord." Her words made no sense to him, but the curl of her lip and the angry sparkle in her eyes jolted him. She was on the crest of a wave of anger and continued remorselessly. "There is nothing wrong with my logic, sir. Let me tell you that I am beginning the way I mean to go on—a maxim I learned from you. You shall have your heir, but nothing more from me. Is that plain enough speaking for you, or would you like me to go on?"

"Don't trouble, my dear," he bit back, goaded to a fury as great as her own. "A husband can always find consolation when he finds himself mated with an ungenerous wife."

She was stung into a retort. "Oh, a mistress, I know, does not have the burden of breeding every year!"

His voice was like ice. "You are misinformed, ma'am. Some do." And he left abruptly, shutting the door firmly behind him on a seething, tearful Catherine.

* * *

Take A Trip Into A Timeless World of Passion and Adventure with Kensington Choice Historical Romances! —Absolutely FREE!

Enjoy the passion and adventure of another time with Kensington Choice Historical Romances. They are the finest novels of their kind, written by today's best-selling romance authors. Each Kensington Choice Historical Romance transports you to distant lands in a bygone age. Experience the adventure and share the delight as proud men and spirited women discover the wonder and passion of true love.

Get 4 FREE Books!

We created our convenient Home Subscription Service so you'll be sure to have the hottest new romances delivered each month right to your doorstep—usually before they are available in book stores. Just to show you how convenient the Zebra Home Subscription Service is, we would like to send you 4 FREE Kensington Choice Historical Romances. The books are worth up to $24.96, but you only pay $1.99 for shipping and handling. There's no obligation to buy additional books—ever!

Save Up To 30% With Home Delivery!

Accept your FREE books and each month we'll deliver 4 brand new titles as soon as they are published. They'll be yours to examine FREE for 10 days. Then if you decide to keep the books, you'll pay the preferred subscriber's price (up to 30% off the cover price!), plus shipping and handling. Remember, you are under no obligation to buy any of these books at any time! If you are not delighted with them, simply return them and owe nothing. But if you enjoy Kensington Choice Historical Romances as much as we think you will, pay the special preferred subscriber rate and save over $8.00 off the cover price!

We have 4 FREE BOOKS for you as your
introduction to
KENSINGTON CHOICE!
To get your FREE BOOKS, worth up to $24.96, mail
the card below or call TOLL-FREE 1-800-770-1963.
Visit our website at www.kensingtonbooks.com.

Get 4 FREE Kensington Choice Historical Romances!

YES! Please send me my 4 FREE KENSINGTON CHOICE HISTORICAL ROMANCES (without obligation to purchase other books). I only pay $1.99 for shipping and handling. Unless you hear from me after I receive my 4 FREE BOOKS, you may send me 4 new novels—as soon as they are published—to preview each month FREE for 10 days. If I am not satisfied, I may return them and owe nothing. Otherwise, I will pay the money-saving preferred subscriber's price (over $8.00 off the cover price), plus shipping and handling. I may return any shipment within 10 days and owe nothing, and I may cancel any time I wish. In any case the 4 FREE books will be mine to keep.

Name_____

Address_____Apt._____

City_____State_____Zip_____

Telephone (____)_____

Signature_____

(If under 18, parent or guardian must sign)

Offer limited to one per household and not to current subscribers. Terms, offer and prices
subject to change. Orders subject to acceptance by Kensington Choice Book Club.
Offer Valid in the U.S. only.

KN123A

4 FREE

Kensington
Choice
Historical
Romances
*(worth up to
$24.96)
are waiting
for you to
claim them!*

*See details
inside...*

‖‖‖...‖.‖.‖...‖‖.‖..‖.‖.‖.‖..‖‖..‖..‖‖.‖..‖..‖‖...‖

KENSINGTON CHOICE

Zebra Home Subscription Service, Inc.

P.O. Box 5214

Clifton NJ 07015-5214

But she did not stay at home that night. Shortly after Rutherston left, a noisy happy party, including Lucy, Norton, Henderson, and her brother Tom, who had posted all the way from Breckenridge, was shown in to Catherine's drawing room.

"The little devil has finally put in an appearance, Kate! Mary's third boy was born last Tuesday morning," Tom cried exultantly.

"And how is our sister Mary?"

"Not so well this time, but Ma is with her, so you're not to worry. I was sent to bring the glad tidings, but I stay for only a day or two."

Tom's news troubled Catherine. Her sister, Lady Mary, was only one year older than she, and until her marriage to Viscount Haughton, had been her closest confidante. In four years of marriage, this was her third child. She remembered briefly Mary's happiness when she had seen her last in Breckenridge, and longed to be with her now. She questioned Tom closely, but his uncertain replies did nothing to satisfy her.

"Lady Rutherston?" She heard Henderson's voice address her and she brought her thoughts back to the present. "We are engaged to go to the theater tonight. If you care to join us, I would deem it a great honor." His voice was warm and inviting, and as she looked into his eyes, Catherine saw the understanding reflected in them. It seemed to her that he had sensed her unhappiness and was reaching out to comfort her. When she thought of Rutherston's cold sneer as he had left her alone to her misery, her mind was made up. She did not want to be left alone with her unhappy thoughts, and with forced gaiety, she set out with her friends in Henderson's carriage to see the great Kemble in Shakespeare's "Macbeth."

* * *

Henderson's family was well connected, and although he had little money of his own, barring what he made as a portrait painter, he never seemed to want for anything. The box that they occupied that evening belonged to his aunt, Lady Blakney, but since she was rarely in town, Henderson had it for his own use.

Catherine found herself in the front row, seated between Tom and Henderson, Lucy and Norton sitting directly behind them. It was in the first interval, when she was left alone with Henderson while the others promenaded in the corridors or visited acquaintances in their boxes, that she caught sight of Rutherston, and the smile on her lips froze. He had just entered the box opposite, in which a beautiful woman was holding court surrounded by a group of admiring gallants. As he looked across the theater idly, his glance came to rest on Catherine, and she saw the shock register on his handsome face. She bowed to him with a slight nod of her head and turned her attention back to Henderson, forcing herself not to look in Rutherston's direction again. She flicked open her fan with a flutter to half cover her face, and asked her escort the identity of the lady in the opposite box who was attracting so much masculine attention. She knew by his knowing expression that Henderson had seen everything that had passed between Rutherston and herself and had guessed the significance of their stiff little bows to each other.

"That lady," he said in an undertone, "is Lady Pamela, old Symington's widow—but I am given to understand that her title is by way of being a courtesy."

Catherine forced herself to laugh and lifted her chin a little higher in case Rutherston should be watching.

"Why have I never seen her at any of the assemblies? She has a face and form that one would not easily forget."

Henderson considered her question, a look of embarrassment on his face.

"Tell me, Adrian! From you, at least, I expect honesty."

"My dear, she is accepted in some circles and not in others. Obviously, you and she move in different circles."

"And which circles does she move in?"

"Oh, the highest—she is a camp follower of the Carlton House set."

Catherine tried to control the shaking of the hand in her lap, and Henderson, seeing it tremble, covered it with one of his own.

It was at that moment that Rutherston entered their box, his aristocratic features a cool mask of civility.

In one graceful, unhurried movement, Henderson released Catherine's hand and stood up to greet the new arrival. The two men acknowledged each other with affable courtesy, but Catherine was conscious of a forced indolence in Rutherston's manner, like a panther approaching its prey before it springs to attack.

"My dear, I see that Shakespeare succeeded where Euripides failed. Your headache is better, I trust?" he drawled in a cool, indifferent inquiry.

Catherine was barely aware that she nodded in assent. From the moment that she had observed him with the stunning Lady Pamela, she had been engulfed by a sense of desolation, and she was afraid to speak lest some quality in her voice betray her. She was grateful for Henderson's presence of mind as he engaged Rutherston in conversation, giving her time to regain some of her composure. The thought that her husband had lied to her when he had said that he was to be at Carlton House now began to fan her fury, and she found it the perfect antidote for self-pity. She knew that Rutherston was not well pleased to find her alone with Henderson, but she had no intention of divulging that there were five in their party.

He stayed for only a minute or two, and shortly afterwards Catherine saw him enter the divine Pamela's box and sit down in a vacant chair beside her. She watched their heads close together in intimate conversation and a stab of fierce jealousy shook her to the core. For the rest of the interval her eyes traveled involuntarily to Lady Pamela's box, and it was not long before she saw Rutherston depart. She felt Henderson's eyes watching her with pity—an emotion that she despised—and from that moment on exerted herself to be as lighthearted and gay as she could manage, but when she finally set down at Berkeley Square and Henderson had walked her to the door, his words, softly spoken, "Catherine, he is a fool!" all but undid her.

Rutherston did not come home that night, and Catherine was sure in her mind that he had found consolation in the arms of the seductive Lady Pamela, whose virtue, if Henderson was to be believed, was highly questionable. She thought of the extreme emotions of Euripides's abandoned Medea, and she determined that Rutherston would not see how deeply she had been affected.

The portrait painting was not going well. The preliminary sketches had been completed and Henderson had begun to assemble the palette of colors that he hoped would capture the rich autumn tints and translucent quality of Catherine's complexion and costume. He had chosen her gown—a lustrous cream-colored satin cut low in the bodice, and over it had flung with apparent carelessness a golden taffeta pelisse, which he took infinite pains to drape around her shoulders. He had tilted her chin in her familiar pose and had moved her head this way and that, each time standing back to survey the whole, but it was evident in his silent, impatient demeanor that nothing pleased, and when she moved her head slightly to watch him better, his irritation broke through.

"Catherine, Lady Rutherston, you must stop fidgeting, else we'll be here all day!"

"Yes, Mr. Henderson. I do beg your pardon, but I'm getting a crick in my neck from holding my chin at this awkward angle. I don't think I can keep it up for long."

"I assure you, it's your characteristic pose."

"Is it? Then how ridiculous I must look, with my nose in the air like this. I wonder that I don't fall flat on my face whenever I try to cross a room." She was trying to humor him and was rewarded by seeing a slight slackening of his jaw.

"I meant, of course, when you are angry and the sparks flash from your eyes. Think angry thoughts, my lady, and you'll soon catch the pose." When he saw the stricken look that crossed Catherine's face, he muttered a curse and was at her side in a moment, his arms around her.

"My dear, forgive me. I did not think."

Catherine held him off, her hands pressed hard against his chest, and shook her head, forcing a wan smile to her lips.

"Adrian, please don't or I cannot bear it." She increased the pressure of her hands, warding him off, and he stepped back a couple of paces.

"Do I have your permission to speak, Catherine?"

"No! You must not, now or ever." At her look of alarm, he closed his lips in a grim line.

"You need not be afraid—I can protect you if ever you need a friend."

Catherine looked at him in astonishment.

"Adrian, if you are developing a tendre for me, let me disabuse you of the sentiment at once. I am under my husband's protection. Believe me, there is nothing that you can do to make things right. It is only a silly quarrel between husband and wife."

He looked as if he might have said more on the subject, but changed his mind, and became the professional artist once more.

"I've done as much as I can in this house, my lady." He had begun to pack his materials with some ferocity into his artist's valise. "The light is all wrong. We must work in my studio from now on." At her look of unease, he went on, "Lord Rutherston has agreed. You will, of course, be chaperoned by your maid."

"How ungracious of you to imagine that I even gave that a thought, Mr. Henderson! That was not what I was thinking!"

"No? Then what did you think?"

He had read her mind accurately, but Catherine was determined to put their relationship back on a surer, less personal footing.

"I merely thought that some days you are beyond being pleased, and you will be just as cross with me in your studio as you are here. Tell me, Mr. Henderson, do all artists abuse the subjects of their portraits when their stiff fingers or dull eyes are at fault?"

"To a man, ma'am," he responded in the same bantering tone. "We are, as you say, an ungracious lot."

They continued their conversation in a similar vein for the few moments longer that it took Henderson to retrieve his things and take his leave, and Catherine kept him at a distance with a bright, birdlike chatter that he made no effort to penetrate, but when she was left alone, she sat down to make sense of her disordered thoughts.

Rutherston had warned her that Henderson was dangerous to women and a rake. She could not believe it. His blond good looks and gracious, engaging manners won him friends of both sexes very easily. He had a natural, inborn charm, which her husband lacked, and he genuinely liked people, whereas Rutherston, except for a few intimates, found them mostly a bore, and made no effort to please. She liked Henderson very well, but her heart was quite untouched.

For good or ill, she loved the arrogant, insufferable, selfish, odious Marquis of Rutherston who, even if he did not know how to love, regarded her with a fierce pride of possession which would brook no overtures from other males.

Catherine shivered involuntarily when she remembered that Rutherston had said her good sense and his marksmanship with a pistol would keep Henderson at a distance. She did not believe that Henderson cared a button for Rutherston's marksmanship. But she did, and she intended to use the good sense that her husband had credited her with to see that no harm came to one of the few people in London who had taken her interests to heart.

Henderson was, she decided, far more the victim than the predator, the chivalrous romantic whom predatory females might easily ensnare. Why, he is like Hippolytus, she thought with surprise. On reflection, Catherine was not so sure that her conclusion was quite accurate. Mr. Henderson was a little too warm-blooded to be exactly like the perfect Hippolytus, but like Hippolytus, he needed protection, and she would not see him come to harm.

She was about to mount the stairs when the front door opened and Rutherston sauntered in. Catherine had not seen him since the theater the night before. She would have liked to wipe the sardonic look off his face, but her butler, George, was standing by to relieve his lordship of his things, and Catherine knew better than to commit the unforgivable solecism of having words with her husband in front of the servants.

"M'dear." Rutherston bowed formally as he slipped his evening coat off his broad shoulders into George's waiting grasp. "All-night session at Carlton House. Ran into Freemont and was obliged to give him my word that I'd be in the House tomorrow to support his bill on Ireland. Nuisance, that!" He turned to George in dismissal. "Thank you, George, that will be all."

When George had retired, leaving them alone, Catherine half turned to mount the stairs, addressing Rutherston over her shoulder.

"If you would excuse me, my lord, I am going to change."

"Where's Henderson?" he asked abruptly.

"Gone home, in a bad humor. He says that he can do nothing with the light in this house." She forced herself to speak naturally. "From now on we are to work in his studio."

Rutherston nodded absently, regarding her costume with close scrutiny. "Where are your pearls?"

Her hand flew to her throat.

"Henderson doesn't want me to wear jewelry. He said it's distracting."

"I daresay he does, but I want you to wear the pearls. See that you do." His tone was curt and cutting.

"Yes, my lord," Catherine responded through clenched teeth.

"Catherine—a moment of your time." He held out his hand and she was obliged to put her icy hand into his warm one, and he walked her, unresisting, to the room she had newly vacated.

He led her to a chair beside the empty grate and stood, one foot on the fender, looking down at her, a circumstance which, in Catherine's opinion, gave him an unfair advantage.

"I saw Norton this morning."

Catherine said nothing, not putting herself about to make the interview any the easier, and Rutherston, recognizing the stubborn set of her chin, went on doggedly.

"You did not tell me that your sister Mary had been delivered of her child."

"My lord, I have scarcely seen you! You had barely left our box last night when I recalled that I had not told you. And when I would have followed you to Lady Symington's box, Mr. Henderson forbade me to go." There, let him make what he liked of that veiled piece of malice.

"Would he not?"

"I thought to tell you this morning, but you were not home, and I did not know where to find you." Her face was a mask of innocent blandness.

"I see that I have been at fault." He moved to stand beside her chair.

"I have been with Norton, Catherine. He left this morning with Lucy for Breckenridge."

"He what? For what reason?"

"What reason could there be? To apply to your father for Lucy's hand." Rutherston smiled to see her prim look dissolve as her mouth gaped open in astonishment.

She jumped out of her chair and began walking about, wringing her hands in agitation.

"What are they thinking of? Papa will never countenance such a match! Why didn't they tell me what they were about? They should have eloped!"

"Eloped?" Now it was Rutherston whose face registered shock. "You cannot be serious! I thank God that my cousin has better sense than that!"·

"Sense? Do you call it sense to offer for a girl when there is no hope of your suit being accepted? It will break Lucy's heart, and I call that nonsense!" Her flushed face, sparkling eyes, and heaving bosom made Rutherston, momentarily, forgetful of what he was about to say. He was tempted to pull her into his arms, but he collected himself, not wishing to precipitate a new quarrel.

"His suit will be accepted, Catherine, I have no doubt of it. There is no need for this wild talk and extravagant emotion."

"I think I know my father better than that. I tell you, he will be adamantly opposed."

They were standing face-to-face, Catherine looking up at him, her eyes brimming with unshed tears.

"My dear!" He caught hold of her hands and spoke gently. "I have made a settlement on Lucy provisional to her marriage to Charles. She gets Branley Park—an estate I have no use for anyhow. It will mean a comfortable living for them and the kind of life that Charles most enjoys."

"A settlement! On Lucy? Why did you not give the estate to Charles? He is your kinsman."

"A man's pride, my little goose. Charles would not accept a farthing from me, but Lucy is my sister-in-law. I am in duty bound to provide for my wife's relations. I finally made Charles understand that."

"But why didn't they mention any of this to me? Lucy has always confided in me!" Catherine's voice was puzzled and a little forlorn.

"I think they meant to last night, but found you somewhat preoccupied. Tom said that you were distressed to hear about your sister Mary. And besides, they could not speak freely with Henderson present."

Catherine sat down, her mind trying to digest all that Rutherston had told her.

"There is no need for us to remain longer in town, Catherine. Lucy has gone. I have no business here. I shall arrange our removal to Fotherville House by the end of the week."

"What about the portrait?" Catherine asked absently.

"Henderson will come down in a week or two to complete it. There is no hurry."

"But Richard." It was the first time she had used his name in a long while, and he was well pleased. "These things take time to arrange—settlements, journeys. When did it all come about?"

"My decision to give Lucy Branley Park was by no means sudden. I had it in my mind since before our marriage. Their decision to go to Breckenridge was hastened, I believe, by the departure of your brother Tom this morning. They made up their minds on the instant to go with him—and Charles found me at White's early this morning to put me in the picture."

She looked up at him, but with the light behind him, she could not see the intensity of his regard.

"You are a strange man." He heard the weariness in her voice, and put out a hand to caress her face, but she shook it off.

"Let me think, Richard. Give me a little time. Somehow, I never thought you would lift a hand to help them." She rose and stood with a preoccupied air, smoothing the folds of her dress.

"You never did have a high opinion of me, did you, my

love?" He spoke lightly, but there was an implacable set to his jaw.

"But . . ."

"Yes?"

She had been about to say, "I love you," but she choked on the words. He did not love her, and it would give him the upper hand again. He would only despise her for it. She was too weary to think, and the symptoms of her pregnancy, for she was sure it was that, were taking their toll.

"I must rest for tonight. But I do thank you for what you have done for Lucy and Charles. It was uncommonly kind. Sometimes, I don't think I know you at all."

He wanted to say so much more, but the look of strain on her white face halted him.

"You need not go to Carlton House tonight. I shall convey your apologies to the prince, if you wish it, Catherine."

"No, I want to go. I don't think I could bear another evening of Medea's company."

"You could always settle for Hippolytus."

They were falling into their former way of address, and it brought them very close to a reconciliation.

"Have a care, my lord, I may meet my Hippolytus at Carlton House tonight."

"I have no fear of that, my sweet wife. Amongst the Carlton House set, manners are always thought superior to morals."

It was an unfortunate remark, and although Rutherston saw the shutter close on Catherine's face, he was at a loss to know what meaning she had attached to his words. It made him angry to see the feigned indifference in her expression, but he was too concerned for her welfare to confront her with that anger, and he watched helplessly as she left the room with her little chin raised a few degrees in that pert, unself-conscious posture that told those closest to her that one more word and she would do battle.

Chapter 18

As soon as Catherine passed through the Grecian portals of Carlton House, she knew that it had been a mistake to come. Nervous exhaustion and fits of nausea had left her weak and trembling at the knees, and her dark suspicions about Rutherston and Lady Symington teased her mind. She missed the steadying presence of Lucy and Norton, for Rutherston, silent and remote, seemed like a stranger at her side.

She entered the great house with a dread sense of foreboding, and steeled herself to an outward display of tranquillity that she was far from feeling. The heat in each successive chamber was oppressive, as she had known it would be, and the brilliant lights of the glittering chandelier in the vast interior of the Circular Room intensified the throbbing in her temples. She moved, dreamlike, from group to group, aware of Rutherston's guiding hand at her elbow. But it was not long before he was hailed by some crony, and although he left her in the care of Lady Arabella, Catherine felt that he had abandoned her to pursue his own pleasure.

In normal circumstances, she would have enjoyed the spectacle, but she was too conscious of her own misery to care. There were more men in regimentals to be seen at Carlton House than almost any other residence. Here, at least, one was made aware that a war was in progress, and that these gallant young men would soon depart to meet their fate with careless chivalry. Most of them were younger sons, Catherine reflected, for only seldom did the heir to any fortune or title of distinction cast care to the winds and risk everything for king and country. But younger sons had everything to gain and nothing to lose—but their lives. It was because of these reckless young men that she and Rutherston could live untroubled on their estates, and Catherine wondered if he ever gave it a thought.

From time to time throughout the evening, Rutherston came to her side, drawing her away from the society of the dowagers and debs to make her known to men of widely different stamp. He was on familiar terms with those who formed various coteries in government circles, and although it was evident that his support was courted, he confided to Catherine that most of those present were noteworthy in only one particular—their mediocrity. But those few whom he did admire, he introduced to Catherine, and although at any other time she might have been flattered, her emotions were too raw from the slights he had inflicted upon her to appreciate the gesture.

As the evening progressed, Catherine found it increasingly difficult to force the smiles to her lips, and her spirits flagged even further. She longed for a tranquil place where she could sit in quiet seclusion without having to make the effort to appear interested in the inane comments and Court gossip of the fashionable elegance around her. In her hand she clutched a glass of iced lemonade that Rutherston had procured before he was carried off by Lord Liverpool, and Catherine wandered about, well within sight of her husband, until she spied an empty sofa beside a fronded palm where she sat down to rest, holding at bay the nausea that had settled to a vague unease in the pit of her stomach.

Her eyes traveled dully over the crowded assembly, coming to rest on a merry circle of Hussars in blue and gold regimentals who were attracting attention to themselves by their noisy hilarity. One young man, not in uniform, his hand resting lightly on the shoulder of a companion, threw back his head to laugh, showing the gleam of white teeth, and Catherine saw that it was Adrian Henderson. For the first time that evening, she smiled in genuine pleasure. He turned at that moment, and catching sight of her, raised his hand in salute, and almost immediately detached himself with lazy grace from his companions and made his way toward her.

So thick was the crush that Catherine stood up so that Henderson might not lose sight of her. She took a few cautious steps forward, but by some mischance, the glass in her hand tipped, cascading the lemonade in a stream of silvery droplets to the back of the elegant lady who barred Catherine's way.

Lady Pamela Symington spun round, her beautiful face contorted by fury, and Catherine, in one fearful glance, recognized Rutherston's theater companion of the night before. Catherine saw venom in the narrowing eyes, and although the lips smiled, the voice that spoke was contemptuous.

"Lady Rutherston, is it not? Richard's little country-bred wife." She turned to the exquisite at her side. "Percy, this is the little chit of a thing who carried off the unattainable marquis."

The elegant fop, his high, pointed collar touching his ears, raised his quizzing glass in a languid hand and stared at Catherine in mild curiosity.

Catherine was scarcely aware of the malicious words

or the indolent stare. Her gaze was riveted to Lady Pamela's soft white neck and the dazzling diamonds that encircled it. She stood incoherent, transfixed, her face paper white, and instinctively her hand flew to her own breast to finger the chaste bridal pearls, and she wanted to tear them from her throat, but some vestige of pride restrained her. He had given this woman, his mistress, the diamond necklace that she, in her naïveté, had imagined was meant for her!

Her breath quickened in her body, making her shoulders heave with her deep gasps, and she felt the nausea rise from the pit of her stomach to engulf her. The glass slipped from her nerveless fingers, shattering on the floor, and all conversation in the immediate vicinity abruptly ceased. Catherine looked around wildly, her hand clasped tightly over her mouth, the nausea shaking her body in uncontrollable spasms. Out of the corner of her eye, she saw Rutherston, white-faced, forcing his way through the throng toward her, and wild panic surged through her veins.

She tried to scream a name, but it came out as a whisper. The room went spinning around her head and she fell, dazed, to her knees. Then Henderson was by her side, sweeping the Symington woman out of the way, and his arms went round her, lifting her up and out of Rutherston's reach to safety. A path was made for them through the crowded chambers, and a liveried footman, hurrying to assist, ushered them into a small saloon, and on Henderson's curt instructions went in search of Lord Rutherston.

Catherine strove for composure, gathering the remnants of her waning strength and distracted thoughts. How could she ever have supposed that she had the wit and beauty to hold a man of her husband's temperament?

She had been living in a dreamworld, and now it had been turned into a painful nightmare.

A blessed numbness crept over her as she listened to the soothing words of Henderson's anxious voice, and she closed her eyes, trying to blot out the picture that came to torment her of a dark beauty, an Aphrodite, and on her breast the priceless token of a man's love and esteem.

She was dimly aware of Rutherston's presence and his cold, uncivil words of gratitude to Henderson, then she was in strong arms, her head crushed against his chest as he carried her to the waiting carriage to take her to Berkeley Square.

The doctor confirmed Catherine's pregnancy, and forbade all parties and balls. He further advised Rutherston to put off the proposed journey to Fotherville House, until his wife should be over the attacks of nausea which, in Dr. Strang's opinion, almost never lasted more than two or three weeks.

Catherine was glad that their removal to Fotherville House had been delayed, for she felt that in that particular setting she would be overwhelmed by a house that was the ultimate expression of Rutherston's fastidious personality.

His frequent absences left her in no doubt that he was pursuing his pleasures with the rapacious Lady Pamela, and the knowledge left her wretched beyond bearing. Her emotions hovered between depression and fury, but pride compelled her to conceal her feelings from Rutherston by assuming a polite but preoccupied air. She knew that it angered him and was glad of it.

Cut to the quick by his blatant neglect, she became less

than discreet in encouraging Henderson's attentions, pushing Rutherston, she knew, to the limit of endurance, and she waited with bated anticipation for the storm to break. She knew instinctively that he would try to assert his mastery over her—that he regarded her as one of his possessions—and she was determined to show him the error of his arrogant turn of mind.

Rutherston stepped out of White's and felt the late night breeze warm against his cheek, and on the spur of the moment decided to walk to Berkeley Square. Ignoring the line of hackney coaches along St. James Street waiting for prospective fares, he swung right and directed his steps toward Piccadilly and home.

His thoughts turned to Catherine and the estrangement that had sprung up between them, and he wondered if it was folly to absent himself every evening and spend so much of his time at his various clubs. It was not as if he enjoyed the interminable round of gambling and drinking, he mused, nor the fatuous conversation of toad-eating bores, but his pride had been wounded by Catherine's out-of-hand rejection of his lovemaking, and he had been stung into retaliation. One word, one gesture from her, he thought morosely, would have kept him by her side, but she had never once given him any sign that his presence or absence was of the least interest to her, and he smarted under her cool indifference.

His manner toward her was everything that was proper in a husband's conduct toward a wife, and he was cautious to say or do nothing, in her overwrought condition, that might shatter the fragile truce. Perhaps, he reflected wryly, he had been too cautious. In one week, he would carry her off to Fotherville House, and in that secluded setting he would not tolerate the wall of civility with which she contrived to keep him at arm's length.

There were too many distractions in London, he thought irritably, as he turned briskly into Berkeley Street, and Lady Pamela and Henderson could not too soon be left behind for his peace of mind. The lady was one embarrassment that he believed he had removed, but when he remembered that she had said some few words to Catherine before she swooned, his jaw set in an implacable line. He could not believe that the lady would be so foolhardy as to court his enmity, but he would leave nothing that touched Catherine to chance. If Lady Pamela's conduct to his wife had been remiss in any way, he would take steps to ensure that in future she acted with due decorum.

The strength of Henderson's attachment to Catherine left him in some doubt. He had seen Catherine's look of pleasure when she had first caught sight of him at Carlton House, and a white-hot jealousy had been aroused in Rutherston's breast. He uttered a harsh profanity when he recalled that Henderson had been a moment before him to snatch Catherine when she fell, certain that his rough passage toward her had been observed by them both.

The portrait painting had been postponed indefinitely, Rutherston giving as his excuse that Catherine's condition forbade her traipsing all over town or sitting unmoving for hours at a time. Nor was he well pleased when she had tried to argue the point. He had become unnecessarily curt, and the hostility he had fleetingly observed in Catherine's eyes before she had lowered her lashes to conceal it had raised his hackles.

But Henderson's visits to the house he could not, with any grace, curtail, and he was acutely aware that Catherine basked in his admiration. It irked him beyond bearing to open the door of his own house to the sounds of their laughter, and to find, on entering the drawing room, their two heads bent together in conspiratorial conversation. Nor was he present for more than a few minutes before Henderson would rise to take his leave, and, thought Rutherston savagely, with him went all the glow of Catherine's warm nature.

If it had not been for Catherine's pregnancy, he would have ridden her with a tighter bit. But the lady was much mistaken if she thought he would dance long to her tune. He was no callow youth to be treated in such a cavalier manner, but a husband who meant to be master in his own house, and if his Catherine did not yet recognize that fact, he meant to teach it to her gently but inexorably.

Lady Pamela Symington's house was situated at the edge of Richmond, that village on the edge of London that had been at one time the residential district of the aristocracy, until the monarch had removed his Court to Kensington Palace. In the wake of the courtiers' exit had come an influx of diplomats, politicians, merchant bankers, and the occasional professional artist or writer. It was an expensive and interesting area, and most agreeable to Lady Pamela, whose flamboyant lifestyle would have been tolerated less well in the more exclusive and sedate Mayfair.

She was dressing at a leisurely pace when her maid tapped urgently at the door and on entering imparted the welcome news that Lord Rutherston waited impatiently below, and Lady Pamela received the information with a small smile of triumph. The abundance of dark hair, piled high on her head, she now undid and shook loose about her shoulders, and the riding habit she had been about to don was thrown carelessly aside and a slip of violet silk hastily drawn on. As her maid did up the tiny row of buttons at the back, Lady Pamela turned to the looking glass to scrutinize her reflection. Her large violet eyes were deepened to amethyst, absorbing the color of her gown, and with her glossy raven tresses framing the lily-white perfection of complexion and rounded breast, Lady Pamela's sensual beauty smiled confidently back at her.

"Quick, Sarah, the amethyst earrings. Mind, the ones Lord Rutherston gave me." A small blue velvet box was brought to Lady Pamela and she quickly fastened the gems to her delicate ears.

Her entrance into the blue saloon was all that she had hoped for. Lord Rutherston turned to greet her, his eyes smiling his approval.

"Pamela, your beauty quite unmans me." He bowed over her hand. "And as always, your taste is exquisite." He lightly fingered the amethyst drops at her ears.

"And your gallantry, as usual sir, is excessive," she replied archly, tapping his outstretched hand with a playful finger. She moved to a small sofa against the wall and patted the place beside her. "Sit down, Richard, and tell me what brings you to Richmond. I thought the charms of Berkeley Square had cast a spell on you." As she saw the frown crease his brow, she thought that perhaps she had gone too far, but his voice was bland in its reply.

"Did you? No, it is not Berkeley Square that charms me, but my Berkshire estate. To tell you the truth, Pamela, I shall be very glad to remove myself from all my . . . encumbrances here." As he spoke, he moved to a chair adjacent to the sofa, ignoring the blatant invitation in Lady Pamela's eyes, and the smile hovering on her lips became hard and fixed.

"Indeed, and do you take your wife to Fotherville House, or is she one of the . . . encumbrances that you speak of?"

He ignored the question, and looked thoughtfully at her for a moment or two, lightly tapping the tips of his fingers together.

"Pamela," he began, and so kindly did he say the name that she stiffened, knowing now that the words he would say were not the words she wanted to hear. "Pamela, you were beside . . . Lady Rutherston when she fainted at Carlton House. Tell me what happened."

That he had called his wife by her formal title rather than her Christian name fueled Lady Pamela's anger, for she knew it was his way of protecting Catherine from the curiosity of those whom he regarded as outsiders.

"Are you implying that I said something to upset your wife?" She strove to keep her voice light.

"Did you not?" So soft and menacing were his words that Lady Pamela looked at him with startled speculation.

"Lady Catherine, sir, was unwell before she fell against me." Her reply seemed to relieve his mind, and she waited only a moment before continuing with malicious sweetness, "I remember that she gave one glance in your direction before she stumbled and then . . ." she broke off in confusion, as if reluctant to continue.

"And then?" He had not moved, but his fingers locked together, and she was aware of his close attention.

"And then she cried out for someone called Adrian. She said his name twice, so I am not mistaken, and some young man, I don't know who, carried her off. That's all I know." She glanced sideways at him to see the effect of her words, but his impassive countenance told her nothing of what was in his mind, and his silence provoked her to spite. "Perhaps it was her brother she called for?"

"Perhaps it was." Still his face remained bland, and she could not tell whether the barb had found its mark or not. His coolness goaded her into indiscretion.

"Then, when next I meet Lady Rutherston, my lord, I shall ask after the health of her brother Adrian. He visibly blanched when his sister cried his name in so piteous a tone. Such an attractive-looking man." She was unprepared for the violence of Rutherston's response. He reached out his hand to grasp her wrist, and spoke through clenched teeth.

"If you try to further the acquaintance of my wife, my dear Pamela, I shall make you sorry. Do I make myself clear?"

She tried to wrench away from him, her eyes blazing with anger. "You are transparent, my lord! Your anger is not for me, but for your wife! What is it you suspect? That perhaps she prefers another?"

The words hung in the air, and although he held her wrist as if to silence her, her fury could not be abated. She hissed the words at him, her face contorted with malice.

"It did not escape my notice that the gallant gentleman who carried off your bride was also her attentive escort at Covent Garden. You fool . . ."

Before she could utter another word, Rutherston pushed her back violently and stood towering over her, and for a moment, as she looked into the remorseless anger in his eyes, she felt pure terror.

"Have a care, my lady. I will not hesitate to break you and bring you down if you say or do one thing that could harm Catherine. Whatever that fertile imagination of yours has conjured up, I advise you to forget it. I came here for only one purpose—to protect my wife from any indiscreet disclosures about our relationship that you may feel compelled to utter. That, I will not tolerate."

Lady Pamela strained back into the sofa, wrenching her wrist out of his fierce grip, and in her nervousness the laughter was torn from her like convulsive sobs. "What fools men are! She knows already! No, don't give me one of your murderous stares. I did not tell her—but I tell you she knows. Did you think that you could keep it from her?"

The derisive scorn in her voice lashed him, and he stood clenching his fists, disbelief written on his face.

As the lady watched him warily through narrowed eyes, some of her confidence seemed to return, and she tried a more conciliatory approach.

"Even if she does know, Richard, what of it? Is she such a green girl that she does not understand that a husband may weary of domestic bliss?" His thoughtful silence emboldened her to reach out and touch the edge of his sleeve. "Richard!" The word was spoken with sensual pleading, but Rutherston, lost in thought, neither saw nor heard. Presently, he seemed to come to himself, and cursing softly under his breath, strode out of the room without a backward glance.

Chapter 19

Some time after Rutherston set out in his curricle to execute some small matter of business, the nature of which he did not divulge to Catherine, she took the opportunity of having the carriage brought round. She implied to her butler that the seclusion imposed on her by an overanxious husband had been a trial to bear, and that she wished to make an excursion to Richmond Park merely to take the air. But Catherine's motives were far from pure.

Four days had passed since she had received a cryptic message from Henderson saying that he was sorry to absent himself from town on some pressing matter, but that he hoped to return in a day or two. It was Catherine's intention to make a small detour to Chelsea where Henderson's house was located, to ferret out news of her friend, for she hardly dared mention his name to her husband or disclose that she felt uneasy on Henderson's behalf.

She knew that if it came to Rutherston's ears that she had disobeyed him, he would be infuriated, but she was made reckless by his own evasive attitude, since he never disclosed where he had been or what he was about, and she had determined to practice a small deception of her own. It did not seem likely that he would ever be apprised of her visit to Henderson's house, but she was careful to pack her pearl necklace in her reticule, reasoning that, if he challenged her, she would give as her excuse that Henderson was eager to sketch her with the pearls that Rutherston was adamant would grace her throat for his portrait. Had she but known that Rutherston was at that very moment already tooling his curricle through Richmond, Catherine would have abandoned her scheme, for she had no wish to run even the smallest risk of being discovered anywhere near Chelsea.

It was with a disapproving sniff that Simpson, Rutherston's groom, pulled down the steps of the carriage and gave his mistress his hand to help her alight, and at that moment Catherine looked up and was momentarily arrested. The front door of Henderson's house stood wide open, and two burly men in leather aprons were in the process of negotiating a large canvas out of the door. They were taking their instructions from a small, portly man whose sober mode of dress informed Catherine that, although he was not elegant enough to pass for quality, he was at least a member of the middle class.

Catherine watched in puzzlement as the men maneuvered the canvas down the stone steps, carefully avoiding the wrought iron railings, and into the entrance of the adjacent house, and after one quick scrutiny Catherine alighted. She advanced upon the little fat man, and he turned smartly at the tap on his shoulder, startled to see a lady of such fashion at his elbow. His hooded lizardlike eyes flitted quickly over her elegant person and the carriage with liveried coachmen standing by, and his manner became immediately alert.

"My lady, you are looking for Mr. Henderson, perhaps?" The sly, knowing smile that spread across his lips offended Catherine greatly, and she turned to snap an order to her disapproving groom.

"Wait here, Simpson, I shall return directly." She moved toward Henderson's house, pushing brusquely past the beady-eyed man with the intolerable sneer, but he followed her footsteps with dogged persistence.

"But my lady, Mr. Henderson is not here. I am his landlord, Mr. Kemp."

Catherine halted on the threshold and turned a haughty face upon him. "What is going on here?" she asked in her most imperious manner. "Who gave you permission to remove these canvases from Mr. Henderson's house?"

His small lizard eyes blinked at her rapidly, as if he could not understand her overbearing manner, but his mind was quickly calculating how he could best turn this chance encounter to his advantage.

"My lady," he began again, smoothly trying not to give offense, "the law is on my side, I do assure you. I am impounding Mr. Henderson's chattels for nonpayment of rent and board. I am quite within my rights." He noted her attentive expression and pressed on. "He is fortunate that he has a few assets, otherwise he would have found himself in debtors' prison. If he has other creditors, and I have no doubt that he has—for what young man isn't in debt to his tailor or bootmaker—he may yet find himself in the Fleet."

Catherine's rising anger was quelled by the sinister words, and her face paled. Many a young man, she knew, was frequently left to cool his heels in jail until his friends relieved him of the burden of his debts, and if his friends or relations were unobliging, then he might be left there to rot.

She became aware of several pairs of eyes watching

her speculatively and the indelicacy of her situation began to embarrass her. "Mr. Kemp, I would speak with you privately." The words were exactly what Kemp had been hoping to hear, and he gave his best bow of servility, almost prostrating himself, and with a wave of his hand indicated that Catherine should enter his "humble home."

It was then that Simpson coughed discreetly in an effort to gain her ladyship's attention, but she appeared not to hear.

"Your ladyship," he broke in apologetically, embarrassed to have to call her to a sense of her indelicacy, "you wish me to accompany you?"

"Don't fret, Simpson. This will take only a moment. Why don't you walk the horses or something." And turning her back on her shocked coachmen, she entered Kemp's house without benefit of a chaperone.

She was shown into a small office on the ground floor, and refusing the proffered chair, came to the point directly. "How much does Mr. Henderson owe you?"

Mr. Kemp looked pained at such preemptory, unladylike tactics, and withdrawing the account of Henderson's debts from his desk, prattled on about rentals and laundry, wines and dinners, cleaners and hackneys, until Catherine called a halt.

"How much?" she asked again, bluntly.

"A little over three hundred pounds!"

"Three hundred pounds?" Catherine repeated stupidly, appalled at such a vast amount, and she listened vaguely as Henderson's landlord gave her an itemized account of the arrears that Henderson had accumulated in just over a year.

She had no money of her own, apart from small sums of cash that she could draw on, for like all ladies of quality, Catherine simply charged anything that took her fancy and left her husband to pay the bills. Nor could she touch a penny of her marriage settlement, and she did not see immediately what was to be done to help Henderson.

"Mr. Kemp," she cut in rudely, as he was still talking, "if you give Mr. Henderson a little time, I am sure he will clear his debts. He is not without friends."

"If only I could, my lady, if only I could." He sighed and shook his head morosely, as if it pained him to be the harbinger of bad news. "But you see, I have creditors of my own who are pressing me for payment. I am sorry to have to tell you, but I find myself quite embarrassed at my own lack of funds." He waited for a moment before continuing. "Now if your husband were willing to . . . ?"

"No!" Catherine exclaimed emphatically.

"Ah! Well, perhaps not."

Each was lost in thought. Kemp knew that all society ladies were usually short of the ready, but careless of other valuable property that could be easily disposed of. He played his last card.

"Now if your ladyship had some small trinket or other that could be exchanged for Mr. Henderson's account, I would be glad to call it quits."

Catherine remained unmoving, her brow furrowed in thought. Kemp's suggestion had come almost immediately after she had thought of her pearls, so that she evinced no surprise. She had already made her decision, and with calculated deliberation, reached into her reticule and extended the blue velvet box. She would think of some way of getting them back, she reasoned, but she had no choice if she wanted to protect Henderson from ruin. He was her friend, and she would find a way to make Rutherston understand.

"Will you accept this in payment?"

He opened the box and regarded the pearls with avaricious eyes. The lady, he observed to himself, was an innocent. She had no conception of what they were worth. He could tell that they were of the finest quality and perfectly matched, probably worth twice as much as Henderson's debts. He had no doubt that Catherine's husband would pay very handsomely to have them returned.

He knew better than try to dispose of them elsewhere. All that he had to do was to take them to the firm of jewelers whose name was conveniently emblazoned on the box, and they would negotiate for him. He should come out a couple of hundred ahead on this little enterprise, he thought gleefully.

Nor did he doubt for one moment that this supercilious lady who was so high in the instep would be soundly horsewhipped by her husband for her rash behavior, and the thought cheered him greatly. How he detested these aristocratic toffs who gave themselves airs and graces, while all the time they were no better than they should be. He smiled benignly at Catherine.

"Yes, my lady. I would be happy to accept this little trinket in payment of Henderson's debts. I shall probably still be out of pocket, but beggars can't be choosers."

"In that case, Mr. Kemp, would you please mark Mr. Henderson's account paid in full, and sign your name to it. I shall, of course, keep the receipt." Catherine spoke coldly, her dislike obvious in her disdainful tone.

He could hardly restrain the laughter on his lips. So the little baggage thought that she was a shrewd businesswoman, did she? Well, let her think it! In a few days her folly would come home to roost and then she would think of him with a new respect!

"But of course!" he replied obligingly, and signed his name with a flourish. Catherine scanned the account and thrust it into her reticule with a sigh of relief. Kemp extended his hand. "It is a pleasure to do business with you Lady . . . ?"

Ignoring the proffered hand, and the inquiry in his voice, Catherine moved to the door. "See that all Mr. Henderson's belongings are returned forthwith," and giving Kemp the slightest of nods, she swept out to her waiting carriage.

The desire to continue to Richmond Park had left Catherine, and she told a granite-faced Simpson that she wished to return to Berkeley Square, and as the carriage moved off sedately along the embankment, Kemp followed its progress with his eyes, lost in a delightful reverie, contemplating the retribution that would befall a proud lady within a few days at the latest.

In this, Henderson's landlord was mistaken, for Catherine's movements were observed by Rutherston as he made his way home from Richmond and his interview with Lady Pamela. He recognized his livery and carriage moving slowly ahead of him on the road, and he reined in hard, making his fidgety grays rear violently in their traces, almost oversetting the unsteady curricle.

He cursed under his breath and turned them aside to an inn that lay just off the road. He had no wish to overtake Catherine with his faster team, for it would take her only a moment to guess that he had come from Richmond. He was compelled to delay for an hour or so, and he fumed in impatience.

"Where the devil has she come from?" he wondered to himself. Certainly not Richmond, for he would have overtaken her on the road out, and there had not been enough time for the slow-moving barouche to make it out there and back. He gave the matter some consideration, and was not well pleased with the result of his speculations.

It was a grim-faced Rutherston who returned his

sweating team to the stables and sought out his equally grim-faced groom. Nor was Simpson voluble on his mistress's movements that afternoon, but after much thrust and parry, Rutherston learned some small part of the story, and when he had given his orders to harness a fresh team, he set off once more toward Chelsea, with a reluctant and reticent groom perched behind.

Her ladyship, thought Becky as she helped Catherine dress that evening, was in a distracted mood. She had watched her jump at every small sound, as if she expected disaster to strike at any moment. Nor did her ladyship show the slightest interest in what she should wear to go to the theater with the Earl and Countess of Levin, and Becky had been left to choose her gown.

She had selected a pale yellow silk with ivory underslip and matching ribbons tied under the breast and embroidered profusely at bodice and hem with the same matching thread. Lord Rutherston had excellent taste, thought Becky approvingly, for left to herself, her ladyship would never take the time or trouble to dress herself well. She would spend hours traipsing through libraries and bookshops, but ask her to give up one afternoon for fittings and to choose and match silks or ribbons and she became restless and bored. It was Lord Rutherston's doing, Becky acknowledged gratefully, that in her mistress's wardrobe there was nothing that did not suit her ladyship to perfection—not that Miss Catherine cared overmuch.

Becky stood back to survey her handiwork and offered a small suggestion.

"The pearls, I think, my lady?"

Catherine's hand flew to her throat and her cheeks turned a guilty pink.

"Good heavens, Becky, I am sick of the pearls! If I wear them one more time, I'll be put down as a pauper. Fetch me my grandmother's sapphire brooch."

There was not much to choose from in her jewel box, thought Catherine wryly, but the small trinkets that any young woman collects throughout her maiden years. She knew well enough that the Rutherston jewels, although by rights belonging to her husband, remained temporarily in the keeping of the dowager marchioness. Rutherston had never discussed when or how the collection would pass to his wife, and Catherine had to acknowledge that until that moment she had never given it a thought.

Should she produce a son and heir for Rutherston, she observed disconsolately, he would probably give her the famous Rutherston emeralds, but if you, poor child, are only a girl, her thoughts ran on mournfully, your mother will probably be deemed worthy only of more pearls.

She smoothed her abdomen with a tender motion of her hands in a protective gesture, and into her mind came a picture of Rutherston, through a long wedded life, presenting her with one set of pearls after another, and the humor of the situation made her giggle nervously until the tears ran down her cheeks.

"My lady?" asked Becky in astonishment.

Catherine shook her head, consumed in uncontrollable mirth. "It's nothing, Becky. Just a foolish notion that caught my fancy!"

Becky attached the sapphires to Catherine's bodice. She did not think that his lordship would approve the adornment, but she knew her place and said no more.

At that moment they were informed by the butler that the earl and countess awaited below, and Catherine made haste to find her fan and a suitable wrap should the night air turn chill.

Rutherston entered the room soundlessly, unobserved by Catherine, and with a curt nod to Becky indicated that she should withdraw. Catherine was in the process of extracting her fan from a drawer low on her dresser, when some sixth sense made her conscious of a threatening presence. Although her back was still turned upon him, she knew that he was there and in a dangerous mood, and her heart began to hammer unevenly against her ribs. She had time to compose her features, and turned to face him with a semblance of confidence.

"My lord? Have you decided to accompany me to the theater tonight? If you do you will probably provoke the ton to scandal, for no one expects so noble a lord to grace his wife's side." She spoke merely to cover the threatening silence and to distract his attention from her neck as she drew her shawl securely over her bosom. "The Levins are below. Did you speak with them?"

Still he said nothing, but reached out one lazy hand to grasp her shawl and pull it off her shoulders to reveal her naked throat.

"Really, my dear," he drawled, making Catherine quake in her shoes, "I have tried to impart a modicum of taste to you. You surely don't intend to wear sapphires with that dress? It has tiny pearls sewn into the bodice. Does that not suggest something to you?"

"Yes, I see what you mean, Richard." She brazened it out. "I should have chosen another gown to wear, since I particularly wanted to wear my grandmother's sapphires tonight. It won't take me a moment to change. Would you send Becky to me?" She moved away from him toward the wardrobe and began frantically to search for something that would suit sapphires.

"You are late, Catherine. It would be much simpler to change the sapphires than the dress. Let me help you." He turned her around and she felt his hands brush against her breast as he slid his fingers down the bodice of her gown to release the catch of her brooch. Then he dropped it with a clatter and reached out to grasp her by the elbows and pulled her down to sit before her dressing table. She looked into the mirror and she flinched to see the iciness in his eyes. He placed his hands lightly on her shoulders.

"Where are your pearls, Catherine?" His voice was low and even, but Catherine heard the menace behind the soft words and she gazed at him speechlessly.

"You won't tell me?" He smiled then, as if he were entertained by the charade he was forcing her to go through. "No matter, my dear!" The drawl was back in his voice, and Catherine stilled her breathing, wishing she could drop her eyes from his, but she was afraid to. He slipped his hand into his coat pocket and withdrew a box that Catherine recognized at once, and removing the pearls, he fastened them around her neck.

"How beautiful you are, my love, like a virgin queen, with just a touch of sensuality glowing in those tawny eyes. How desirable you look. No man gazing at you would know whether to protect you or ravish you." He noticed her chin lift, but did not find the gesture charming, as he might normally have done, but merely another sign of a wanton and rebellious disregard for a husband's authority, and he dug his fingers cruelly into her arms. Catherine gasped in pain and wrenched herself free, knocking over the chair in her alarm. At that moment there was a light knock at her door and before he could reach her, she called out sharply, "Enter."

"The earl and countess are anxious to leave, my lady."

"Thank you, Becky. Please stay and tidy my room. I was on the point of joining them."

She turned to Rutherston, a small smile of triumph hovering on her lips.

"If you will excuse me, my lord, I must go now."

Becky looked in consternation from one to the other and hastily removed herself to the far end of the room where she averted her eyes and made a pretense of tidying up.

"You have merely won for yourself a short reprieve, madam." She was at the door ready to bolt if he made one move in her direction, and he relaxed his tense posture. Her cool, unruffled demeanor needled him into an attempt to provoke her to anger or jealousy.

"You can have no objections if I seek other . . . um, diversions, my dear?" He spoke in a nonchalant undertone so that her maid would not hear.

Emboldened by Becky's presence in the room, and incensed by Rutherston's veiled reference to his mistress, Catherine tossed her head and with a rapier thrust slipped under his guard. "My lord, would a wife put restraints on a husband that she is unwilling to accept for herself? It would be monstrous unjust!" And flashing him her sweetest smile, she flounced out of the room and hastened downstairs to escape and safety.

200 AN INNOCENT BRIDE

Chapter 20

When Catherine entered the house later that evening, her pulse began to quicken, and she delayed in the dim interior of the vestibule, her eyes and ears straining for any indication that Rutherston might be about, but she could detect none.

"Has his lordship come in yet, George?" she asked, with as much unconcern as she could command.

"I don't believe so, my lady. He advised me not to wait up for him." George's stoic demeanor in the face of every eventuality was still a source of wonder to Catherine and she strove to emulate his example.

"But he did go out?"

"Oh yes, my lady. Immediately after you left." George's tone evinced a faint surprise at Catherine's query and she became instantly more circumspect.

"Thank you, George. Then perhaps you had better follow his lordship's instructions. I need nothing more tonight."

If Catherine's butler was conscious of the note of strain in his mistress's voice, he gave no sign, but merely bowed in acknowledgment of his dismissal and turned to move off sedately in the direction of the domestic quarters. His lordship and her ladyship might think that they had no need of his services, he intoned to himself, but he hoped he knew his duty better than that. He would maintain his unobtrusive vigil until his lordship returned.

Catherine remained unmoving for a moment or two, stripping the gloves delicately from her fingers, and the wretched state and uncertainty of her feeling were borne in upon her. Her extravagant impulse on Henderson's behalf paled to insignificance in comparison to Rutherston's infamous conduct with Lady Pamela. Whilst she had no wish to encounter her husband for what must be, she thought fearfully, a stormy interview, she felt that his absence from the house to be with his mistress was an intolerable insult, and it left her angry and confused. Deep in thought, she crossed the hall and began to mount the stairs toward her room.

She remembered her bold taunts thrown carelessly at his head as she had left him that evening and she cursed her rash stupidity. But when she recalled the insult that had provoked her to such anger, her sense of injury grew, and tears filled her eyes. She was besotted with a man who regarded her as nothing more than a chattel, a possession, and as a woman she had no recourse to redress the wrongs of a husband. She reached her door and flung it wide open and slammed it ferociously behind her, as if it could relieve the fury of her mind.

"My dear, one would think that the hounds of hell were after you. Shall I give the alarm?" In the flickering gloom, she saw a dark form detach itself from a chair and move toward her. Catherine froze. He moved to within a step of her, and she could smell the brandy on his breath.

"R . . . Richard! Are you *here?*"

"Indubitably, my love, though I have no doubt that you are fervently wishing me elsewhere."

The feigned drawl in his voice roused her to anger once more, and she looked boldly into his indolent stare.

"What's this?" she asked scathingly. "No diversions in London to distract the noble Marquis of Rutherston? And do you think, my lord, to be diverted by me?" She moved to push past him, but he caught her by the shoulders, and turned her to face him.

"No more evasions, madam. You have had your respite. You will tell me the whole story, if you please, of this afternoon's ridiculous adventure." He stood watching her closely, waiting for her to begin, but the intimacy of the darkened room and the warmth of her skin under his touch inflamed his senses and he was acutely aware of how long it had been since she had admitted him to her bed, and he knew that he would tolerate her refusal no longer.

"Catherine," he murmured, slipping his arm around her waist, "none of it matters."

She twisted from his grasp. "No! I will not. . . ."

At the unexpected movement and her denial of his claims upon her, Rutherston's self-control gave way. Catherine saw the fury blazing in his eyes and she shrank backwards across the room, keeping just out of his reach until her shaking legs came hard against a chair. She twisted behind it, using it as if it were a shield to protect her from his attack.

"What a fool I have been! I told you once, did I not, my dear wife," he said with biting sarcasm, "that one sigh from you could bring me to heel? By God, from now on, I will teach you to be a docile wife and come to *my* heel when I give the command."

He flung the chair aside in his mad lunge toward her, and seized her by the waist, swinging her into his arms. Catherine pushed futilely against his chest with her hands, but his grip tightened ferociously and she stilled. He twisted her till her head tilted back, and his mouth came down savagely upon her lips, his tongue ravaging the soft recess of her mouth.

He moved toward the bed and threw her hard upon it, and as he knelt beside her Catherine cried out with fright. With unhurried deliberation, he slid his hands around her back to undo the buttons of her gown, and she could hear his breath rasping in his throat as he disrobed her till she lay naked beneath his hands.

"Richard, do not do this!" She put out her hand in a gesture of appeal, but the movement seemed to enrage him further. She heard his muffled oath as he threw off his dressing gown and pulled her roughly to lie under him.

His hands, brutally compelling, moved across her body with a fierce possessiveness, demanding her submission, and she steeled herself to lie unflinching beneath his weight. But the urgency of his need and longing communicated itself to her, blotting out her feeble resolve. She sensed the deep hurt within him and could not bear it.

"Don't, love, don't!" she whispered against his ear, and her hands slid over his shoulders to caress his neck in a comforting gesture. Rutherston felt her soft and yielding beneath him, and his anger instantly abated.

His touch gentled to a caress and his warm lips teased her mouth to open and accept his tongue. Then, patiently and relentlessly, he seduced her to passion and at last heard her deep-throated gasps of pleasure. But he moved back, waiting for her clear response that she would welcome him.

"Catherine?" She heard the hesitancy in his voice, and she reached for him, moaning his name against his mouth. He needed her, and she wanted only to heal his lacerated heart. She went to him willingly, and all the uncertainty and pain were forgotten in his arms.

But Rutherston delayed the final moment of their rapture, cherishing Catherine's uninhibited response to his lovemaking. Nor would he take possession of her until she returned his softly murmured endearments of love and longing. They moved as one, and their sweet yearning was finally assuaged in the wave of wondrous ecstasy that washed over them.

She lay with her face turned away from him, her eyes gazing unseeing into the darkening room. For the first time it occurred to her that he had come from his mistress's bed to hers, and she could not endure the thought. His hand reached out to touch her shoulder and she shook him off.

"Catherine?" His voice was disbelieving. She hardened her heart against him and slipped out of bed to find a wrapper to cover her nakedness.

"Catherine, what do you want me to say?" There was an edge of exasperation in his voice, and still she stood mute.

"For God's sake, Catherine, is it only your pride that is wounded? Was not my pride wounded also when you gave my bridal gift to clear another man's debts?" He reached for his dressing gown and shrugged into it, gazing all the while at her rigid back. "I did not take you against your will."

She turned on him furiously, directing all the anger that she felt at herself onto a more fitting object. "But you would have, my lord, would you not? In your maddened rage, what would you have done? Gone away quietly? I think not!"

Her contemptuous words made him shift uncomfortably, for he was appalled at the unreasoning jealousy that had provoked him to such fury against her. But he knew of a certainty that he would never have harmed her.

"You cannot believe that I would hurt you, Catherine. For God's sake, you are carrying our child!" His voice finished on an incredulous note. Presently, he went on more quietly, "I wanted only to love you, and you wanted our lovemaking just as much as I did. You cannot deny it."

"It was fear of your brute strength," said Catherine hotly, "that made me submit to you."

He knew that it was not true, but it angered him to hear her say so.

"Did it please you, my lord? A docile wife is what you said you wanted, I believe?"

"What is Henderson to you, Catherine?"

"Henderson?" she asked warily, startled by the sudden change of topic.

"I think you heard me the first time. The man for whom you were willing to risk my wrath. Those pearls have cost me dearly, for I have paid for them twice over."

"Adrian," she retorted with emphasis, "is no more to me than Lady Pamela is to you, my lord." She saw the flush of color suffuse his face and felt the desolation of a hollow victory.

"He is my friend," she went on earnestly. "I had nothing to give to save him from ruin but my pearls. I would have told you, but you discovered it before I had the chance." When he made no reply, she added wearily, "I knew you would not believe me."

"And do you believe me, Catherine, when I tell you that Lady Pamela belongs in my past, and that she means nothing to me?"

His outright lie hurt her more than if he had confessed the whole to her, and she wanted only to give him pain.

She waited a moment until the lump in her throat had dissolved.

"It is not of the slightest interest to me what Lady Pamela is to you. Please do not feel compelled to set aside your mistress on my account. And now, my lord, if you have nothing more that you require from a docile wife, I would sleep."

They stood facing each other, Rutherston angry and bewildered, Catherine regarding him with calm contempt.

"As you will, ma'am. It would be unchivalrous of me not to accept your generous offer respecting my mistress. You may keep your chaste bed."

Catherine turned away so that he would not see the hot tears on her cheeks, and a moment later she heard the bedroom door slam as he let himself out.

It was a subdued and courteous Lord Rutherston who handed his wife into his carriage one wet and dreary August morning as she embarked on a solitary journey that would take her to Branley Park and Breckenridge. Her strained, deep-shadowed eyes looked up at him with perfect composure, and Rutherston felt his heart constrict. This white-faced stranger was not the Catherine he had brought to London a mere three months before.

"I shall be down in a se'enight, more or less, my dear, and after Lucy's wedding we shall remove to Fotherville House." He smiled kindly.

She gave him her hand to kiss, but he ignored it and bent his head to brush her cold lips lightly with his own. If only she would come a little way to meet him, he thought in exasperation, the absurd breach between them would soon be healed, but Catherine would not bend.

As the carriage moved off with its spate of coachmen and outriders whom he had instructed well, he watched with satisfaction. There would be no attempt from any highwayman to interfere with such a well-protected equipage, unless that highwayman happened to be a fool, for all the outriders were armed and knew how to use a pistol.

Rutherston turned back into the house and made for the breakfast room where a pot of fresh coffee was waiting for him. He ensconced himself in a deep armchair and stretched out his highly polished Hessians to rest comfortably on a low table.

He hoped that he was doing the right thing—giving Catherine this short interlude to be on her own without him. When the letter had arrived from Lucy asking them to come down for the wedding, Catherine had become quite animated, and seeing it, he had concurred in her desire to leave for Breckenridge as soon as possible. Only one small matter of discord had ensued. She had wished to put up at Ardo House, but he had insisted that she stay at Branley Park, her husband's residence until Lucy and Norton were legally married.

He was determined on a reconciliation and felt his goal could be sooner achieved if they had some little privacy. Ardo House was not the setting for what he had in mind, for he intended to court his Catherine all over again.

Nor was he without hope, he mused as he drank his coffee, for whatever Catherine might say or try to imply, their last lovemaking, although it had had a stormy beginning, had concluded on the deepest tenderness.

He smiled wryly to himself. Catherine had much to learn in the art of pleasuring a husband, and he intended to be her teacher, but in the few short months that they had been married, she had revealed things to him that he had never experienced before. He knew much about the art of sensual pleasure, but it was Catherine who knew about love itself. He knew how to seduce her senses to passion, but it was she who imbued his desire with some quality, some grace, that lifted it high above mere carnal lust.

Her regard for Henderson was something of a puzzle, but he had finally discarded the notion that there was anything serious to be feared in that quarter, on her part at least. She had responded to her husband's lovemaking in a way that convinced him that her heart was entirely his. But something had occurred to mar her happiness and he intended to discover what it was.

One week was all the time he would allow her to pursue her maidenly pleasures and enjoy the company of her family and friends. And then he would join her. But in the meantime, a whole empty week of utter boredom yawned before him; seven days and nights without Catherine, and already he was in a fever of impatience to be quit of London and carry her off to Fotherville House.

Chapter 21

Three days after Catherine set off for Breckenridge, Rutherston dined with his mother in Green Street. The ladies had but recently returned from a sojourn in Brighton, a resort made fashionable by the prince regent. It was a family gathering, with only four people present, Beaumain, who had come up to town to convey his duchess and her mother to his seat in Kent, Rutherston himself, and the two ladies.

The arrangement suited Rutherston very well, for he had yet to impart to his family the news of Catherine's pregnancy, and he knew better than to allow his mother to come by the information secondhand. He waited till dinner was over and the ladies were about to retire, and since he had no inclination to be thoroughly bored by that clod of a brother-in-law, Duke Henry, he asked if they might dispense with the after-dinner port.

His grace was a stupid man but shrewd, and when they rose to accompany the ladies to the drawing room, he clapped his brother-in-law heartily on the shoulder, and uttered, in what was meant to be a whisper, "So that's the way of it!" And when he saw Rutherston's look of pained surprise, he went on persistently, "Stands to reason. Knew you wouldn't dine with us just for the pleasure of our company!"

The dowager marchioness, seeing that her son was on the point of making a stinging rejoinder, cast him a warning look and asked for his arm, and as he led her dutifully upstairs to her private sitting room, he was conscious of a feeling of déja vû.

"Well, Richard, dear," the dowager began encouragingly when everyone was comfortably settled, "tell us of Catherine. Has she recovered from her attack of influenza?"

"Well, no, Mama," he replied, smiling broadly at his mother, whom he held in the deepest respect, "Dr. Strang has advised me that this particular condition will last six months more, until it runs its course."

The dowager regarded her son fondly, the deepest contentment shining from her eyes, and he rose, moving toward her quickly to plant an affectionate kiss on her cheek.

"I am the happiest woman alive," she said tenderly, clutching his sleeve.

"Well, I never heard of influenza lasting six months, 'pon my honor!" The raucous voice of the duchess made mother and son wince simultaneously.

"My dear Jane, Richard is advising us that Catherine is in a delicate condition. Their child, my grandchild, is expected in . . . February?" She looked for confirmation to Rutherston, who nodded his assent.

"Catherine? In a delicate condition? Well, the sly puss! Did she know when I asked her? She practically denied it!"

"You asked Catherine if she were pregnant?" asked Rutherston, dumbfounded. "And pray, when did that interview take place—for Catherine said nothing to me."

"Oh, it was just before the Carlton House soirée. I remember it well. You remember, Mama, I had a bilious attack that evening and you stayed home to nurse me." The duchess was quite unaware of the turmoil she had created in her brother's breast or his bellicose expression, and she turned to her husband fondly.

"Told her how I presented you with our firstborn nine months almost to the day we were wed, my dear."

Rutherston spoke quietly and calmly, only half conscious of his mother's restraining hand on his sleeve.

"Pray continue, Jane. What else did you say to Catherine?"

"What? Oh, not much. She seemed quite agitated, for some reason or other. She didn't even wait for tea."

"Good God, Jane, tell me what you said to Catherine," Rutherston exploded.

Duke Henry rose and took his stand by his wife's chair. "Look here, Rutherston, no need to take on like that. Why shouldn't Jane ask Catherine if she was in a delicate condition? Women are interested in that sort of thing."

The dowager marchioness, aware that her two offspring were about to become embroiled in the kind of quarrel she had so detested as they were growing up, now took firm control.

"Henry, Richard, sit down! Jane dear, try to remember what you said to Catherine. Obviously you offended her in some way—without meaning to, of course," she added hastily as she caught Beaumain's movement out of the corner of her eye.

Her grace looked properly pensive. "But Mama, I cannot think *what* offended her. I told her how *happy* we all were now that Richard had given up his ramshackle way of life to start his nursery."

Rutherston groaned, a phrase of Catherine's coming to mind that he had glossed over at the time. "Not our child, but your heir," was what she had said, and it had held no menace, no warning for him.

"Yes dear, go on," said the dowager encouragingly,

who after years of practice knew just how to handle the duchess. "What more did you say?"

"I told her how *relieved* we had all been when Richard gave you his solemn promise that he would marry in his thirtieth year and how we had left him to be as wild as he pleased, since we knew that a Fotherville *never* reneges on a promise. Perhaps it was unwise of me to have mentioned Lady Harriet, but what harm in that?"

"What harm indeed?" interjected Rutherston bitingly, a comment that was lost on his sister.

"And is that the whole of it?" asked the dowager.

"I did mention that we were surprised at how quickly Richard got himself leg-shackled, for nobody expected him to gratify your wishes so soon, Mama. You know it's true." The duchess now appealed to Duke Henry. "So you can see, I said nothing at all that could give Catherine offense."

"Quite right, my love," said her husband stolidly, glowering at Rutherston, who now held his head between both hands.

"Does it matter, Richard?" the dowager asked in concern.

"Yes, Mama, it matters a great deal. But at least I know now what I have to contend with."

"But what did I do?" wailed her grace.

"Nothing," snapped her brother, "but make my life a misery for the last number of weeks." His words startled the company, for it was the first indication that all was not well between the marquis and his lady.

"Mama," he said presently, "will you see me out?" And taking his leave of his crestfallen sister and his belligerent brother-in-law, Rutherston conducted the dowager marchioness downstairs.

He took his mother's hand in his. "May Catherine and I expect to see something of you later in the autumn?"

"At Fotherville House?"

"Where else would I be?"

"You are so like your father, dear. That house means a great deal to you, does it not? It is a great showpiece. I hope Catherine feels at home in it. I never could."

"But, Mama," he protested, "the house is perfection itself. It cannot be improved upon."

"Yes, dear, that is exactly how your father felt. But that is just what I mean. It is rather . . . impersonal. I never felt like the mistress of Fotherville House, merely a guest in it. If I were you . . . Well never mind. You're old enough to conduct your own life."

"No, go on, Mama. If you were I . . . ?"

She turned to him impulsively. "Give Catherine a free hand, Richard. If you can bear it, let her change things. And if you can't bear it, then don't make Fotherville House your principal residence. You have other estates. Let her have some say in her future home. You'll never regret it if you do, not if her happiness means anything to you."

He looked steadily into his mother's inquiring eyes. "Her happiness means everything to me!"

The dowager marchioness kissed him softly on the cheek. "Then it *is* a love match! I hoped it was, but you never confided in me. Do you know, my dear, when I heard how soon after your thirtieth birthday you had chosen a wife, I wondered."

"Yes, and if you did, my dearest Mama, you may be sure that Catherine is wondering, too."

"Then you must convince her that her conjectures are nonsensical! You'll find a way."

"Oh, I mean to, Mama. I mean to!"

* * *

"My lord?" said George apologetically, entering Rutherston's library later that evening. Rutherston looked up from the book he was reading.

"Yes, what is it, George?"

"Mr. Henderson is here and insists on being admitted. I tried to dissuade him, my lord, but he says the matter is urgent."

"Does he now?" said Rutherston, rising from his seat and laying aside his copy of Euripides's "Hippolytus." "Then don't keep him waiting, George. Show him in, and see that we are not disturbed."

George departed, to reappear a moment later with a bemused and smiling Henderson at his heels.

"Evening, Rutherston," Henderson began amiably. "I had hoped that I might find Cath . . . that is, Lady Rutherston with you, but your butler tells me she left for Surrey three days ago."

"Yes, for her sister's wedding to my cousin Charles Norton. I join her next week. But don't stand on ceremony," Rutherston said, waving to a leather armchair by the smoldering grate. "Will you join me in a brandy?"

Henderson disposed himself comfortably and accepted the proffered glass.

"You are a cool customer, Rutherston," Henderson began provocatively as he tossed off the brandy at one gulp.

"Am I?" Rutherston settled himself and raised his brows in faint surprise. "I would have thought that *that* description was better suited to yourself."

Henderson laughed and eyed Rutherston ruefully. "Perhaps I am. I had half expected to find you ranting and raving and demanding immediate satisfaction for an episode that even I don't understand."

"No! Did you?" Rutherston remarked noncommittally

as he held out the decanter to pour his guest another drink. Henderson sipped his second brandy slowly, and reaching into his pocket, withdrew a slip of paper which he extended to his host. Rutherston scanned it and saw that it was a bank draft for just over three hundred pounds.

Henderson continued, "I'm afraid you are still out two hundred pounds. That bank draft covers my debt to my landlord, but I'm not in a position at the moment to refund the difference you paid to retrieve Catherine's pearls. I'm afraid her impetuous gesture has put me in your debt."

"It's no matter," said Rutherston levelly. "I really don't want this, you know, but I suppose you will insist that I take it?"

Henderson nodded. "Oh, I do."

"Very well then, but under no circumstances will I accept the difference I paid to retrieve Catherine's pearls. That piece of folly on a wife's part is more properly the burden of a husband, so we will say no more about that, if you please!"

"Isn't she a trump, though? What a warmhearted girl." Henderson did not notice the slight stiffening of his host's spine, and went on musingly, "You know, she's a damn difficult subject to paint. It's hard enough to portray that unique coloring—but next to impossible to capture that vibrancy which comes from her generous spirit." Henderson put down his glass.

"That's one of the reasons I came to see you—and Catherine. I won't be completing that portrait for some time. I'm off to join Wellesley." He saw Rutherston's start of surprise. "My fond and generous aunt, Lady Blakney, has given me the funds I need to start fresh. I shall be purchasing a commission in the Seventh Hussars, so you see, it may be some time before I can get back to complete Catherine's portrait."

Rutherston's spine relaxed, and he poured himself another drink. "But why? You never struck me as the sort who was the least interested in adventure."

"Didn't I? Perhaps you didn't try to find out what sort I was!" Rutherston looked affronted, but Henderson went on easily, "No, no, I don't mean to insult you, I'm just stating a fact. Anyway, I'm not interested in glory. I want to become a better artist, and paint subjects that are worth painting. To put it simply, I'm bored with what I'm doing."

"Then I hope you find what you're looking for, although naturally, I'm disappointed that Catherine's portrait will be delayed."

"You shouldn't be, you know. I intend to continue with it when I've learned my art better, but whether I'll part with her portrait or not is another matter. I may decide to keep it, or I may decide to make a present of it to Catherine."

"What the devil do you mean by that?" asked Rutherston, a menacing note creeping into his voice.

"Why, what should I mean, except that I intend Catherine's portrait to be the best piece of work I shall ever complete?"

The two men sat imbibing their brandies, casting wary glances at each other, like two dogs circling each other before a fight.

"Look here, Rutherston," Henderson began at last. "Let's stop fencing and speak man to man." He uncrossed one long leg and put up an idle hand to rub his ear. "When my landlord told me of what Catherine had done, I was aghast—not because of the gesture itself. I found that rather touching—but because I was alarmed at the interpretation you might put upon it. God, in your shoes," he exclaimed forcefully, "I would be livid!"

"Well you're not in my shoes," said Rutherston smoothly. "And I did not jump to conclusions," he continued, conveniently forgetting how he had been furious enough to go so far as to think of calling Henderson out. "I believe I know Catherine's character better than that. She considered you her friend, and merely did what she thought would save you from immediate ruin." The words were those Catherine had used and seemed entirely reasonable on his own glib tongue.

"And Catherine hasn't been sent off in disgrace?" Henderson was not wholly convinced.

"Certainly not! I told you, she goes down to be with Lucy, and I join her next week."

Henderson was on the point of saying more, but changed his mind. He would have liked to have warned Rutherston of Catherine's unhappy state of mind, but he was perfectly sure that Rutherston would regard it as an unmitigated piece of interference on his part, and no good would be served by it.

"Well, then, if I don't see Catherine before I leave, you will convey my warmest regards to her?"

"Of course." The interview was at an end and both men rose for Henderson's leavetaking.

"You know, Rutherston, it could have been worse." Henderson chuckled. "What if you had insisted that Catherine wear the diamonds for her portrait instead of the pearls? Think how much more out of pocket you would have been!"

"Diamonds?" A puzzled frown creased his lordship's brow. "What diamonds?"

Henderson looked embarrassed. "I suppose there's no point in trying to wrap it up in clean linen. I'm afraid I behaved rather badly when I was your guest at Fotherville House. Catherine and I came upon the secret drawer in your library desk, and I'm sorry to say that I let my curiosity get the better of me. The fault was entirely mine. You see, Catherine found the box and I insisted on opening it. I collect you haven't given Catherine the necklace?"

"What?" Rutherston looked like a man who was choking on a fish bone. "What did you say?" he repeated dazedly.

"Are you all right, Rutherston?" Henderson regarded him in concern and puzzlement, and Rutherston made a supreme effort to regain his composure.

"Yes, yes!" he replied testily. "I'm fine, and no, I haven't given Catherine the necklace yet."

"Then I am sorry," Henderson went on airily, without the least appearance of remorse. "But it was a damned stupid place to choose for a hiding place. Catherine must be eating her heart out by now. She thought it was the most beautiful thing that she had ever seen."

"Yes, I can see that she would." Rutherston spoke more to himself than to his companion.

The two men had walked to the front door, and, when George had handed him his gloves and cape, Henderson held out his hand.

"Good-bye, Rutherston. Perhaps one day I shall learn to do justice to Catherine's portrait, but it's beyond my skill at present."

Rutherston shook the proffered hand. "Goodbye and good luck, Henderson. You're not the only one who has lacked the skill to do justice to Catherine!"

"Really?" Henderson digested Rutherston's words. "Then I hope we both may succeed."

And for once, husband and artist smiled into each

other's eyes, in perfect agreement on the subject of Catherine. But it was Henderson who had the last word.

"You're a lucky fellow, Rutherston, and I hope you know it."

Chapter 22

Catherine made herself comfortable on the garden bench overlooking the Ardo House lawns and flower beds and shaded her eyes to look up at her companions.

"If you would rather I take myself off and leave you two lovebirds alone, you have only to say the word. I begin to feel that my presence here is de trop, and I'd as lief read a book as play chaperone to a couple of mutes."

"Oh fudge!" said Lucy, smiling at Catherine affectionately as she detached herself from Mr. Norton's clasp to sit beside her sister.

"Charles will soon have you all to himself," Catherine went on cheerfully, "and I have missed our cozes. Now children, do tell me all!" She looked expectantly from one to the other. "What did Papa say?"

Mr. Norton disported himself on the grass at the feet of the two ladies and sat shredding a blade of grass negligently between his teeth.

"What could your father say, or mine, for that matter? Things have turned out rather well, thanks to Richard. I knew he would try to do something for me, and I was set to thwart his good intentions, but he outmaneuvered me. I could not object to any settlement he chose to make on his own sister-in-law, now could I?" He flashed a grin.

"You tried!" retorted Lucy indignantly. "When Richard first put the proposition to you, you looked the picture of outraged dignity."

"Ah well, all's well that ends well," said Mr. Norton philosophically.

"Oh yes!" Lucy's voice held a tremor as she turned to Catherine. "What changes have come about in our situation since we last sat on this bench on the eve of our first London Season!"

"Mmmm . . ." offered Mr. Norton enigmatically.

"What does that mean?" his beloved inquired.

"I was merely thinking of two carefree bachelors who not many months past retreated from the wiles of experienced town wenches to be befuddled, bewildered, and finally bagged by a couple of country innocents." He gave a resigned sigh.

"A couple of country innocents!" the ladies exclaimed in unison.

Norton looked up and grinned broadly at the two scowling faces above him.

"Bagged," he repeated unrepentantly, "by two country innocents who looked as if butter wouldn't melt in their mouths!"

"Unchivalrous!" cried Lucy, affronted.

"Ungentlemanly!" teased Catherine with a wag of her finger. "Nor is it true. Come now, Charles, admit it! You offered for Lucy simply to get possession of *my* library— you told me once how much you admired it—and Richard offered for me because of . . ." she faltered, the jest going out of her voice as she saw where the sport had led her, but after a momentary hesitation concluded gaily, "because of his promise! Did you know of it? Yes, I can see from your faces that you did."

Nr. Norton looked nonplussed, but he rallied quickly. "Oho! So you discovered Richard's dark secret, did you—that promise he made to his mother! I'm glad he told you. Females can be such featherheads if they think a fellow is practicing a deception, however harmless. Why, if he hadn't told you, you might have believed he offered for you to get his hands on your vast fortune." Norton cast a beseeching glance in Lucy's direction, and she came to his aid with alacrity.

"Or for her blue blood. Don't forget that, Charles!"

"Or for her breeding, Lucy. Her air of propriety."

"No, Charles! You have gone too far. Everyone knows of Catherine's temper!"

"You're both wrong," interrupted Catherine. "It was to spite his family."

"To spite his mama?" Norton asked in astonishment. "That he would never do! He dotes on her; leastways, he did till he got shackled to you."

Catherine burst out, "Don't tease me! Why did he choose *me?*"

"He was ailing," Norton intoned solemnly.

"Sick," Lucy added mournfully.

"Struck down with a terrible, wasting disease."

"Love!" completed Lucy, with a sage nod of her head.

"Of course!" observed Norton, reaching up and squeezing Catherine's hands in his.

"Thank you," Catherine replied. "But how can I believe you? Where is this lovesick swain now? He's in town, with those very wenches who know how to ensnare a man."

Lucy and Norton looked thunderstruck.

"How can you even believe it, Catherine?" Norton burst out. "Who has been telling you such lies?"

Catherine shook her head miserably, wishing that she had never opened her mouth to unburden herself to her friends. "Just rumors, Charles. Things I've overhead in conversation. Women I've seen him with—at the theater, at the park—you've seen them, too."

"Catherine!" Norton drew his hand distractedly through his hair. "How can I explain it to you? If you were up to snuff, you would understand such things. There isn't a man alive who doesn't have such women in his past." He could see that she was far from convinced and went on purposefully, "I know for a fact that Richard has long since given up his, well . . . all that sort of thing." He waved his hand vaguely in the air.

Catherine looked toward the house and saw that her carriage was waiting with her groom, Simpson, to convey her home to Branley Park. She rose and assumed a carefree pose as she turned to take her leave.

"Thank you for putting up with my fit of the sullens. I expect, when Richard arrives in person, I shall pull out of them. You see, I miss him so." And she was surprised at how much she meant it.

They watched Catherine walk with head erect in the direction of the house, and when she was out of earshot, Lucy turned back to Norton.

"Every man, Charles?" she asked plaintively.

Norton did not even pretend not to understand her. He glowered her down. "Lucy, my pet, on that subject I will not be drawn."

"No?" she coaxed softly, as she fingered the lapels of his dark coat.

"No, my love, I will not!" And with masterful aplomb, Norton folded his arms tightly around his betrothed and kissed her soundly.

* * *

"Humbug!"

"Flummery!"

"What twaddle!"

Richard Fotherville, the sixth Marquis of Rutherston, paused, one hand on the doorknob of the Branley Park library, arrested by the exasperated accents of his beloved's voice on the other side of the door.

He was dressed in a many-caped driving coat, and his mud-spattered boots and dusty, disheveled appearance indicated that he had at that moment arrived from an arduous journey.

"Fustian!"

"What rubbish!"

"I don't believe it!"

The marquis raised his brows, highly diverted, and gently pushed open the door. He entered silently, throwing his coat over the nearest chair, and gazed in the late summer light at the love and bane of his life who at that moment was curled up in a deep armchair engrossed in a book. He approached in a few rapid strides, but the lady gave no sign that she was aware of his presence, and he heard the growl deep in her throat as she continued to read what evidently afforded her no pleasure at all.

He moved to obscure her light, casting a deep shadow across the page she was reading, but the effect that this produced was not the one that his lordship desired. Catherine shifted her position to catch a better light. The shadow moved with her, and Catherine looked up. Amber eyes widened and gazed into gray, and for an infinitesimal moment, Rutherston discerned a welcome in them, before his lady had the presence of mind to guard her expression.

"My dear," said Catherine's husband in a light and bantering tone, pulling the book from her unresisting fingers, "what in the world is giving you so much offense?" He glanced at the title and let out a laugh, which startled his bristling wife. " 'Andromache'? Oh God, no, Catherine! I absolutely forbid it!" and he tossed Euripides's offending play carelessly to the other side of the room.

The lady, a deep scowl marring the beauty of her face, attempted to scramble to her feet, but her lord pushed her back and leaned his two hands on either arm of the chair, effectively imprisoning her. She scowled up at him. "I thought you would approve, my lord," she began primly, her lips pursing in anger. "The insipid Andromache is a model of docility, and just the sort of woman that you idealize!"

"Really?" said his lordship with galling levity, at least to the lady's ears. "I hope you don't mean to emulate that pattern of passivity, Catherine, for an Andromache wouldn't suit me at all!"

She regarded him with uncertainty, conscious of something in his demeanor, a confidence or a boldness that had been absent in the last number of weeks. "Indeed? And when did you form that opinion, for it is not how you expressed yourself to me."

His lordship took his time in answering, for he had discovered at that moment that he was getting a crick in his neck, and without so much as a by your leave, he gathered his lady into his arms and sat down in *her* chair, holding her fast in his lap. Catherine decided that this was the outside of enough and made a gallant effort to remove herself from his clasp, but as his only response was to tighten his grip and laugh at her struggles, she gave up the attempt and remained stiffly in his arms.

"Quite settled, sweetheart?" the odious man asked,

with disarming amiability. "No, really, my love, did I say I wanted a docile wife? It seems to me that in the last number of weeks we have both talked a good deal of nonsense, wouldn't you say?" He was tracing the outline of her scowling brows with his fingers, and Catherine was hard put to concentrate on their I conversation.

"You don't want a docile wife, my lord?"

"I want you, Catherine, and only you, as I have told you on numerous occasions. Why don't you believe me?" The heartless man now began to nuzzle her ladyship's ear, and when she would have pulled away, his hand moved to her neck to still her movements. She could bear it no longer.

"How dare you? How dare you come from her to me with your artful lovemaking? You . . . you rake! You cad! Kakiste! Echthiste!!" she continued, breaking into Greek, which seemed to relieve the ferocity of her emotions.

"Catherine!" said his lordship sternly. "The only thing I have come from is a cold bed, and believe me, I am damned tired of that! Now who is this lady whom you seem to think I am enamored of?"

Catherine's eyes blazed anger at him. "You know who it is! Lady Pamela Symington!"

"Was, Catherine," he said emphatically, *"was* my mistress!"

"I don't believe you! Do you forget, sir, that with my own eyes I saw you dancing attendance on the divine Pamela at Covent Garden when you had only an hour before left my side, reluctantly, so you said, to attend the prince at Carlton House?"

The marquis kept his voice sweet and reasonable as he replied to his outraged wife. "And did I not see Henderson dancing attendance on you on the very same evening when you had intimated to *me* that nothing could drag you from the house?"

Catherine played her trump card. "I have incontrovertible proof of your knavery, sir! You cannot deny it!"

The marquis kept his calm countenance. "And what is this incontrovertible proof, pray?" He smiled in a knowing way and absently curled a wisp of his beloved's locks around one finger. "Won't you tell me, Catherine?" he coaxed. The lady shook her head sourly. "Then I shall tell you. Henderson came to see me last night and confessed all!"

"He confessed?" Catherine asked in a very small voice.

"Oh yes! I know that you discovered the diamond necklace in the secret drawer of my desk."

"Oh!" was all that Catherine could say as she sat frozen with chagrin on his lordship's lap.

"I don't blame you, love. How could I? It was crass stupidity on my part to leave it there for anyone to find. But what's done is done, and I see that I owe you an explanation."

Catherine rallied her anger which had been on the point of dissipation, for with his lordship's arms folded around her, she was finding it hard to remember the cause of all her spleen.

"You don't deny then that you gave that woman such a gift, and *after* you had wed me? And before you say anything in rebuttal, sir, let me tell you that I saw the necklace on her throat the night we went to Carlton House!"

"I had thought as much, my love. I've done a good deal of reflecting since Henderson came to see me." His lordship secured his clasp more firmly around his beloved's waist before clearing his throat to explain his indiscretion.

"I had hoped that you would never know the sordid details of my past, but I see that I must tell you the whole, for these half-truths have wreaked a terrible vengeance on our life together. You won't like what I am about to say, Catherine, and it will give you an even poorer opinion of my character than you hold at present." He regarded her with a troubled expression, and she shook her head and would have protested that for the most part she had formed an excellent opinion of his character, but Rutherston pushed on, determined that she should know the whole.

"When I first came here, when I met you right here in this very room, I had left in London my *two* mistresses." Catherine gave a gasp and Rutherston tightened his grip. "Even before I met you, Catherine, I had decided to give these ladies their congé, for I had promised my mother that I would marry in my thirtieth year. Did I tell you about that promise, my love? No matter! It had no bearing on what happened between us. Catherine, will you believe me when I say that when I met you, I wished I had been the Hippolytus you dreamed about? But I could not, cannot turn the clock back!" He tried to read the expression in Catherine's eyes, but she was giving nothing away, and Rutherston went on resolutely.

"When I returned to town, before I paid my addresses to you, I sought out my mistresses to pension them off." Catherine turned her head away and Rutherston read disgust in her gesture. "No, ma am! Do not avert your head from me! You wanted the truth, and you will have it all!" She turned to look at him, surprised at his harsh tone and wondering why he should be more angry than she.

"My dear, to cut a long story short, you saw my parting gift to one of these Cyprians. It was the phaeton and pair I drove when you saw us in Hyde Park. The other lady was not in town at that time. I had purchased the diamonds for her, but I had no way of getting them to her until after I was wed. You witnessed that scene also, Catherine, when you went with Henderson to Covent Garden. So you see," he said bitterly, "the Fates have been against me from the start."

At that moment there was a discreet knock at the door, but before it could open, Rutherston thundered, "Go away, damn you!" and the shuffling of footsteps could be heard receding.

Catherine was indignant. "It was only Mrs. Bates with my tea. You need not bring your arrogant manners down here with you, my lord, for I won't have it!"

"Have you forgotten Andromache so soon, my sweet?" purred Rutherston.

"I never said I would emulate Andromache, for you know perfectly well that I never could."

"Shall we say adieu forever to Hippolytus and Andromache both? I shall think myself well rid of them."

His beloved seemed not to hear, but was regarding him with frank curiosity.

"Two mistresses?" asked Catherine at last. "And did they know about each other, Richard?"

He had always been sensitive to Catherine's use of his first name, and he breathed more easily, aware that his position in her affections was still secure.

"I don't know! I don't care!"

"And could you not even be faithful to your mistress?"

His lordship groaned. "Catherine, this is not a fit subject between husband and wife."

"You began it, my lord," she retorted hotly.

"Only because I had no choice!" He picked his words

carefully before continuing. "I told you once that mistresses are paid to please. But I was beyond pleasing. It was . . . an empty ritual." He seemed to see a speck on Catherine's chin and rubbed at it with his thumb as if to remove it, but his eyes were watchful. He saw her pensive expression. "Catherine, will you not believe me when I tell you that I have never met a woman whom I love and admire more than you!"

"Yet you gave *her* diamonds," Catherine expostulated, "while to me you gave only pearls!"

His lordship spoke with maddening calm. "I cannot abide that sort of glitter. I thought you had learned something about my taste. The matchless pearls were for a matchless woman; the gaudy diamonds for one of quite a different ilk."

Her ladyship pursed her lips together, and Rutherston smiled to see it. "No, don't sulk at me, you little baggage. I am quite willing to indulge your taste, if it runs to that sort of thing. I dragged my mother out of her bed late last night just so's I could fetch you the whole damned collection of Rutherston gems. There are enough diamonds in that strong box to deck you out as the most expensive Cyprian in all of England, if that is what you wish."

"No!" Catherine said in awed accents. "That was not well done! I won't have your mother thinking that I had designs on her jewels, for I never wanted, never expected them! Was she very angry?"

"Why should she be? She never wears 'em. Mama's taste runs to the same sort of thing as mine. She wasn't in the least angry, only curious."

"And what did you tell her?"

"Nothing! A man doesn't have to explain himself to his mother."

"But he must to his wife?" Catherine's eyes began to sparkle.

"Of course!"

"Then I feel that I must reciprocate. Oh, Richard, you have been so honest with me. I cannot, no I cannot conceal the sordid details of my past from you any longer." Her ladyship struggled to her feet, evading her husband's grasp, and paced the room wringing her hands.

"Catherine," exclaimed Rutherston, devastated, "what are you saying? Surely not Henderson!"

"Oh no, dear! It happened long before that! I'm afraid I quite lost my heart to him, although he was the most ramshackle kind of rake imaginable. He could never be faithful to any one female."

Rutherston sprang to his feet and reached his wife in one long stride. "Who was he, who was he?" he thundered, gripping her shoulders tightly.

"His name was Jason!" whispered Catherine, dropping her eyes. "And I have never forgotten him. I never shall! You remind me of him in some ways."

Rutherston looked suspiciously at Catherine's bowed head, but when he saw her shoulders begin to shake, he put his arms around her to console her, his chest constricted with pain.

"Who was he?" he managed on a soft note.

"The meanest stallion my father ever possessed," Catherine gasped between convulsive sobs of laughter.

"Catherine!" roared his lordship like a wounded lion. "Why are you doing this to me?"

"To teach you a lesson, you conceited man," she retorted quickly. "Jealousy is a hateful emotion, is it not? It is as palpable as a physical pain. Do you know what I have been experiencing these many weeks past, wondering how I could compete with the seductive Pamela?"

"I don't want you to compete with her!" Rutherston responded roughly. "Did I not tell you that our loving is different?" His arms tightened around her. "Oh, Catherine," he moaned against her ear, "it is I who am the novice. You know so much more about love than I. You must teach me!"

A thought suddenly occurred to Catherine, and she looked up at him accusingly. "Your promise! You married me because of your promise to your family. The Marquis of Rutherston must beget an heir."

Rutherston grinned wickedly. "But the Marquis of Rutherston already has begat his heir!" His hands moved over her body with deliberate possessiveness. "How do you explain my amorous attentions, my love, now that my base purpose has been served? And I warn you, I have no intention of allowing you ever again to bar me from your bed." His hands moved to her back in a gesture she knew well, and she felt her gown loosen.

"Do not! Oh, stop! Richard, what are you thinking of?"

"What I am thinking, my love, is that I will be an earnest pupil. Teach me about love, Catherine, please?"

What could she do? An earnest desire for learning must be encouraged. So Catherine complied. She twined her arms around his lordship's neck and returned his warm embrace.

Extra Bonus!
Please turn the page for
Elizabeth Thornton's
delightful short story
SHEER SORCERY

SHEER SORCERY

Chapter 1

Sheer Sorcery, she thought, and smiled.

She was almost past the milliner's shop window in Milsom Street before the confection of feathers and flora registered in her consciousness. Jessica retraced her steps and gazed with total absorption at the most frivolous piece of nonsense that had ever been devised to sit atop a lady's head.

A bonnet? she conjectured, and felt the strangest pang as her eyes made a thorough inspection of the creation which was named—so a small, gilt-edged card informed her—*Sheer Sorcery.*

The bonnet was of the softest green velvet. On the crown was a coronet of holly with red berries. A profusion of green satin ribbons, elaborately tied in loops and bows, adorned the whole to fall away in streamers. And most amusing of all—she blinked and blinked again—perched on the brim was a tiny stuffed blue bird of indeterminate species with enormous tail feathers which curled forward at a saucy angle. There was no doubt in Jessica's mind that it was a Christmas bonnet and meant to be worn only for the festive season.

Without more ado, Jessica walked straight into the shop and bought the absurd object.

"Sheer Sorcery," reiterated the milliner as she wrapped it in tissue paper and placed it in its hatbox.

It was aptly named, thought Jessica. She must surely be bewitched to go against her own principles and succumb to the sin of vanity.

It was, she later repented, one of those insane purchases for which there was no accounting and which would remain hidden away forever at the back of her clothes press. A sober and respectable schoolmistress at Miss Plowden's Seminary for girls did not make a spectacle of herself by sporting such capricious attire, and especially not in the staid city of Bath. Moreover, what her guardian would say if he ever discovered her folly, she scarcely liked to contemplate. He would, in all probability, laugh himself silly. He was used to his sensible ward spending her quarterly allowance on books, and blue stockings, and things of that nature.

For a whole week, the bonnet did not see the light of day. It was not until the carriage which had been sent to convey Jessica home for the Christmas holidays had left Bath well behind that the hatbox was opened and the bonnet reverently unwrapped and set on Jessica's lap.

The only other occupant of the carriage, Mr. John Wynchbold, a pleasant-faced young man of thirty summers or so, watched curiously as Jessica, rather defiantly if a little guiltily, removed the serviceable chip-straw from her head and carefully set the other in its place.

Mr. Wynchbold regarded his companion in grave silence. Jessica had no difficulty in reading his mind. He would be thinking that the bonnet was completely out of character for a spinster lady approaching her twenty-first birthday, and one, moreover, who never indulged in such frivolity. And he would be right. She could not now think what rash impulse had provoked her at the very last moment to retrieve the hatbox from her clothes press and carry it with her into the waiting carriage. *Two impulses in the space of one week?* thought Jessica, and wondered if she was, in very truth, bewitched.

Her fingers toyed absently with the ribbons under her chin. She wished, rather fervently, that she could remove the bonnet without losing face. Since this was impossible, Jessica tilted her head and pretended there was nothing untoward in the prim and proper Miss Jessica Holtby, schoolmistress, sporting the most outrageously extravagant bonnet which had ever graced a lady's head.

"It's very becoming. Truly," said Mr. Wynchbold, breaking into Jessica's reflections.

"Thank you."

"I had no notion that your eyes were green."

"They are gray," corrected Jessica.

"And the color does something for your red hair."

"I don't have red hair."

"No?"

"It's auburn," stated Jessica.

"That's what I meant, Cousin Jessica," returned Mr. Wynchbold diplomatically.

Cousin John was a paragon, thought Jessica, not for the first time, and tried not to resent him simply because he was a messenger for that other gentleman, whom she disliked intensely and who never put himself to the bother of escorting her to Villard in person.

At the thought of her guardian, Roger Moreton, fourth earl of Villard, her face took on a pinched look. She tried to banish him from her mind, and succeeded for all of half a minute. As a last resort, Jessica used all her powers of concentration to substitute a more acceptable image than the provoking image of Roger Moreton. She thought of his parents, the third earl and his countess, and her eyes grew misty.

If only the old earl had lived, things might have been so very different. It was he who had become her guardian when she was orphaned. Truth to tell, Jessica scarcely remembered her parents. They could never settle in one place for long. Her father had been something of a scholar. And while her parents traveled the world, their infant daughter had been left to the care of a succession of indifferent relations until her parents had succumbed to a fever in India. And at the age of ten, Jessica had come to live at Villard.

Villard. It was the only real home she had ever known, and she had loved it. The very air around Villard, to her child's way of thinking, had seemed fresher, sweeter than any air she had ever breathed. The earl and his countess had gone out of their way to make her feel at home. Only one son of all their offspring had survived childhood— Roger, and he was away at university. It was only natural that she should be treated as a daughter of the house.

But she wasn't a daughter of the house. At sixteen, that fact was borne in upon her when the old earl died, the year following the death of his countess. Jessica had been in shock, and so very grateful that Roger was there to comfort her. Roger, whom she saw only in the holidays, whom she had looked up to as if he were a Greek demigod, and who was always so very forbearing of all her childish foibles. She could not have loved him more had he been her real brother, and she had wished with all her young heart that it were so.

She suddenly found herself fighting an absurd urge to weep, and studiously affected an interest in the passing scenery. She would not cry one more tear for Roger Moreton, she promised herself. Five years had come and gone since she had discovered his true colors. She had done all her crying years ago.

She was not wanted. That much had become very evident. And at sixteen, just when she was more in need of a secure foundation than she had ever been in her young life, the new earl of Villard had packed her off to Miss Plowden's Seminary in Bath. He had made no secret of the fact that he was glad to see the back of her.

As though it were yesterday, she could feel herself burn with the humiliation of it. Roger wanted no part of her. The very sight of her irked him. And if he had not promised his father that Villard would always be her home, Jessica was sure that he would have closed its gates to her long since.

"It's snowing." Mr. Wynchbold let down the window and peered up at the sky. A moment later, he pulled his head back and rolled the window tight against the chill blast. "This will slow us down a bit. We may have to spend a night on the road. Roger won't like it."

"We could return to Bath," offered Jessica half hopefully.

Mr. Wynchbold treated her words as a jest. He laughed. "Don't fret. I'll get you home for Christmas."

"Villard isn't my home," said Jessica, and could have bitten off her tongue for the betraying remark. She liked John Wynchbold, but she had never once confided in him, not in all the times Roger had sent his cousin to fetch her home for the holidays. Cousin John was too much in Roger's pocket for Jessica ever to regard him in the light of a friend.

John Wynchbold studied the slight form of his companion with thoughtful eyes. The solemn-eyed waif who, to all intents and purposes, had been adopted into Roger's family, had grown into a beautiful woman. It was regrettable, he thought, suppressing a shudder, that she had turned into a confirmed spinster, and dressed for the part. Nevertheless, all the gray of the Atlantic Ocean—and his eyes roamed over Jessica's gray traveling cloak, which he knew covered an equally unprepossessing frock—could not diminish the girl's bewitching good looks. His eyes came to rest on the green confection on top of her head and he chuckled.

"Your guardian is going to wonder about that bonnet," he remarked.

"Roger won't be my guardian for very much longer," said Jessica with a small self-congratulatory smile. "I come of age on Christmas Eve."

Mr. Wynchbold shrugged negligently. "That doesn't signify," he said, more brutally honest than he meant to be. "As long as Roger is the trustee of your father's estate, he calls the tune. You must learn to accept that fact with grace, Cousin Jessica, else you'll find yourself riding for a fall."

Jessica pressed her lips together as she absorbed the faint warning in Mr. Wynchbold's words. Apart from the intelligence that her competence was modest after her father's debts had been settled, she knew next to nothing about the state of her affairs. She could thank Roger for that. For some obscure reason, he preferred to keep her in ignorance. She swallowed an unladylike oath. The reason wasn't so obscure. She was a female. Roger, like most of his sex, could not conceive that a mere female could do sums. Cousin John spoke no less than the truth. Roger held the purse strings, but only until she reached the advanced age of five-and-twenty or until such time as she wed, whichever came first.

Even so, Roger Moreton did not have everything his own way. In the last year or two, Jessica Holtby had learned how to circumvent the annoying restraints placed on her by her interfering guardian.

At eighteen, when she had graduated from the seminary, Roger had thought to palm her off with Aunt Sophie in her town house in London. Jessica would have none of it. With pride stiffening her spine, and eyes flashing green fire, she had confronted her guardian. She was done with imposing herself on reluctant relatives, she had told him. She had found a niche for herself. Miss Plowden had offered her a position at the school, and she meant to accept it. It seemed that all the hurt she had received at his hands came out in the most scathing vituperation.

Coldly civil, Roger had finally given way. She had hoped never to set eyes on him again. She was not to be so fortunate. In the holidays, he never failed to send an escort to bring her home to Villard. And partly because she knew that the old earl would wish it, and partly because she felt an indescribable sense of homecoming whenever she entered Villard's welcoming portals, she had persuaded herself that she was not losing face by obeying Roger's peremptory summons.

"A penny for them."

"Beg pardon?" Jessica brought her thoughts back to the present. John Wynchbold was studying her pensively.

"You were miles away," he said. "What were you thinking?"

Smiling, Jessica quickly invented, "I was thinking that in a few years I come into my competence. I'll finally be my own mistress." And because Mr. Wynchbold looked as if he were about to argue the point, Jessica quickly cut in, "You must tell me, cousin, whether or not the rumor I hear about Lady Sylvia Claremont is true."

"By Jove!" exclaimed Wynchbold, clearly startled.

"Bath may be a quiet backwater, but you are not behind in the latest *on-dits,* are you?"

"Am I to wish Roger happy?" asked Jessica pointedly.

Mr. Wynchbold looked to be nonplussed. "Beg pardon?"

"Roger and Lady Sylvia," responded Jessica patiently. "Am I to congratulate Roger on his coming nuptials?"

"That would be premature," demurred Mr. Wynchbold. He chuckled, then coughed as he came under Jessica's hard stare. "Lady Sylvia and her mother are making up two of the party at Villard," he said. "I collect they are most anxious to make your acquaintance."

Assuming an amused air, Jessica quizzed, "Whatever happened to Miss Fairmont?"

"Miss Fairmont?"

"She was Roger's flirt last Christmas. And the year before that, it was Lady Charlotte, as I remember."

"Those other ladies were merely passing fancies," answered Mr. Wynchbold, his eyes twinkling.

Jessica felt a shaft of something she refused to put a name to. She made to remove a small leather-bound volume from a handgrip which she had positioned beside her on the banquette. Before she could object, Mr. Wynchbold had the book in his own hand.

"The Vindication of the Rights of Woman?" he queried, reading the title, and returned the book to Jessica. His lips remained suspiciously grave.

"By Mary Wollstonecraft," answered Jessica quellingly.

"Ah yes. A most . . . original lady who advocates equality between the sexes." Perceiving that his companion was about to embark on a subject which was dear to her heart, he exerted himself to head her off. "How did you come to hear about Roger and Lady Sylvia?"

It looked for a moment as if Jessica was not to be diverted. Suddenly blushing, she looked away and said indistinctly, "Lady Bloom is lately come into Bath. Her daughters are pupils at the school. She has many friends in town with whom she corresponds."

"And this lady has cultivated your acquaintance, I take it?"

"Yes."

Jessica was scarcely flattered. It was her connection to the House of Villard which had inspired the lady's interest. As was to be expected, the earl figured prominently in Lady Bloom's conversation, and never more so than when her only son and heir removed to London to acquire a little town bronze. His letters were full of Villard. It was evident that young Bloom admired that gentleman to excess. Villard's exquisite tailoring, his neckcloths, his enviable whipmanship—all must be described in minute detail no less than the beauties of the *haute monde* who were eager to catch the eligible earl's eye.

But it was the less innocent beauties of the *demi-monde* who, much to Jessica's shame, interested her more. Not that young Bloom referred to them in his letters to his mother. But with his sire, he was not so discreet. And Lady Bloom soon wormed everything she wished to know from that long-suffering gentleman. And passed it along to Jessica in sly insinuations and broad hints. Vulgar woman!

Jessica could not now credit that she had been so naïve. Roger was thirty years old. Naturally, there would be women in his life. She must have known it if she had given it a thought. It simply had never occurred to her. Jealousy did not enter into it. Certainly not! But her antipathy to her guardian was not lessened one jot by Lady Bloom's revelations. Quite the reverse.

Suddenly apprehending that the object of her thoughts was the one person in the world she had resolved would *not* be the object of her thoughts, Jessica promptly applied herself to the volume in her hand, and for the next little while gave herself up to the pleasant prospect of a perfect world where women were truly the equals of men.

Chapter 2

The carriage reached Villard well before the dinner hour, but some time after dark had fallen. Jessica followed one of the maids up to her old chamber, vastly relieved that Roger was not present to remark the ludicrous bonnet perched on her head, knowing that he would not allow it to pass without some acid comment.

She was at a loss to explain the growing unease which had crept up on her the closer they had come to Villard. It was only a bonnet, when all was said and done. But she was coming to suspect that, in some unspecified way, the bonnet betrayed something intrinsic to her nature which she wished to suppress, something she did not wish Roger to divine. *Vanity,* she thought, and was glad to let it go at that.

"You're new here," she observed amicably as the young maid began to unpack her boxes.

"Yes mum."

"What's your name?"

"Mary, mum."

Jessica moved about the room, smiling as her eyes lit first on one well-remembered object then another. Here was a painting of the Parthenon which Roger had sent her from Athens when he was on his Grand Tour. And here was a sword he had brought with him from Spain because he had known that she was fascinated with stories of El Cid. But that was in happier days, before Roger had revealed his true nature. Not liking the train of her thoughts, frowning, she removed her new bonnet, packed it in its box, and set it on a shelf at the back of the dark mahogany clothes press.

"What ever happened to Alice? Did she marry her Tom?"

"That she did, mum. Fancy you remembering her!"

"Why shouldn't I remember her? This used to be my home. I know all the members of staff. I'm Jessica Holtby, Lord Villard's ward."

The maid's lips formed a round O.

"Why does that surprise you?" asked Jessica.

"I'm sure I don't rightly know, except . . ."

"Yes?" encouraged Jessica.

"It must have been the bonnet, mum. I wasn't expecting you to be a lady of fashion." Suddenly conscious that she had inadvertently insulted her master's ward, young Mary flushed to the roots of her hair and promptly returned to the task at hand.

Jessica was left to consider that, below stairs, she had become an object of speculation. No doubt Mary would tell the other servants about the bonnet. She wondered what they would make of it.

"Tell me about Alice," she said at last, trying to relieve the poor maid of some of her embarrassment.

Mary was glad to follow the pretty lady's lead. In a matter of minutes, Jessica had formed a clear impression of Alice's favorable circumstances. After a long courtship, and only when the master had made a cottage on the estate available to Tom, one of his gamekeepers, the couple had finally married. And to crown their happiness,

Alice was soon to present her Tom with the first fruits of their union.

"A baby," said young Mary rapturously.

A baby, thought Jessica, and felt a sudden constriction in her womb. Before she could pursue the reason for this odd pang, a lackey was at the door with a message from his lordship. Roger wished to see her in his office before dinner was served.

It took only a moment to run a comb through her short crop of feathery curls. She leaned forward toward the cheval mirror and gazed steadfastly at her reflection. Jessica had no notion of the startling effect of milky white skin against auburn hair. The heart-shaped face held no interest for her. She stared into the huge eyes that stared back at her as if she could see into her own soul.

"I have gray eyes, not green," she told the surprised maid before she swept out the door.

Roger's office was on the ground floor. A burst of masculine laughter came from the music room, farther along the hall. There was never any question that Christmas at Villard was a pleasant prospect for those fortunate enough to be invited.

For a moment, Jessica hesitated with her hand on the doorknob. She knew that she ought to knock before entering, but some impulse to catch Roger unawares provoked her to omit this common courtesy. She pushed open the door and entered.

He was standing with his back to her at one of the long windows gazing out at the dark night. There was something about the way he held himself, something about the set of his shoulders, which gave her pause. The vague impression of determination was lost the moment he became aware of her presence.

"Jess," he said, straightening.

And because she felt something clench deep inside her at the familiar diminutive which only Roger ever used, she said crossly, "I wish you would call me Jessica."

He gave her his wickedly roguish grin which never failed to annoy her. She suspected that he knew it and was more than a little pleased with herself when she managed in a marginally warmer tone, "How are you, Roger?"

"Better for seeing you, Jess," he answered, and the grin intensified as Jessica's brows winged upwards.

"Please be seated," he said, gesturing to an upright chair, and moving toward her, lounged against the flat-topped desk in an attitude of arrogant grace.

Seating herself as Roger indicated, Jessica tipped back her head and returned stare for stare. Once upon a time, Jessica had reckoned that Roger Moreton was the sum and substance of a maiden's prayer. Through half-lowered lashes, she made a slow inventory and was forced to the grudging conclusion that, to all outward appearances, the earl was unquestionably worthy of any woman's admiration.

A Corinthian among Corinthians, young Mr. Bloom called him. Jessica had no difficulty in understanding why. To her, Roger had always seemed something of a latter-day Roman centurion. Hair the color of sable clung to his head in curling disorder. The tight-fitting dark coat and pantaloons merely emphasized the muscular physique. *Pagan,* thought Jessica, and swept down her lashes to clear her mind of the disturbing picture.

"Why do you persist in dressing like a nun?"

At the clipped tone, her eyes flew open. "Scarcely a nun," she protested, trying to sound amused. Coolly, sedately, and rather shockingly, she baited, "I'm not one of your birds of paradise, Roger. I'm a schoolmistress. For my profession, I don't require elaborate gowns."

"Birds of paradise?" Those intensely blue eyes lightened. "What do you know about birds of paradise, Jess?"

What Jessica knew about birds of paradise—and all of it from Lady Booth—could be written on the head of a thimble. What she said was, "You may take my word for it, there is quite as much of *that* going on in Bath as anywhere else."

His brows lifted. "In a girls' seminary?"

Jessica made a small sound of exasperation. "I do have a circle of friends outside the school, you know." Mentally, she ticked off Lady Bloom and the library clerk at the circulating library, wondering if two might legitimately form a circle.

"So," he said, and the glitter of laughter in his eyes grew brighter. "You've heard about my 'birds of paradise,' have you, Jess? I wonder who told you?"

If she had been caught red-handed going through his private correspondence, Jessica could not have been more mortified. That she managed to suppress her blushes, she counted a major victory.

Musingly, he went on, "I shouldn't have supposed that a lady who prides herself on the lofty tone of her mind would spare a thought for my . . . low amusements." Jessica knew when she was being baited, and she schooled her features to remain politely indifferent. His voice softened to the caress of velvet. "Does it disturb you, Jess, to know that some women, present company excepted, of course, are susceptible to my . . . person?"

Jessica's mouth went slack. She hardly knew where to look. This was not the sort of conversation she was used to hearing from Roger. She was to blame. It was she who had opened the door to this salacious form of conversation by referring to his birds of paradise. She wondered how she might turn the subject.

"Or perhaps you *are* susceptible, and this is your way of letting me know it?" drawled that hateful voice.

"No!" she gasped. "No!"

"No, Jess? Truly?"

Her mouth opened and closed and her eyes fell away from his. She was appalled at the picture his words had impressed on her mind. Roger as her lover? It was not a role her mind was willing to accept. As the forbidden picture persisted, a shiver of alarm danced along her spine.

She jerked back as his hand shot out and captured her chin, holding her face up for his inspection. Confusion, embarrassment, and something like dawning awareness were starkly evident in her eyes. He patted her cheek. She recoiled as if his touch burned her. The gesture was not lost on the earl.

"Do you still hate me, Jess?" he asked ruefully.

"A-amazingly so!"

He released her and Jessica sank back into her chair. There was no levity in him when next he spoke. "When do you intend to give up playing school, Jess?"

It took a moment before she could collect herself, and not all her efforts could keep her voice from shaking. "We've had this conversation before, Roger. As I've told you, you did me a great service when you sent me to Miss Plowden's Seminary. I'm with my own kind. I'm a useful member of society. What more should I want?"

"No thoughts of marriage, Jess? No secret ambition to be mistress of your own establishment? No hope of children?"

For a few seconds, blue eyes locked on gray, and it was as though a duel of wills was being fought in that quiet room. Finally, Jessica said, "You know my sentiments on the subject of marriage. A woman stands to lose . . ."

With an abrupt wave of one hand he waved her to silence. "I'm familiar with the sophistry, Jess. You've repeated it ad nauseam. You value your independence above all things."

"Yes."

"Piffle. I know you better than you know yourself. You're not so very different from other women."

Her look spoke volumes and he laughed, not pleasantly, but derisively. When he straightened from the desk, she rose with him.

"So," he said, "you reach your majority in less than a fortnight. You'll be free of me at long last. That day you've longed for above all others has finally arrived."

Before she could frame a reply, he went on in a different tone of voice, "For both our sakes, I suggest that we call a halt to hostilities. This is Christmas, Jess. You know, 'peace and goodwill to all men'? It's more than time to forget our differences and expiate the past."

"I hope I am never uncivil to you before your guests," she answered stiffly.

"That's not what I meant and you know it. My dear, the present state of affairs cannot continue indefinitely. Did you suppose that I would permit it?"

She digested his words in silence. She heard the threat, but was at a loss to understand what he meant by it.

"Truce, Jess?" he murmured in that curiously mesmerizing tone he could command when the mood suited him.

To reply in the negative would have betrayed a childish intractability. "Truce," she agreed, then added, challenging, "But that doesn't mean I am surrendering."

The laughter was back in his eyes. "All in good time, Jess, all in good time."

Before either of them could speak again, there was a knock at the door. Roger pivoted as the door opened, and a dark-haired vision in pale muslins floated toward him with outstretched hands. "Roger," trilled the vision breathlessly, "I came as soon as I could slip away.

Jessica coldly appraised the newcomer and for some inexplicable reason, her heart sank. She knew at once that the statuesque beauty was Lady Sylvia, Roger's prospective bride, and she thought that she had never beheld a more dazzling and utterly feminine female in her whole life.

With his usual practiced grace, Roger captured the proffered hands and, stepping aside, said formally, "Lady Sylvia, may I make known to you my ward, Miss Jessica Holtby?"

Lady Sylvia checked her forward movement as she became aware of the other girl's presence. A mask of polite interest settled on her beautiful features. "Miss Holtby," she said, "I am delighted to make your acquaintance. Roger has told me so much about his . . ." she hesitated for a moment, laughed lightly, and concluded, "clever little ward."

Jessica took instant umbrage to the knowing smiles which her companions exchanged. She was being dismissed as an oddity. Her hackles rose. But something in Roger's eyes warned her to tread carefully.

The vision was speaking. "You must call me Sylvia and I shall call you Jessica, since we are soon to be more closely connected." A delectable blush stole across Lady Sylvia's complexion. Half-laughing, addressing Roger, she continued, "Or do I tempt the fates by divulging our little secret before time?"

Jessica did not hear Roger's reply. There was a sudden roaring in her ears. It took a moment or two before her head cleared. She knew that she was smiling and that she replied suitably if vaguely to the polite flow of small talk which ensued. But it was only when she was in the privacy of her own chamber that she was finally able to get her breathing under control.

"Mum? What ails ye?" asked Mary anxiously, noting Jessica's paper-white face and trembling form.

"Fatigue 'tis all," said Jessica, and she threw herself on the bed. *Fatigue,* her thoughts echoed. What else could it be? And wracked by emotions so unfamiliar that she could not put a name to them, Jessica turned her head into the pillow.

Chapter 3

Jessica approached the door to her chamber lost in a brown study. She was dressed in an old riding habit of an indeterminate green, a relic from former days when she had permitted her guardian to select and furnish her wardrobe. Her eyes were bright, her cheeks were glowing with health. She had lately spent a pleasant hour or two in the most agreeable company, riding over a small section of Roger's estate.

It was Cousin Jason, Viscount Deveryn, and his wife, who had invited her to go riding. Jason was no stranger to her. He was related to Roger and John Wynchbold through a maternal grandmother. But his little wife, Maddie, had taken Jessica completely by surprise, to say the least.

Even on first impression, Cousin Jason's little wife was unexpected. The girl was pretty enough, but no beauty. And Jason was . . . well . . . simply divine. Jessica had taken it for granted that the gilded Adonis would choose for his consort a diamond of the first water. Shock soon followed upon shock. Behind that little wren exterior, the girl concealed one of the sharpest, shrewdest intellects that it had ever been Jessica's privilege to encounter.

Her thoughts drifted to the conversation at the dinner

table the night before, the liveliest in Jessica's memory. It was Jason who had thrown down the gauntlet, and his young wife had not been slow to pick it up. The subject was of the keenest interest to Jessica— the lot of women in society. Within minutes, the battle lines had been drawn, the gentlemen on one side, and the ladies, as was to be expected, on the other. How was it possible that such a serious subject had generated so much . . . hilarity? Jessica had rarely enjoyed herself more.

And as the humorous debate had raged around her, Jessica had found herself watching the interplay between the viscount and his clever wife. It stirred something in her—not envy exactly, but an ache, a longing for something to fill her own empty life. There was a tenderness there, a caring, which she wanted for herself. Maddie must be the most fortunate girl in the world, thought Jessica. She had a husband who adored her, she was the mother of his child, and if she was a bluestocking, no one thought any the less of her for it, quite the reverse. But then, Maddie was an unpretentious girl. It was easy to like her. Whereas she . . .

Jessica gave herself a mental shake. Sternly, she told herself to snap out of it. She was sure she did not know what had come over her of late. As a rule, she was not one to wallow in self-pity. It was Roger who had done this to her. He could not say two words to her, it seemed, but he must introduce the subject of her future now that she had almost come of age. It was only natural that he should do so, she supposed, but, oh, it made her feel restless and quite out of sorts.

She pushed open the door to her chamber and came to an abrupt halt. There, in the center of the room, was the perverse object of her reflections, and in his hands was her Christmas bonnet.

Unrepentant, grinning wickedly, his gaze locked with hers. "What the devil is this?" he demanded.

In tight-lipped anger, Jessica stalked him. "How dare you! How dare you!" she fairly sputtered.

She backed him up against the wall till they were toe to toe. Not that it made a jot of difference. Roger held the bonnet aloft in one hand, well out of her reach. It would have been undignified to try and wrest it away from him. Undignified and futile.

Exasperated, she flounced away. In the next instant, she was dragged round to face him. There was a reckless glitter in his eyes which had her trembling.

"Please, Roger, please," she implored as one arm locked around her shoulders.

"I'll tell you what this is," he said, and he held her steady as he forced the bonnet on her head. "This is Jessica Holtby as she sees herself in her most secret dreams, all feminine and prettied up to bewitch the *man* of her dreams. Jessica Holtby, you're a fraud!"

"No," she said, and tried to pull away from him. He clamped both hands on her shoulders and forced her to the cheval mirror.

"Look at yourself, Jess, and tell me what you see."

She kept her head averted, but one rough shake from those powerful masculine hands brought her gaze quickly up to the glass.

Soft. Alluring. Intriguing. A female confident of her femininity. Jessica shrank from the false image.

"You're a beautiful woman, Jess. Why does that make you afraid? My God, don't you see what this means? There's hope for you yet."

If the ridiculous bonnet had not been perched on her head, she would have made some scathing rejoinder. As it was, she was a good deal subdued when she said, "It's only a bonnet, for heaven's sake. It means nothing at all."

"Does it not, Jess? Does it *not?* I beg to differ. Look at yourself. When did you last pretty yourself up like this?"

For endless moments, Jessica stared at her reflection in the looking glass. Panic began to pulse through her body. In spite of the picture she presented, she had no wish to attract the notice of any gentleman, especially not Roger Moreton. He had rejected her, once, in the most humiliating way. He would not be given the opportunity to do so again.

When she felt his grip slacken, before he could stop her, she pulled out of his arms. The laughter in his eyes died when she rounded on him. "This stupid bonnet was nothing more than a dare!" she burst out.

"A dare?"

Her mind worked furiously to invent the next lie. "A dare," she repeated, struggling to find her composure. "From one bluestocking to another. Do you suppose I'd normally be caught dead in anything so, so . . ." she searched for the right word.

"Feminine," he helpfully supplied.

"Decadent," she immediately corrected.

The laughter was back in his eyes. "When I think of it," he said, and his fingers tugged gently on the saucy feather which brushed one flushed cheek, "you do put me in mind of a 'bird of paradise,' Jess."

Horror-struck, she stared at him. "It was a d-dare," she stammered.

"Was it?" She could see that he didn't believe her. "And just what was the nature of this dare, Jess?"

To gain some time, she removed the bonnet and deliberately put some distance between them. *What was the nature of the dare?* The deceitful words, rather shockingly, came to her easily. "Why, what should the dare be, Roger, but simply to wear the stupid thing for a whole day?"

"And you wore it inside the carriage, with only Cousin John to witness your folly? You never used to be so craven, Jess."

She ignored the taunt and responded angrily, "He told you, I suppose?"

"Did you doubt that he would?" When she made no answer, he went on softly, "Never to be worn again, Jess? *Never?*"

She did not know what game he was playing. She only knew a curious urge to protect herself. "The day you see me don this stupid bonnet . . ."

"Yes?" he challenged.

She laughed lightly, and ended, "you'll know that I've come into my dotage *or,*" pausing for effect, "that I've prettied myself up to bewitch the man of my dreams." There, she had struck just the right note, she congratulated herself.

"Be sure they are not one and the same day, Jess, or you may find that the man of your dreams is already bespoken—or in his grave."

"Oh you!" she disparaged, and moved to the clothes press to stow the horrid bonnet. "What . . . ?" She could see at a glance that her own garments had been removed and replaced with a set of something quite different— pale muslins and silks, velvet pelisses in richer, warmer shades. Her blood began to boil. The angry words rushed onto her tongue as she pivoted to face him. "How dare you remove my things without asking my permission!"

She sucked in her breath as he pounced on her. He no longer looked amused or calm. She knew that the hands which were clamped on her shoulders would leave bruises by morning.

His voice was as dark and threatening as his eyes. "I dare for a very good reason. I'm still your guardian, Jess. It suited my purpose to allow you to go your own way these last number of years. But as I told you earlier, that state of affairs will no longer be allowed to continue."

When she opened her mouth to protest that she would soon cease to be his ward, he administered a rough shake, silencing her.

"You will wear the garments I have purchased for you, else I swear I'll tear the clothes from your back and put you into them myself."

With an impatient curse, he released her and took a step back. He studied her in silence. Her eyes were wide and tear-bright. Her lower lip trembled. Color was high on her cheekbones.

"Jess," he said, curiously gentle, then seemed to think twice about what he was about to say. He moved away, giving her breathing room. "Jess," he repeated, but this time his voice was controlled, "we were interrupted yesterday before I had a chance to tell you. This is no ordinary holiday. The whole damn clan of Moretons and Darnleys will be descending upon us. There is to be a special celebration. I won't have you dressed for the part of the proverbial poor relation." He flashed her a cozening smile. "It reflects on me, you see."

Out of everything he said, Jessica's mind locked on only one thing—there was to be a special celebration. "Your betrothal," she said, before she could stop herself.

Surprise flared in his eyes.

Suddenly, it became very important to her to appear as calm and cool as he. "You are to be congratulated, Roger.

Lady Sylvia is a lovely girl." She summoned a creditable smile.

"Lady Sylvia?"

Nodding, she went on determinedly, though the words almost choked her, "She's just right for you. I'm sure you'll be very happy together."

One eyebrow quirked. "What makes you say so?"

Why was he pressing her like this? "She's beautiful," she answered simply.

He smiled ironically. "I am not such a coxcomb as to choose a wife merely for beauty, Jess. One can weary very quickly if that is all a woman has to recommend her." Gently, he prompted, "Is that all you can find to say about Lady Sylvia, Jess, that she is beautiful?"

"Well," she said, floundering, "she's very . . . charming."

"Charming?" His eyes took on a faraway look. "Yes, Sylvia is certainly one of the most charming ladies of my acquaintance. It is my considered opinion that she would defer to her lord and master in all things. What do you think, Jess?"

Lord and master? The very words were polemic. Jessica smirked unpleasantly. "You'll have everything your own way, if that is what you wish," she readily agreed.

Musingly, he murmured, "It sounds like . . . paradise. What man wouldn't envy me?"

It was too much to bear. "But I wouldn't be in *her* shoes for all the flax in Flanders."

"Wouldn't you, Jess?" He was so close that she could smell the faint scent of his cologne. Absently, he toyed with one of her wayward curls. "Don't you think I'll make an unexceptionable husband, Jess?" he asked, and he turned the full force of that provokingly roguish grin upon her.

Jessica tried to check her temper and succeeded fairly well. "A good husband? Not by my lights!"

"No?" he drawled whimsically.

Why did she have the feeling that he was toying with her? Without appearing to do so, she tried to inch her head away to dislodge his fingers from her hair.

"Is it because of the birds of paradise, Jess?"

Her cheeks bloomed. His eyes smiled.

Before she could find her voice, he went on in an altered tone, "You should know me well enough to know that, once I wed, those bird of paradise will become ancient history. I intend to be a faithful, loyal husband, Jess. My wife will never have cause to complain of her husband's infidelities, I promise you."

That he would play the part of the attentive husband with aplomb, she did not doubt. Hadn't he done as much when he had played the part of the indulgent, older brother? But it was all a sham, as later events were to prove. And she was a fool to waste one moment in regret for the Roger she had known as a young girl.

That other, younger Roger had filled her whole life, though she only saw him in the holidays. But in the months when he was in town, doing whatever it was young bucks did in town, scarcely a week went by when a letter did not arrive at Villard addressed to her. She had hoarded those letters as if each were a fifty-pound note.

She shrank, remembering the nature of her own letters to Roger, where she had spilled out her heart, describing in great detail the half-understood longings that could only be experienced by an adolescent girl. After that never-to-be-forgotten night, during all her years at Miss Plowden's, she had never once written to him.

"Jess, what is it?" His eyes searched her face as his hand came up to cup her chin.

She didn't like him touching her, not since the night he had spoiled everything between them and sent her away from Villard.

"It is not to me you should be making these promises, Roger, but to Lady Sylvia. I have no interest in your little *affaires.*"

"No interest, Jess? Are you sure, my dear?"

"None whatsoever," she answered emphatically.

He laughed, and let her go. "Don't tempt me to put you to the test, Jess." He spoke lightly, but there was something in his voice which frightened her. And then, he was speaking normally, and Jessica wondered if she had imagined it.

"You'll wear the garments I have chosen as long as you are still my ward. Agreed?"

She signified her assent with an abrupt nod of the head.

"Only one more week, Jess, and then you need never again humor your wicked guardian." And with a smile he was gone.

Chapter 4

The muslin gown which Jessica selected to wear that evening was more ivory than white and did something flattering for her pale complexion. Roger, she supposed, had considerable experience in purchasing garments for his birds of paradise. He would know what colors suited birds of widely different feathers. Deplorable, thought Jessica, and snorted resentfully.

Nevertheless, as her eyes took in the costumes of the other ladies who sat down to dinner, the resentment gradually faded. Her own gown did more than pass muster. It was a picture of simple elegance, and suited her tastes exactly. She angled a sidelong look at her guardian and noted the approval in his eyes before he turned his head away to converse with the lady on his right.

The conversation that evening was quite unlike the debate which had raged round the table the evening before. Jessica surmised that this was so because the gathering had now grown to a sizable number. Jessica was acquainted with nearly all of Roger's guests, most of whom, like the Deveryns, were distant relatives, or close friends of their host. By Christmas Eve, the numbers, so she had been informed, would swell to fifty or more. It seemed that Roger intended to introduce his betrothed in grand style. Someone made the observation that Christmas was not what it used to be.

"That will soon change," answered Aunt Sophie, a widowed lady who admitted to being no more than "something over forty" when everyone knew she was sixty if she was a day.

"How so, Aunt Sophie?" asked Roger.

Aunt Sophie set down her cutlery before replying, "You young people are all beginning to marry off, and not before time, if you want my opinion. In another year or two, you'll be stocking your nurseries. And then these ancient halls will fairly ring with the sound of children. Christmas is nothing without children, you know."

Coming from Great-aunt Sophie, the comment was a surprising one. Though she was twice widowed, she had no children of her own and did not seem to repine overmuch for their lack. She had a whole army of grown-up stepchildren in Italy, where she had made her home for a number of years, having married a member of the Italian nobility. Since becoming a widow for the second time, she had settled in London in a town house in Cavendish Square. Villard was like a second home to her, and Roger like the son she had always wanted but never had.

"We do know," responded Viscount Deveryn, exchanging a meaningful glance with his wife. As everyone knew, the Deveryns' infant daughter had been left in the care of her grandmother in Oxfordshire. By Christmas Eve, they would be reunited, as Deveryn's family was expected to arrive at Villard.

Something about the exchange set Jessica to thinking. Her eyes chanced to brush Roger's and her glance was held, inexorably, painfully, until Roger was distracted by someone else.

When she was able to marshal her thoughts, she found that the conversation was all of former Christmases, and the fun and games which had enthralled them in their salad days. It came as no surprise to anyone when the suggestion was made that, in lieu of the more usual conversation and musical entertainments after dinner, they should get up a few lively games such as charades and blindman's buff and others of that nature.

Jessica tried to enter into the spirit of the thing with as much eagerness as anyone, but behind that carefully assumed smile she felt utterly wretched. Roger was showing every deference to Lady Sylvia, and was making a great show of including her in every conversation. Jessica remembered a time when he would have done as much for her. But in those days, she had been the cherished little sister. At present, she was merely the poor relation. Lady Sylvia was destined to become mistress of Villard.

And for so paltry a reason, Jessica had taken the girl in dislike. It put her quite out of patience with herself. The girl had done nothing to deserve her reprobation. In point of fact, Lady Sylvia was nauseatingly *nice*.

During a break between games, Roger sauntered over and spent a few minutes in idle conversation with Jessica. "That girl," he said, referring to Lady Sylvia, "has all the virtues any man could wish in a wife."

Jessica's eyes came to rest on the subject of their conversation as Lady Sylvia angled her head back and laughed prettily at one of Mr. Wynchbold's sallies. The girl did everything prettily, thought Jessica. The only bad thing one could say about her was that she had a battle-ax of a mother. Jessica's eyes shifted to take in the lady in question. Lady Mounteagle was in quiet conversation with Aunt Sophie.

Mounteagle by name and eagle by nature. The woman even had the look of an eagle, with that beaked nose and those prominent eyes. Lips quirking, Jessica essayed, "You know what they say, Roger. If a man wants to know what his wife will be like in twenty years or so, he should take a good look at her mother."

For a moment, his eyes gleamed brightly at the hit. But Jessica was given only a moment or two to savor her victory. "And what about you, Jess? What will you be like in twenty years?" he drawled, and having delivered this cruel thrust, he wandered off.

The evening went from bad to worse, for in an unguarded moment Jessica came within hailing distance of the two elderly ladies who had set themselves up as chaperones, and she was obliged to join their select company.

And listen, ad nauseam, as Lady Mounteagle extolled the infinite virtues of her young chick. It became almost laughable, for it was soon evident that Aunt Sophie regarded this high praise, in some sort, as a reflection on her own unfledged chick—Jessica.

"Oh yes, Sylvia was the undisputed toast of the *ton* in her first Season," confided Lady Mounteagle at one point.

"That honor might very well have been Jessica's if Roger had been able to persuade her to make her comeout," countered Aunt Sophie.

Jessica slanted Aunt Sophie a quelling look. She had no wish to pick up that particular bone of contention. She had refused a come-out for the simple reason that Roger had made it very plain that she was not, nor ever had been, a member of the family. She was not one to accept a grudging charity.

As if reading her mind, Aunt Sophie said placatingly, "That was the year you decided you wished to continue at Miss Plowden's as a teacher, dear. Roger said that your mind was set against a Season in town," and turning to Lady Mounteagle, Aunt Sophie played her trump card. "Jessica is a very clever girl, you know. It runs in the family. Her parents were both scholars of some note."

Lady Mounteagle did a fair imitation of turning up her beaked nose. Her gaze roved over Jessica, making a frank inventory. "You did well to train for a profession," she said, finally. "Once your guardian weds, you would not wish to be in the way at Villard."

Jessica sucked in her breath. Aunt Sophie let out an infuriated hiss. Before either could answer this set-down, Lady Mounteagle went on relentlessly, "As I understand, you were originally the ward of the third earl?"

Jessica's answer was forestalled by Aunt Sophie. "Jessica's great-grandmother was a Moreton. Her father named my nephew—that's Roger's father, by the way—as her guardian in his will."

What Aunt Sophie kept to herself was the knowledge that the third earl had not even known of Jessica's existence until the lawyers had approached him with the intelligence that he had been appointed her guardian. It seemed that when her parents were abroad, she had been left in England to the care of her mother's people, none of whom really wanted her. The earl could not, in all conscience, decline his duty to a member of the family, however distant the connection. And so, Jessica had come to live at Villard.

"And," continued Lady Mounteagle, "on his death, you

became Roger's ward when he was no more than a young man in his twenties?"

Evidently, the old battle-ax had been making inquiries. Jessica did not like the lady's tone. "What of it?" she demanded.

Lady Mounteagle sniffed. "It scarcely seems proper."

"Stuff and nonsense!" exclaimed Aunt Sophie. "There was nothing improper about it. Jessica was away at school. And when she came home for the holidays, I was always sent for to act as her chaperone. I take leave to tell you, Lady Mounteagle, that my great-nephew needs no lessons in deportment. Jessica's reputation is blameless, yes, and she has Roger to thank for it."

Having discovered what she wished to know, Lady Mounteagle tried for a conciliation smile. "I never meant to suggest anything else," she said.

Jessica was not sorry when Lady Sylvia swooped down and carried her off for the next game which was starting up.

"I hope Mama said nothing to annoy you," offered Lady Sylvia shyly.

The girl was covered in confusion, and it came to Jessica that she had a very good idea of what her mother had been implying. She wondered if anyone else had harbored similar suspicions, and flushed to the roots of her hair.

"You mustn't let anything Mama says overset you," said Lady Sylvia in a low tone.

With her cheeks blooming like roses, Jessica could hardly deny that Lady Mounteagle had said something to overset her. She remained silent.

Rather miserably, Lady Sylvia went on, "She's a trifle overzealous when it comes to observing the proprieties.

No one who knows you or Roger puts any store in what she says."

Slightly mollified, Jessica said, "My guardian, no less than your mama, is perfectly stuffy about preserving the proprieties."

And for the first time ever, it was borne in on Jessica that to have remained permanently at Villard with a guardian who was only nine years her senior would have occasioned the most salacious form of gossip. Though she had told Roger often enough that he had done her a service by sending her to Miss Plowden's, it was only in that moment that she came to examine the truth of her own words.

"You're most generous," intoned Lady Sylvia, and Jessica could see that she meant it. For all of quarter of an hour, she felt quite in charity with the girl until Roger, with a blindfold over his eyes, caught the beauty in his arms during the game of blindman's buff.

It was all perfectly proper and above board. For obvious reasons, the rule was that only the hands of the person caught were to be examined to determine that person's identity. Lady Sylvia, blushing rosily, gave Roger her hands, and Jessica's heart stopped beating.

"Soft," he said, and circumvented all the rules by bringing them to his face and rubbing his cheek against them. The gentlemen, wise to his game, gave out whoops of appreciative laughter. The ladies giggled nervously. Jessica trembled.

Roger turned over one of Lady Sylvia's small hands and pressed his lips to her fingertips. Jessica could feel the jolt of that kiss from her own fingers all the way to her toes.

"You're coming within a hairsbreadth of having your hand slapped," shouted Lord Tony, one of Roger's

Corinthian friends who had, against all expectation, succumbed to matrimony a six-month before.

Jessica sliced a quick look at Lady Mounteagle, expecting that high-stickler, at any moment, to put an end to this masculine deviltry. Far from showing annoyance, Lady Mounteagle was beaming her approval.

Ignoring the catcalls and jests, Roger continued to examine Lady Sylvia's hands. "This lady has a gentle disposition," he said. "She is sweet-natured."

"Well that disqualifies my wife," cut in Lord Deveryn outrageously. "Maddie has a ferocious temper." And for his demonstrable lack of gallantry, he had his toe trodden on by the lady he had insulted. He let out a howl.

When the laughter had died down, Roger went on. "You're not Aunt Sophie."

"How can you tell?" someone shouted.

"Aunt Sophie's hands are as warm as her heart."

"Incorrigible boy!" said Aunt Sophie, pinkening with pleasure.

"You can't be my ward," mused Roger.

"Why can't she?" queried one of the ladies.

It was only a game, but Jessica found that she was waiting nervously for Roger's reply.

"Because," said Roger consideringly, "Jessica would never allow herself to be caught by a mere male. Am I right, my ward?"

"Once caught, twice shy," she rejoined airily and everyone laughed.

"This has gone on long enough," interrupted Mr. Wynchbold. "You must guess who the lady is, Roger, or go down to defeat."

"Oh I knew at the outset who the lady was," was the provoking rejoinder. "But I could not resist the temptation, you see, of holding the lady's hands with no brows raised. Lady Sylvia," he said, "your perfume goes before you. Gardenia, I think?" And he removed the blindfold with a flourish.

"Trust a practiced flirt like Roger to make the most of his opportunities with the ladies," one wit complained.

To which another immediately responded, "Poor fellow. His bachelor days are coming to an end, as I hear tell."

The ladies frowned. The gentlemen chortled. The game started over, but this time, Jessica did not take so many pains to ensure that she evaded capture.

Chapter 5

The day was perfect. During the night there had been a fresh fall of snow. By morning, the skies had cleared to bright sunshine, and though there was a nip in the air Villard's guests were not slow to avail themselves of the amusements which were laid on for their enjoyment out of doors.

Those of an athletic bent, and who moreover were not above losing their dignity, went skating on the frozen duck pond. Others, of a more timid nature, chose instead to make forays into the woods to gather holly, ivy, and mistletoe to decorate the main rooms. The old sleigh was taken out of storage and harnessed to a team and put at the ladies' disposal. And just before dusk, everyone entered into the spirit of the thing by making snowscapes on the front lawn. Most of those were demolished shortly after when the gentlemen challenged the ladies to an impromptu snowball contest. By the time evening rolled round, everyone was too lethargic to participate in anything more strenuous than conversation and a quiet game of cards.

Jessica sat in the great stuffed armchair before a blazing fire. Her feet were tucked under her. The guests were now on such familiar terms that no one looked askance at this undignified posture, not when Lady Mounteagle had long since retired for the night.

A few of the gentlemen had wandered off to play a game of billiards in the billiard room. For those whose appetites could still be tempted, a late supper had been laid on in the dining room. Only half a dozen or so people sat about the drawing room, and of those, most were drifting into sleep. Conversation was desultory and frequently died altogether.

Startled, Jessica looked up as Roger dropped to his haunches in front of her chair. "Here, brat," he said. "Your favorite brew."

Jessica obediently cupped her hands round the proffered goblet and inhaled deeply. "Mmm. Villard's famous negus." The aroma of clove, lemon, and nutmeg filled her nostrils. "I still can't understand why this wonderful libation is reserved for Christmas only," she said, voicing a childish complaint she had never tired of repeating over the years.

"That," said Roger, "is so that Christmas will be a memorable occasion."

And as he was used to do in days gone by, he sat on the floor, bracing his back against her chair, his long legs stretched out in front of the fire. She had only to reach out her hand and she could comb her fingers through his dark hair. Jessica quickly brought the goblet to her lips and took a long swallow.

It was Lady Sylvia who took up the thread of conversation. She looked up from the game of piquet she was playing with Mr. Wynchbold, and said softly, "I think this is the most memorable Christmas holiday I've ever enjoyed. I had no notion people could be so . . . informal. At home, we don't really do much more than go to church services on Christmas Day and sit down to dinner.

When I marry," and she blushed charmingly, "I shall want to celebrate Christmas with as many of my friends as I may. We don't have too many visitors to Mounteagle. It's so out of the way, you know."

Jessica, thinking of Lady Mounteagle, shrewdly inferred that Mounteagle's inaccessibility was not the only reason people stayed away.

After an interval, Lady Deveryn, Maddie, as Jessica now thought of the girl, stirred in her chair and said drowsily, "Christmas Day in my home—that's Scotland, by the by—is held to be a holy day. We don't have parties and such like as you English do. But Hogmanay . . ."

"That's New Year's Eve," interjected Jason by way of explanation.

". . . Hogmanay is positively riotous."

"I'll say," answered her husband with feeling. "And lasts till the end of January. So don't feel sorry for the Scots because they forego the Christmas season. One way or another, they make up for it. January is just one long round of parties after another."

"I like parties," said Maddie challengingly.

"I know," said her husband, leaning over to tweak her ear.

There was something about the gesture, something about the exchange between Maddie and Jason which made Jessica acutely conscious of the vast emptiness in her own life. Her eyes rested on the back of Roger's head and she was overcome by an overwhelming sense of melancholy.

Gradually others contributed to the conversation, stirred by the idle words which had been introduced.

"A memorable Christmas," murmured Aunt Sophie. "There have been so many over the years. Well, I'm an old woman. One would hope that there would be many memorable Christmases, wouldn't one?" Her voice faded as her thoughts drifted back in time. She came to herself gradually. "There was one, though, that stands out in my memory. Roger, you must remember it, too."

"Must I?"

"It was the first Christmas that either of us met Jessica. Don't you remember? It was also my first Christmas in England in years. I was complaining bitterly about the weather . . ."

"Lord yes," interjected Roger, "and extolling the virtues of Italy ad nauseam."

". . . when your carriage lost a wheel. We had to put up at Salisbury for the night."

There was an interval of silence before Roger replied, "Yes, I remember. You are right, Aunt Sophie. It was a most memorable Christmas." And as if he were lost in memory, he inclined backwards until his head was resting against Jessica's knees.

It was a monstrous liberty. Jessica half expected someone, everyone, to make an outcry. It must be the effects of the negus, she thought, or the debilitating heat from the blaze in the grate, or the intimacy of the half-darkened room, lit by only a few flickering candles, which had dulled everyone's senses. Yes, her own included, for she could not seem to summon the energy to dislodge Roger from his comfortable position.

"Tell us about it," said someone.

Aunt Sophie embarked on her tale, and as her voice droned on, Jessica allowed herself to drift with the words.

Her knowledge went beyond Aunt Sophie's recollections of a young girl mourning her parents' sudden demise. Her parents had been strangers to her. She could scarcely remember them. If she had been the quiet little waif Aunt Sophie described, the reason was not hard to find.

No one had ever wanted her, not her parents, and certainly not the succession of relatives who had the care of her over the years. She had been sure that in a few months' time the Villards would tire of her also, and pass her along down the line. And knowing this, she had refused every offer of friendship. She'd made friends before. It always ended the same way. She was to go on a little holiday, she was always told. And her things were packed and she was bundled into a coach and sent off to the next set of relatives. Just thinking about it made her swallow.

"The transformation was nothing short of miraculous," Jessica heard Aunt Sophie say. "This unsmiling, difficult child who never had her head out of a book suddenly blossomed into a normal, mischievous girl. Do you remember, my dear? I've often wondered what happened."

Jessica shifted uneasily. As if recognizing her discomfort, Roger captured her hand and laced his fingers through hers. He raised his head and turned so that he was facing her. "Yes. What happened, Jess?" he asked quietly.

For a moment, it was in her mind to offer some evasion. She could not say what provoked her to tell the truth, unless it was Roger's softened expression. How dared he pretend to care for her after everything that had happened? Almost defiantly, she said, "What happened was this. I wasn't eavesdropping, but I overheard Roger in conversation with the earl. He referred to me as his little sister. You can't imagine how that affected me. It meant, you see, that I was a member of a real family—a mother, a father, and . . ."

". . . a brother," someone finished for her, when she hesitated.

"Yes."

Abruptly, Roger dropped her hand and rose to his feet. Jessica's gaze followed him as he moved to the punch bowl to replenish his glass.

"And did it matter so much to you?" asked Lady Sylvia, pausing in her game to look over her shoulder at Jessica.

"I once thought so," answered Jessica.

"Jessica was my father's ward," said Roger, the harshness in his voice raising a few eyebrows. "Jessica was my father's ward," he repeated, controlling his tone. "She wanted for nothing. She still wants for nothing. It is sheer perversity that makes her earn her living as a schoolmistress."

There was something in his words or manner which seemed to disturb the pleasant inertia which had settled on the company. Jason yawned and suggested that it was time to retire for the night. He rose and helped Maddie to her feet.

Lady Sylvia, thinking only to smooth the curious ripples which she sensed were eddying below the surface, offered mildly, "I'm sure, Roger, that everyone here thinks of you as Jessica's brother, or as close as makes no difference."

It was John Wynchbold who answered for Roger. "Don't be a goose, Sylvia," he said. "How could Roger ever think of Jessica as his sister? He was twenty or so when he first set eyes on the child. And since your attention has been wandering from our game this last half hour, I suggest we pack it in and follow Jason's example. I'm for bed."

His words acted as a signal on the other guests. One by

one, they made their goodnights and slipped from the room. When Jessica made to follow them she was stopped by a quiet aside from Roger, requesting her to remain behind.

Aunt Sophie was the last to leave. She gave her nephew a very straight look, shook her head as if in reprimand, and exited quietly, carefully leaving the door halfway open.

A log cracked in the fireplace, sending sparks shooting up the chimney. Jessica became involved in arranging the folds of her skirts. The silence unnerved her. Finally, she looked up.

Roger was watching her intently. "I had not known," he said softly, "that I ever referred to you as my sister."

She swallowed before answering. "I always thought of you as my brother. It was wishful thinking on my part, I daresay."

His eyes and voice were guarded when he answered, "You heard what John said. How could I think of you as my sister? It was impossible."

He moved closer. Jessica inched back into her chair. "When you were sixteen," he said, and his eyes slowly searched her face, "you didn't want me for a brother. Don't you remember, Jess?"

She did, and the memory scourged her. Weakly, she got out, "It was all a misunderstanding. I was only sixteen, for heaven's sake. I don't remember what happened that night."

There was no pity in him. "Then let me refresh your memory."

She closed here eyes trying to shut her mind to the pictures his words evoked. It was wasted effort. As though she were that girl of sixteen again, she experienced everything as if she were experiencing it for the first time.

It was the day of the earl's funeral, and she was still in shock. But Roger was home, and that was all the consolation she needed. Roger, who understood her better than she understood herself. The gap in their ages signified nothing. Nor did it make a jot of difference that they scarcely ever saw each other. Everything was confided in their letters. They were like two sides of the same coin. Hadn't Roger said so?

In the middle of the night, she had awakened from the worst nightmare she had ever endured. It wasn't the earl's coffin that was being lowered into the grave, but Roger's. She was beside herself. If she lost Roger, she knew she would not wish to go on living.

She didn't give a thought to the wisdom of what she was doing. She didn't wait to don her dressing gown. In only her cotton night rail, she hared along the corridor to Roger's room. She opened the door and called his name, not once, but several times.

"Jessica?" His voice was heavy with drowsiness as he raised in his bed to one elbow.

She didn't wait for an invitation. She flung herself into his arms. "Roger," she sobbed, "Roger, don't leave me. I couldn't bear it. I love you so."

For a moment, it seemed as if he would resist her. And then those strong arms wrapped around her and his mouth came down on hers. And as though it were the most natural thing in the world, she twined her arms around his neck and pressed her young body against his. Of their own volition, her lips softened under the fierce demand of his mouth.

It wasn't enough for her. She had wanted to get closer to him. "Please," she'd begged, pulling at the covers. "Please."

"Jess! Jess!" he had groaned. "This is madness!" But

he pulled back the covers so that she could slip in beside him.

Where it might have ended was something Jessica did not dare contemplate. It was the shocked exclamation from the doorway which brought them to their senses. Aunt Sophie, appalled, was demanding explanations, and Jessica was crying and stammering incoherently about her nightmare and having wished only to be comforted in the arms of her brother.

The following morning, her whole world fell apart. She would scarcely have recognized the coldly formal gentleman who bit out a strained apology for his infamous conduct and, on the next breath, informed her that she was no longer permitted to remain at Villard. Two choices were open to her. She could go to Aunt Sophie's in London, or she could go away to school.

It was all so painfully familiar. She wasn't wanted. Her credit had run out, and she was to be passed along to the next set of relatives. And it was all the more frightening because it was Roger who was doing it to her.

In the end, she had chosen to go away to school. She could not bear to impose herself on Aunt Sophie. She would never again put herself in a position where she could be rejected or be sent away.

It was settled. She would be in Bath within the week. Roger left that very morning, taking up lodgings in a hostelry in Salisbury until such time as she removed her polluting presence from his house.

The parting of their ways was bitter indeed. She did not think she would ever forget his last words to her.

"You are not now, nor ever have been, a member of my family. You were a guest in my father's house, his ward, to be precise. *I* am your guardian now, Jess, no more, no less."

And when she had applied to Aunt Sophie, she had received the assurance that Roger was sending her away for her own good. She knew better. She had done something wicked and must be punished for it.

She did not know how long the silence lasted. For a moment she sat with her head bowed, a hand pressed to her eyes. Exhaling a long anguished breath, she looked up at him and whispered brokenly, "I hate you, do you know?"

Temper flared in his eyes but was quickly subdued. He went down on his haunches until they were eye to eye. "You don't hate me, Jess. That is only bravado. Haven't you grown up yet? Aren't you woman enough to know what it is you feel for me?"

All of a sudden, her composure cracked and pain and confusion clouded her beautiful eyes. She was visibly shaking, but when he made a move to put his arms around her, she went rigid.

"Jess," he said, and extended one hand in an unconscious gesture. "For God's sake, answer me! Do you still think of me as a brother?"

She shot to her feet as if his words had burned her. Slowly, careful not to frighten her, he straightened.

"Brother!" she hissed at him, and her bosom began to heave with the turbulence of her emotions. "You don't know the meaning of that word!"

Contrition evident in every line of his bearing, he essayed a cautious, "Don't I, Jess?"

"No!" she declared passionately. "A brother . . ." Unable to keep the hurt and accusation from her voice, she continued, "A brother is someone who enters into your dreams and feelings about things; a brother is someone in whom you can confide your deepest secrets. A brother loves you when you are foolish—yes, wicked, even. A brother is always there when you need him." Her voice broke with the force of her emotion, but she ignored it. "A brother would never *never* send me away. A brother . . ." She shook her head, blinking back the moisture in her eyes.

His head was bowed and, without her being aware of it, he had somehow contrived to catch hold of her stole. "Jess," he said, as humble as she had ever seen him, "I don't think you know very much about brothers." And he pulled on the stole, dragging her closer. "Generally speaking," he said, and his tone was low and very grave, "brothers and sisters don't confide in each other. Oh, they may love each other, but not in the way you describe. Do you know what I think, Jess?"

Before she could prevent it, his eyes had captured her. "What?" she asked hoarsely.

"I think we were closer than brother and sister. We were friends, Jess, friends. Brothers and sisters don't exchange the sort of letters we wrote to each other, you know. Do you still have my letters, Jess?"

"Yes," she whispered, before she had time to think of an evasion.

He smiled whimsically. "You should read them again, Jess. Don't you remember what I wrote you—that all the beauties of the *ton* bored me to tears, and that I could scarcely wait for you to grow up so that *you* could be the one to partner me in the dance? You do remember I wrote that, Jess?"

She stared at him with huge, frightened eyes.

When it was evident that she was not going to answer him, he went on in the same quiet tone, "And didn't I tell you in my letters that I was wearied of the glamorous social whirl, and that the only excitement I craved was to claim the girl of my dreams and make her my bride?"

No response.

"Would a brother tell his sister that her skin was as soft and as white as swansdown and that her hair was like a waterfall of liquid fire? Jess, I ask you, would a brother write poems to his sister?"

His hands had crept quite naturally from the edges of her stole to her arms. He administered a gentle shake to loosen her tongue.

"How . . . how can I say?" she asked tremulously. "I never had a brother."

"No," he said, "you never had a brother, Jess. For if I had been your brother, it would not have been necessary to send you away to school."

"Lady Mounteagle said something . . ."

His vehement expletive silenced her. "Your reputation is spotless," he exclaimed. "I made damn sure of it."

"Oh, I understand that *now.* But, oh, was it necessary to be so *cruel?* Shall I ever forget your words to me that day, or your expression as you uttered them? Nothing will convince me that a friend would speak in such terms to a friend."

Suddenly conscious that his hands were kneading the tension from her shoulders, she gave a jerk and pulled out of his arms. She moved quickly away from him and said breathlessly, "We are not the same people we once were. Too much has happened. We can never be friends now."

Too experienced to give chase when her mind was still set against him, he allowed her to reach the door before calling her name. To her questioning look, he said, "Take this thought with you, Jess. You were the one who ended our friendship. No, my dear, don't try to deny it. *You* were the one who came to my room that night. Good God! Did you really suppose that we could remain friends after we shared that kiss?"

He shook his head at her look of surprised hurt. His lips thinned. There was an unmistakable thread of menace in his voice when he said, "I have your word on a truce, Jess. You shall abide by it, my dear, or you'll suffer some very unpleasant consequences. Do you take my meaning?"

The whole width of the room was between them. Secure in the knowledge that she could take to her heels before he could reach her, Jessica gave free rein to her temper. "Perfectly," she said. "But very soon, I shall come of age. Then we need never again set eyes on each other. Do you take *my* meaning?" And turning on her heel, she flounced from the room.

For a full minute, Roger stood motionless, gazing at the open door. Coming to himself, he sighed, and slumped into the chair which Jessica had vacated. Soon afterwards, a small ironic smile softened his lips. A moment later, he shook his head and let out a laugh.

He was thinking of Jessica's Christmas bonnet. It was saucy, daredevil, and totally captivating. In many ways, it brought to mind a younger Jess—the girl who had revealed herself to him in their long correspondence as she had grown to womanhood. He frowned, wondering how everything could have gone so wrong.

"Jess," he said into the silence, "Jess." He had loved her so long. His friends would laugh themselves silly, he was persuaded, if they had the least suspicion that Roger Moreton, top o' the trees Corinthian, had lost his heart, years before, to a slip of a child who was no more than ten years old!

He'd lost his heart to that engaging child, but four

years were to pass before he was aware of it. Jess was
something over fourteen when she wrote that fateful
letter in which she shyly informed him that she had received her first grown-up kiss from the vicar's son.
He'd damned himself, then, for having invited little
Jess to express herself so freely in their correspondence. His mother, he well knew, would be aghast if
she ever discovered the nature of the girl's letters to
him. But how could he have gainsayed little Jess? The
child was so sensitive, so intelligent, so perceptive, and
so damnably, damnably ardent to embrace life that he
had felt privileged to be the recipient of her most personal reflections and confidences. It was more than
that. He had encouraged Jess shamelessly to hold nothing back from him.

But with this letter, something new was introduced
into their discourse. Little Jess was now a grown
woman, she calmly informed him, and had received
her first kiss. His next thought had struck him with par-
alyzing force. Those kisses had damn well better be
reserved for him.

Horrified, revolted with himself as though he had been
a child molester, for the better part of a month, he had
plunged into every pleasure which was offered. But nothing, neither drinking, nor gaming, nor a succession of fair
Paphians could blot out the thought which had taken
hold. He had fought against it. As God was his witness,
he had fought against it. But Fate, or the Deity, had fashioned his future for him. Jess.

And having reluctantly accepted his destiny, the torment began. The girl was so young that it would be three
years before society and his sire would sanction her marriage. At three-and-twenty, three years had seemed like
an aeon to him. There was also the problem of their rela-

tionship. Jess saw him in the light of a brother. Carefully, determinedly, he began to disabuse her of that notion. And he thought he had succeeded fairly well until the night, two years later, when Aunt Sophie had walked into his chamber and had rescued Jess from his lover's embrace.

Jess had wanted the comfort of her brother's arms, she had sobbed out. Her words had plunged him into confusion. Brother! Surely he had not mistaken the nature of her response to him? He was resolved to marry her out of hand, whether or not she was in a humor to have him, for how could he keep himself from her, having once tasted the beginnings of her surrender?

Aunt Sophie had tried to persuade him against that course. Jessica was only sixteen, she had pointed out. She had lately endured the worst trauma of her young life, having lost both the earl and the countess in a short space of time. In another year or so when the girl was more mature, she would be in a better frame of mind to receive his addresses. And how would it look if he should wed so soon after his sire's demise? The gossip was like to bring infamy to both Jess and himself.

It was the worst mistake of his life. How many times since had he damned Aunt Sophie for her advice? And the only thing that had persuaded him to abide by it was Jess as she had been that morning when he had sent for her. She had flinched away from him and had averted her eyes as if the very sight of him sickened her. And who could blame her?

Against every inclination, he had sent Jess away. And the Jess he knew had vanished as if she had never existed.

She wanted no part of him. And when she had graduated from the seminary, she had begged to be allowed to accept a position on staff. As her guardian, it was in his power to forbid it. But her agitation at the thought of leaving Miss Plowden's was so great that he had not had the heart to insist.

In the deepest doldrums, he had returned to Villard with the Moreton family betrothal ring still in his pocket. He had shut himself up for a week in his chamber with only a bottle of brandy for consolation, chastising himself as the sorriest fool in Christendom. His case was hopeless. It was finally over.

When he had emerged from his chamber a sober and much wiser man, he had done with entertaining flights of fancy respecting Miss Jessica Holtby. She had her own life to lead, so she had told him. Let her get on with it. He had a life of his own.

But the heart, he had discovered, was a contrary organ. It refused to obey the commands of his brain. It made a place for Jessica in spite of his protests. He could never be indifferent to his little Jess. He would never be free of her.

He stopped in his reflections to withdraw a slim cheroot from a silver box on the mantel. Lighting it from the embers of the fire with a taper, he settled himself in his chair and slowly inhaled.

He was thinking of Jess as he had seen her when she had swept in through Villard's front doors, almost a sennight before, with the absurd bonnet perched on her head. He had been in the attics, and about to descend to the floor below when he'd glanced over the well of the staircase. In the next instant, he had been stunned speechless. Like a man bewitched, he'd trailed Jess and her fanciful bonnet with his eyes as she slowly mounted the stairs.

When he had come to himself, he found that he was shaking like a leaf. There was a buzzing in his ears that took several minutes to clear. He felt light-headed, and happier and more buoyant than he'd felt in years. With a flash of intuition, it came to him that he had been given a sign. There was no question that he was going to pursue it, come what may.

His hopes had been somewhat dashed in his subsequent encounters with Jess. She seemed no more ready to admit what was between them than she had ever been. If he had not known about the bonnet, he would have left her to it. But he did know about the bonnet. And he could no longer accept the role she had assigned to him in her life.

Brother. What he felt for Jess was not brotherly. And if he ever had referred to her as his little sister, he had no recollection of it. He wondered if she had made it up, just to keep him at arm's length.

For several more minutes, he gave himself up to his reverie. When he ascended the stairs to his chamber, his step was lighter. He hummed tunefully under his breath. He was thinking that it was time Jessica Holtby learned a lesson. He would give her "brother," and let her see how she liked it.

Chapter 6

At first, Jessica was merely vexed. Soon after, she was affronted. Roger's conduct toward her had begun to verge on the insulting. Only good breeding, she was persuaded, prevented his guests from remarking upon it. And it certainly was not jealousy she was feeling, she assured herself time without ceasing over the next day or so. Certainly not. If her guardian wished to make a cake of himself over Lady Sylvia, she was sure she did not give a straw. No. What stuck in her craw was his total lack of observance toward her.

When they went for a walk in the park, it was Lady Sylvia who must be helped over the stile, and Jessica who was left to fend for herself. When they rested their horses when they went riding, it was Lady Sylvia, yes, and every other lady, who must be solicitously assisted to dismount and mount up again, and Jessica who had to manage as best she might. And when Roger took them for a drive in the sleigh, it was Jessica who had to squeeze into the tiny backseat, while Lady Sylvia and Roger sat up front, conversing gaily and laughing, and only occasionally throwing the odd crumb of conversation her way.

Naturally, when the sleigh drew to a halt and the groom came running to hold the horses' heads, it was

Lady Sylvia who must be assisted to alight. With drawn brows, Jessica watched as Roger's hands spanned Lady Sylvia's waist and swung her to the ground. She could scarcely believe her eyes when they turned to go into the house, completely oblivious of her predicament. In simmering anger, she edged forward.

Roger, throwing her a bemused look over his shoulder, said airily, "You'll manage, Jess?" and continued on, without waiting for her to reply.

Jessica did not deign to answer him. Gathering the skirts of her redingote about her, she jumped. Her ankle turned beneath her and she lost her balance, sprawling face first into a drift of snow. Strong hands on her shoulders drew her to her feet.

The look of concern was quickly wiped from Roger's face when Jessica blew the snow from her nose and glared up at him. Laughing, he straightened her plain, everyday bonnet. It was too much for Jessica. She went stomping into the house.

He caught her in the great foyer, right under the garland of holly and mistletoe, and swung her to face him. Jessica's eyes went wide as she realized her folly. For a whole sennight, she had carefully skirted the kissing bough in order to avoid the very calamity which had overtaken her. Roger must kiss her. At the thought, her skin heated, and a pulse began to hammer wildly at her throat. She closed her eyes.

"Dear, dear," he drawled, addressing Lady Sylvia, who had entered behind him and was eyeing them speculatively. "Brothers do so hate to be caught under the mistletoe with their sisters."

Lady Sylvia giggled as Roger pressed an indifferent kiss to Jessica's cold cheek. "There, brat," he said. "There is nothing untoward in brothers and sisters exchanging the occasional kiss, you know," he grinned.

It was a moment before Jessica realized he had released her. Wordlessly, with great dignity, she picked up her skirts and made to ascend the stairs. She had not meant to look back. When she did, she wished she had ignored the impulse. Roger was kissing Lady Sylvia under the mistletoe, and there was nothing brotherly about *that* kiss.

She went storming into her chamber as if the hounds of hell were after her. She was bitterly angry and, for no reason that she could think of, strangely disturbed by the kiss she had witnessed. Roger, to all intents and purposes, was betrothed to the girl. It was to be expected that an eager suitor would wish to steal the odd kiss.

Not liking the path her thoughts had taken, Jessica ruthlessly brought them round to her own grievances—the indignities she had been forced to suffer in the last day or two. There and then, she resolved to have it out with her guardian. If Roger did not wish her to remain at Villard, and it was clear that he did not, he had only to say so. And those were not tears on her cheeks. Certainly not! That wetness was no more than snowflakes which were melting from the heat of her skin.

She found him in his office at the back of the house. One of his gamekeepers was with him. Jessica made to withdraw but was waved into the room and told to take a chair.

"Tom was just leaving," said Roger, and Jessica recognized the thickset young man as her former maid's husband.

A few pleasantries were exchanged, and Jessica asked after Alice's health.

"Bloomin'," answered Tom, not without a certain pride.

Smiling, Jessica asked, "And when is the babe due?"

When she was informed that the babe had arrived three days since, her brow puckered, but only for a moment. More pleasantries were exchanged, after which the young gamekeeper bowed himself from the room.

Roger closed the door and said dryly, "I can tell by the look on your face that you are doing your sums, Jess."

Rather faintly, she asked, "How long have they been married?"

"Not long enough."

"Oh."

Roger settled himself in the chair behind his desk. "What's the matter, Jess?" he challenged. "Are you like all the rest? Does it outrage your sensibilities to know that I've kept on my gamekeeper in spite of his evident moral laxity?"

"That's not what I was thinking," she protested.

"What were you thinking?"

She looked away, but could not prevent the nervous giggle. His eyebrows rose.

To that questioning look she answered, "What I was thinking was that, according to one of the upstairs maids, you rewarded Tom and Alice for their 'moral laxity,' as you call it, by providing them with a cottage." When she observed his gathering frown, she went on hurriedly, "I'm jesting, of course. You must know that I would not wish you to turn them off for so paltry a reason. I know that Tom was courting Alice for years before this happened. It was impossible for them to marry when his mother was so sickly."

He leaned back in his chair and studied her openly. "You always had a romantical turn of mind," he mocked.

"Sir Lancelot and Guinevere, Abelard and Heloise, Lord Nelson and his Emma—unconventional characters were always the ones which captured your girlish imagination, as I remember."

She was no more immune to his taunts than she had ever been. Eyes heating with temper, she quoted, " 'To err is human, to forgive, divine.' "

"So understanding of human frailty, Jess?" and the derision in his tone was more marked. When she made no response, he went on in the same vein, "Is this the woman who cast my 'birds of paradise' in my teeth?"

Burning with indignation, she answered, "I did no such thing. Your . . . your 'birds of paradise' are scarcely my concern."

They stared at each other across the width of the desk, her eyes shooting green sparks; his half-hooded, watchful, veiling his thoughts.

Into the silence, he said softly, "I am no libertine. In my whole life, I only once took advantage of an innocent girl. Am I always to remain unforgiven, Jess?"

Her eyes widened, but she said nothing.

Gravely, he went on, "I had a mistress, yes. But I swear that I severed that connection long before I left London to come down here."

In contrast to his level tone, her voice trembled, "Why are you telling me all this? As I've told you before, it is to Lady Sylvia you should be making these confessions. She, no doubt, will be gratified to know that she will not have to share your love with another woman."

"Share my love?" Laughter flickered in his eyes. "Do you mean with my mistress?"

The answer was clearly evident in her face.

"Do you think a man loves his mistress, Jess? Good God! I knew that you were naïve, but not that naïve."

"Lord Nelson loved Lady Hamilton," she pointed out frigidly.

"There are exceptions, of course, but I am not one of them. I have only ever loved one woman, Jess. And when I make her my wife, she shall never have cause to question my fidelity. Do you believe me?" She did, and felt numb with despair. Summoning the vestiges of her composure, she said, "That is neither here nor there. Furthermore, this conversation is most improper, and you know it."

"Brothers and sisters don't often stand on ceremony with one another, Jess. There was a time when no subject was too delicate to be admitted to our conversation, or have you forgotten?"

Jessica wasn't about to touch this last provocation with a barge pole. "Why do you persist in referring to me as your sister?"

"I thought it was what you wanted."

There was a pause as she digested his words. "Once, perhaps, but you never did. I can't believe you have changed your mind."

"Look! This is a very significant moment in my life. You must see that the last thing I wish is for Lady Mounteagle to get on her high ropes. You are a beautiful woman. I am a man and far from my dotage. Naturally, she is suspicious. Lady Sylvia is also. I aim to show them that their suspicions are groundless, do you see?"

She did. This significant moment in his life was his betrothal to the only woman he had ever loved—Lady Sylvia. She coughed delicately into her hand to ease the sudden constriction in her throat.

"And . . . and is *that* what you have been attempting

these last few days—to convince Lady Sylvia that we are, to all intents and purposes, brother and sister?"

"What else?"

She sniffed.

"What?" he asked.

"You were never used to treat me in that cow-handed fashion when I thought, in very truth, that you *were* my brother."

He smiled, showing a flash of white teeth. "I knew you would work it out when you gave it some thought, Jess."

She would have quizzed him some more, but before she could do so, there was a knock on the door, and his steward entered.

"Just take your cue from me," Roger told her airily, ushering her out.

And she did. With a vengeance.

In the space of twenty-four hours, she allowed herself to be caught under the mistletoe by every gentleman present, with the exception of her "brother." And when she caught his darkly brooding look she flashed him a sisterly grin.

In the drawing room, after dinner, when the furniture was pushed back against the wall and an impromptu dance was got up, in the most unobliging terms, she was heard to refuse Roger's request to partner her in the waltz. With a saucy smile, she flounced off and, in true sisterly fashion, danced the waltz with someone else.

And when she was asked by Aunt Sophie to hand round the tea things, it went without saying that she overlooked poor Roger altogether. When he made to go riding, she must go for a walk; when he went for a walk, she must go riding. Roger, in like fashion, gave as good as he got. And so it went on.

"What the devil is going on?" demanded Aunt Sophie, having tracked Jessica down in the morning room, where she lingered over a late breakfast.

Roger and most of the younger set had taken themselves off to Salisbury to do some last-minute shopping. As was to be expected, Jessica had much rather not.

"Have you and Roger had a lovers' tiff?"

Truly shocked, Jessica exclaimed, "Aunt Sophie, what a thing to say!"

"Why is it?" Aunt Sophie poured herself a cup of tea and came to sit beside Jessica at the table.

"For one thing, you must know that Roger is on the point of announcing his betrothal to Lady Sylvia."

"I just cannot comprehend the younger generation," averred Aunt Sophie crossly. "I never thought my great-nephew wanted for sense. I can't think he seriously means to offer for the chit." She slanted Jessica a sly look.

"I thought it was all settled," said Jessica, trying to sound brighter than she felt. "Surely he means to announce it tomorrow at our Christmas Eve party?" It was also her birthday, her coming-of-age, when she would at last be shot of the odious man. The day that she'd once thought could not come too soon for her liking had finally arrived.

Aunt Sophie grunted noncommittally. For some few minutes, the two ladies went through the motions of drinking their tea.

Finally, Aunt Sophie set down her cup and saucer and subjected Jessica to one of her hard stares. "Won't you mind if Roger shackles himself to that widgeon?"

"Lady Sylvia is very nice. I'm sure they suit each other to perfection," answered Jessica discouragingly.

Undeterred, Aunt Sophie offered, "As nice as

ninepence, I make no doubt. But she's not the girl for Roger." After an interval, she let out a sigh before continuing, "My nephew, the old earl, I mean, would be bitterly disappointed. He always harbored the hope that you and Roger would make a match of it one day."

Jessica's expression was arrested. "I can't think why."

"It wasn't just wishful thinking," mused Aunt Sophie. "Anyone with eyes in his head could see that the boy virtually doted on you."

From beneath lowered brows, Aunt Sophie studied Jessica's carefully neutral expression. "You have not forgot the night I surprised you in Roger's chamber—yes, and in his bed, no less?"

Jessica choked on the dry toast and was compelled to take a long swallow of tea. Her cheeks burned. "It was all a misunderstanding," she mumbled weakly.

Perceiving her discomfort, Aunt Sophie gave her a commiserating pat on the shoulder. "My dear, I hope you will believe me when I say that you cannot regret that night more deeply than I. As your chaperone, I knew myself to be greatly at fault, knowing as I did how the boy felt about you. I ought never to have permitted you to remain under the same roof, not when you were both so susceptible, what with the strain of the earl's death and everything. In a weak moment, the inevitable happened. I should have expected something of the sort."

"Roger was like a brother to me," said Jessica miserably. Any reference to that night only brought back her feelings of acute guilt and shame.

"Unfortunately, Roger did not think of you as his sister."

Jessica was studiously following the progress of a solitary tea leaf which was floating on the surface of her tea.

Aunt Sophie's voice gentled. "Jessica, painful as it may be for you to recall that unhappy episode, I have a particular reason for mentioning it. My dear, you mustn't allow what happened that night to destroy your young life."

"I wouldn't! It hasn't!"

"Hasn't it? I wish I could believe you. But since then, you've changed, Jessica, out of all recognition."

"I've grown up, 'tis all."

"Mmm." Aunt Sophie was beginning to feel that she was knocking her head against a brick wall. It was not normally in her nature to meddle. But a number of things were persuading her to break one of her own cardinal rules. In the first place, Jessica's twenty-first birthday was on the morrow. It was more than time that the girl put the past behind her. In the second place, she had the forlorn hope that Roger and Jessica might still salvage something of what they had once felt for each other.

With some idea of redeeming Roger's character in Jessica's eyes, she said carefully, "Roger isn't a bad man, you know. True, you were an innocent, and, quite naturally, shocked by what happened. But you will allow, I hope, that the provocation was great?"

"Please, Aunt Sophie," pleaded Jessica.

Relentlessly, Aunt Sophie pursued her course. "And when he came to his senses, his conduct was irreproachable. He left the house at once; you were sent away to school; and since then, whenever you are under his roof, you are hedged about by a score of chaperones and more. Won't you at least give him his due?"

For some time now, ever since Lady Mounteagle had made her snide remarks, Jessica's view of her guardian's conduct toward her had been undergoing a gradual change. But there was one thing that never ceased to fill her with burning resentment.

Her eyes lustrous with the force of her emotions, she said, "He told me that day, when he sent me away to school, that I never had been a member of his family, that he was not and never had been my brother, no, and never wished to be."

"I expect he meant to clear away the one real obstacle that stood in his way. You wanted him to be your brother, and he was determined to refuse the role you had chosen for him."

A thousand thoughts circled in Jessica's brain. She voiced the one that was least shocking. "Why didn't you say something before now, Aunt Sophie?"

About to reach for the teapot to replenish her empty cup, Aunt Sophie's hand stilled. "But I did, my dear, at least as much as you were willing to accept at the time. Don't you remember?"

Jessica tried, without success, to recall Aunt Sophie's words to her after that catastrophic night. "All I remember is asking you why Roger was sending me away. And you said something to the effect that it was for my own good."

"Did I?" asked Aunt Sophie, and calmly proceeded to refill her teacup. "It's so long ago, I scarcely remember. But you still haven't explained why you and Roger are acting so oddly." And she embarked on a catalogue of what she had observed.

Jessica thereupon related Roger's reasons for wishing to lull Lady Mounteagle's suspicions.

"Oh dear," said Aunt Sophie. "Then Roger really is set on having Lady Sylvia. She's a lovely girl, I grant you, but not at all suitable for my nephew. She'll bore him to tears before the ink has dried on their marriage lines."

Jessica was of the same opinion but remained glumly silent. She wasn't aware of the smile which Auntie Sophie hid behind the rim of her teacup.

Chapter 7

As Mary fiddled with papers and hot tongs, painstakingly curling Jessica's fine hair into diminutive ringlets, Jessica gazed wordlessly at the reflection in her looking glass. A girl with eyes too big for her face returned her solemn stare.

It was Christmas Eve. It was her birthday. She had finally come of age. She was dressed in the most becoming gown she had ever had in her possession—Roger's gift to her—and she did not know how she was going to survive the coming ordeal.

She had known, of course, that this Christmas party was of a different order from anything that had gone before. Those other Christmas Eves had been intimate family gatherings. This do was to be more in the nature of a ball. An orchestra from Bath had been engaged. Caterers had taken over Villard's kitchens. Carriages had been arriving throughout the day, disgorging relations, most of whom Jessica had met only rarely, and every bedchamber in Villard, from cellars to attics, was fully occupied. There was a sense of expectancy in the air, for though Roger's betrothal was held to be a secret, no one doubted that an announcement was imminent. Otherwise, why were they all here? Jessica reckoned that she must be the only person at Villard who could not find it in herself to share in the general excitement.

By rights, she ought to have been in transports. That very morning, after a lazy breakfast in her chamber, Roger had sent for her to advise her about her financial status now that she had reached her majority.

He told her in uncompromising terms that he was still to be the trustee of all her monies. It was no less than she expected. What had robbed her of breath, as document after document was put into her hands, was the substantial bequest which had been settled upon her by the old earl. The income from her capital was more than enough to set her up comfortably in her own establishment—if Roger would permit it. She made the suggestion, but he refused to discuss it until a more opportune moment should arrive. And since, at that very moment, he had been called away to settle a dispute between his own chef and the hired caterers, Jessica saw the sense in what he said.

For the next few hours, she went about in something of a trance. The old earl had settled a handsome competence upon her as if she were, in very truth, a member of the family. She hugged that knowledge to her like a beggar clutches a newly minted guinea. It was not the size of the settlement that thrilled her, but the knowledge that she had not been forgotten. Just thinking about it exalted and humbled her at one and the same time.

Her euphoria dissipated by degrees when on every side she overheard speculation about the brilliant future which awaited Roger and Lady Sylvia. Soon Roger would wed, and Lady Sylvia would be mistress of Villard. The prospect must please all their friends and relations. Jessica tried to imagine that happy moment when the announcement of their betrothal was made.

"Ooh, mum!" Mary's face was a picture of consternation. "Did I burn ye with the tongs?"

"No. Why do you ask?"

Mary looked closely at Jessica's reflection in the mirror. "I thought I saw tears."

Blinking rapidly, Jessica managed a wan smile. "No, Mary. You are mistaken. What reason have I to weep?"

What reason, indeed? Unless it was because Lady Sylvia was not the girl for Roger. Hadn't Aunt Sophie said so?

A movement in the glass caught her eye. As Mary curtseyed and made her exit, Roger entered. Schooling her features to betray no emotion, Jessica swiveled on the stool to face him.

He personified—and she could not prevent the small, ironic smile—the answer to a maiden's prayer. Hadn't she always thought so? That pagan profile, those dark locks curling in careless abandon, those intensely blue eyes locking on hers, compelling her to an awareness of everything that was masculine in his nature. He had always had this effect on her.

"You look . . . splendid," she said, forcing her lips to curve even more. This was a special night for him. She was determined that not by one look or word would she detract from his happiness.

"Do you like the gown I chose for you?"

Truthfully she answered, "It's a gown fit for a queen and the most beautiful Christmas gift I've ever received. I don't know how to thank you."

"That you like it and have chosen to wear it is enough for me."

At Villard, the tradition was for close family members to exchange presents on Christmas Eve. In the last number of years, the gifts which Jessica had given Roger, and vice versa, had become almost insulting—a knitted nightcap for him, blue woolen stockings for her, and such like. She was glad that this Christmas she had relented, and had found a special edition of Ovid's poems. Roger was very partial to Ovid.

He raised her with one hand and made a slow inspection. The gown was high waisted and of the sheerest ivory tissue shot through with gold thread at the low square neckline and along the hem. She had an aura of delicacy, he thought, that always tempted him to set her on a pedestal, until he chanced to look into her eyes. Soft. Wary. Hinting of feminine secrets he was resolved would be revealed to him and to no other. But all in good time.

"You are the most beautiful woman of my acquaintance," he said with perfect sincerity. Her cheeks went pink. He smiled. "And the color of your gown sets off your . . ."

"Auburn hair?" she quizzed.

He rewarded her with one of those lazy, roguish grins which never failed to test her temper. She felt like crying.

"Turn around," he said.

In the looking glass, she watched incredulously as he fastened a necklace at her throat. She recognized the emeralds instantly. The necklace had once belonged to his mother, a bridal gift from her husband, and the pride of all her possessions.

"My mother always intended to give you this when you came of age," he said. "And these are from me." And before she could take it all in, he was carefully attaching emerald drop earrings to her ears. "I had them specially made up to match my mother's necklace." He turned her slowly and smiled into her eyes. "Happy birthday, Jess."

Through a veil of tears, she stared up at him. On a

choked sob, she whispered, "Roger, I don't know what to say. I never knew . . . never thought . . ."

"Don't say anything," he said, tilting her head back.

She blinked as his head descended, blotting out the light. Then her eyes widened as she divined his purpose.

The kiss was as unthreatening as he could make it. When he drew away, she gazed up at him with huge, enigmatic eyes. That she had not moved away, he counted as a small victory.

"It's time to go downstairs," he commented easily, and held the door open to allow her to precede him.

From the picture gallery, which also served as the ballroom, came the sounds of revelers and the shrieks of children whose bedtime was long past. For something to say, Jessica commented upon it.

"The children have been allowed to stay up in honor of the occasion," he answered.

"Of course," she murmured, and braced herself to accept the announcement of Roger's betrothal with as much joy as she could muster.

At the doors to the gallery, he halted. "Happy coming-of-age, Jess," he said softly, and swept her inside.

The thunderous applause which greeted her entrance startled her into immobility. Her eyes swept over the throng of people who lined the edges of the great room. Lights seemed to flicker behind her eyes. From every quarter, people were calling out "Many happy returns, Jessica," or offering their congratulations in similar vein. As her eyes lingered, she recognized first one, then another well-wisher.

Jason's parents and their bevy of clever daughters were herding a group of infants who must be the grandchildren, she supposed. Maddie had a babe in her arms, Antigone, as Jessica remembered, and she wondered, inconsequentially, why anyone would wish such a name on an innocent child. Cousin John, Lady Sylvia, Lady Mounteagle, Aunt Sophie, and a host of others she scarcely remembered were all beaming at her. And that could not possibly be . . . ? But it was—Elizabeth Naseby, who had been Jessica's best friend at school and with whom she kept up a desultory correspondence.

Roger led Jessica to the center of the floor and, as if on cue, a battalion of footmen moved among the guests dispensing champagne in long-stemmed glasses. A silence fell.

"Aunts, uncles, cousins, friends," Roger said, raising his glass aloft, "to Jessica, on her coming-of-age."

"To Jessica," a chorus of voices echoed, and as glasses were raised to lips, the lights from the great chandeliers overhead were reflected around the room like the stars in some distant galaxy. Jessica felt light-headed.

"Roger," she whispered, "is this not to be your . . . betrothal ball?"

"This is your night," he answered simply.

"But—but everyone expects that there will be an announce—ment of your betrothal."

"Not everyone. Only you. It was all a hum, my dear. We wanted to surprise you, and I think we succeeded beyond expectation."

"And . . . and Lady Sylvia?"

"She was part of the deception. You were meant to suppose that Cousin John and Sylvia were on the point of becoming engaged. How could we know that your devious mind would make the wrong connection?"

"And are they?" She could not seem to regulate her breathing.

His grin won an answering response from her own lips. "Cousin John," he said with a gravity which belied the twinkle in his eyes, "had almost come up to scratch when I gave him your words on the subject."

"What words?"

He took the untouched glass of champagne from her fingers and gave it, with his own empty glass, into the hand of a lackey who came running. At his signal, the orchestra struck up.

"What words?" repeated Jessica.

" 'If you want to know what a woman will be like in twenty years, take a good look at her mother.' "

"No! You could not be so cruel!"

"Don't alarm yourself, Jess. I have it on excellent authority that Lady Sylvia takes after her sire, so there's hope for that little romance yet." And so saying, laughing like a boy, he swung her into the opening waltz.

Hours later, long after the ball had wound to a close and Villard's guests had trooped off to bed, he found her alone in the conservatory. At his approach, she looked up and smiled.

This is how he wanted to see her, he thought with a ferocity which surprised him. He wanted her in *his* house, with his jewels at her throat, his ring on her finger, and with that intimate smile of welcome reserved for him only.

"Happy?" he asked.

"Sublimely."

"What were you thinking as I came in just now?"

"I was meditating."

He studied her silently. If he had not known better, he would have said that she was slightly tipsy. But Jessica rarely drank, and never more than one glass at a time.

"What was the subject of your meditation?"

Her smile captivated him. "My most memorable Christmas," she said in a languid tone which he scarcely recognized. "And I've decided that this must be it."

He resolved to indulge her playful mood. "How so, Jess?"

She tipped back her head to get a better look at him. "Tonight, everybody loves me," she said. "I'm the best-loved girl in the whole world," and this time, her speech was slurred. "Your father loved me, your mother loved me, Aunt Sophie, Cousin John, Jason, Maddie . . ." she flung her arms wide, ". . . the whole world loves me."

"Why shouldn't everyone love you?" he asked, grinning. *Definitely foxed,* he thought.

"Oh Roger!" She flashed him a superior smile. "I'm not the sort of person that people take to as a matter of course."

"I take leave to doubt that. Look at me. I liked you on sight."

"Pooh! What do you know? I was ten years old. Even then I knew that for every one person who liked me, there were a score or more who could not stand the sight of me."

Her words struck some chord within him—something to do with the sad circumstances of her life before she had become his father's ward. No one had ever wanted her, so his mother had told him. Jess had been left to the care of her mother's people, some of whom had attended her ball that evening. What was it his mother had said? Oh yes. Jess had been passed along from one relative to the next like the proverbial poor relation, never knowing the security of a stable home until she had been set down at Villard.

The next thought struck him with stunning force. In his turn, he also had rejected Jess, or so it must have seemed to her when he sent her away to school.

At that moment, he could cheerfully have put a period to his own existence. There was only one good reason why he should not. In future, it would be his duty, his delight, to ensure that Jess was never again subjected to that sort of humiliation. He would make it all up to her, if only she would let him.

"Everyone who knows you must love you," he said with unshakable conviction.

Sighing, she gazed up at the intricate coved ceiling. When she looked back at him, her eyes were brilliant. "Oh Roger," she said, "I do so want to be the girl you all think me. In fact, I *shall* be that girl."

Smiling, he asked, "What sort of girl is that, Jess?"

"Oh, I don't know." She seemed to consider his question. After a moment, she shrugged helplessly. "I suppose the kind of girl who deserves . . . ," another shrug, ". . . all this."

His expression was serious. "You don't have to do a thing."

She slanted him a sidelong glance. "You must love me very much."

As though he were steering a course through a treacherous quagmire, he said cautiously, "Of course. Can you doubt it?"

"Roger," she said, "why did you do it? Why did you arrange this surprise birthday ball for me?"

"It's no ordinary birthday, Jess. This is your coming-of-age."

"But girls don't have a coming-of-age party," she disclaimed, "only males."

"Ah. But you refused to have a come-out, you see, so we had to think of some way of making it up to you."

At her suddenly doleful expression, he said urgently, "Jess? What is it? What have I said?"

She shook her head and whispered, "I don't deserve it. I don't deserve so much happiness. I don't deserve that anyone should love me. I don't deserve . . ."

"Hush!" he said and held out his hand, palm up. "Come along, birthday girl, it's time for your bed."

She obeyed the implicit command in his outstretched hand without demur. He maneuvered her carefully through the door of the conservatory. In the foyer, she halted and turned to face him. "Roger," she said, "we are under the mistletoe."

"What?"

She dimpled. "A kiss. It's obligatory, I collect."

His eyes searched hers before he drew her into the circle of his arms. Carefully, gently, as if he were handling priceless porcelain, he brought his lips to hers in the softest caress. When he pulled back to study her response, she stared at him with unwavering, luminous eyes.

He spoke with difficulty. "Jess, that wasn't so bad, was it? For God's sake, tell me what you feel."

"I feel . . . wicked," she breathed and drew his head down to renew the embrace.

He could feel the smile on her lips at that first tentative touch. But as their lips brushed, lingered, and sank deeper, the kiss changed into something quite different. He made a small inarticulate sound. She moaned.

His arms clamped around her, drawing her fully against the shelter of his body. Her arms twined around his neck. Her fingers caught in his hair. The blaze to white-hot passion was instantaneous. Within the space of a single heartbeat, it raged out of control.

"Roger!" The couple under the mistletoe pulled apart with a guilty start. Aunt Sophie, leaning over the banister, pinned them with one of her hard stares. "Jessica, retire to your room at once," she ordered.

Jessica's fist was pressed against her mouth.

"Jess!" Roger groaned, and moved to gather her into his arms.

The look of revulsion on her face stunned him. With a little cry, she spun on her heel and went racing up the stairs.

Feeling drained and sick at heart, he watched her till she took the last turn. "Damn and double damn!" he exploded, and went storming into his office.

Chapter 8

He heard the light tap on the door the moment before she entered his office.

"Roger?" Her voice was subdued.

He was stationed at the long window, gazing through the misty windowpane as if the carriages and noisy passengers which were setting out for church services were of the keenest interest to him. The bells of the parish church began to peal, summoning the faithful for miles around on this special day of all days.

He deliberately kept his back to her. He could not bear to surprise that look of loathing on her face.

Clearing his throat, he began on the words he had rehearsed. "I sent for you because I have something of a particular nature which I wish to say to you." Again he cleared his throat and, inhaling a deep, steadying breath pushed on. "I know this subject is a painful one for you, Jess, but you must see that unless we talk about that night, that is, the night you came to my bedchamber, we can never be natural with each other—never be *right* with each other is what I mean."

"Roger, please . . ."

Ignoring her plea, he went on in a low, vibrant tone, "I know how shocked you must have been. How could it have been otherwise? You had led a sheltered existence.

You were only sixteen. You regarded me as an older brother. I betrayed your trust. I don't deserve that you should forgive me. But won't you allow that there were extenuating circumstances, my dear?"

When she remained distressingly silent, he straightened and said more earnestly, "You must think me below reproach. I understand your sentiments. But there is one thing you *must* know." His voice faltered as his courage momentarily forgave him, then steadied as he concluded, "I am not the depraved reprobate you think me."

"But I don't . . ."

"What I did was abominable." For a moment he was silent. "But there was nothing *unnatural* about it, Jess, as you seem to think. I never did regard you in the light of a sister."

"No?" she asked softly.

A shudder passed over him. "No. I was sure you must have guessed long since. I . . . I loved you as a man loves a woman. I still do. And it is beyond my powers of deception to continue in the roles you persist in setting for me. I have no wish to be your brother. I can never be your friend. Do you understand what I am saying?"

She made a small, inarticulate sound and he burst out, "For the love of God, tell me what you are thinking!"

"What I am thinking," she said, and there was suppressed laughter in her voice, "is that if we don't make haste, we shall be late for the Christmas Day service."

Anger, vituperation, even tears, he had expected. But this levity in the face of his anguish was beyond anything. With a roar of rage, he rounded on her.

The words of reproach died on his lips as his eyes took in the vision who smiled up at him.

"Jess?" he said uncertainly.

She tossed her curls, and the absurd bonnet did a little jig on her head. It looked for a moment as if the little bird on the brim was about to take flight. He laughed, and she smiled along with him.

"Jess," he said, and he made an effort to suppress the hope which had sprung to life in his heart. "You told me you would never wear that particular bonnet unless you were in your dotage or wished to bewitch the man of your dreams. And since you are not in your dotage . . ." A thought struck him, and he grasped her wrist with enough force to make her wince. "Who is it Jess? Who?"

She sighed and moved closer. "At last I can say it. It's you, Roger. It always was. It always will be. I've loved you forever, it seems."

His look was frankly skeptical.

"Well," she said, fingering his neckcloth, "almost forever. Do you remember that day when you found me in the stables, crying my eyes out because I was cursed with red hair?"

"I remember," he said. "Some village brats had taken to calling you 'Red.'"

"And you told me they were ignorant little nobodies who didn't know any better?"

"And that your hair was auburn, not red."

"And I was gullible enough to believe you. And fall in love with you."

"But Jess," his brow wrinkled, "that was years ago. You were no more than a child of ten."

"True," she said demurely.

He pressed her hands against his chest and slanted her a credulous smile. "You never even hinted that you loved me, no, not once during all the years of our long

correspondence. Every single one of your letters be-
gins, 'My dear brother.' Sometimes I thought I would
go mad."

"Roger," she said, and the knowledge of Eve was shining in her eyes. "It's taken me a long time to work
everything out, but I've finally done it. I never did want
you to be my brother, you know."

"I take leave to doubt that," he answered emphatically.

"Roger," she said, "would a sister tell a brother that the
vicar's son had kissed her when it wasn't true?"

"What? You can't mean . . ."

"And would a sister inveigle a brother into writing
verses for her by pretending that this same vicar's son had
composed a sonnet in her honor?"

"Jess! You didn't!"

"Think about it, Roger."

He did, and a light flickered to life in his eyes.

"And would a sister take offence when her brother
treated her as brothers are wont to do?"

"Aha! I hoped to teach you a lesson by that little charade. So! You did not care for it when I neglected you and
flirted with the other ladies?"

"Not one jot," she freely admitted, and lowered her
lashes. "And would a sister be crazy with jealousy when
she thought her brother was on the point of announcing
his betrothal to a perfectly wonderful girl?"

"It was no less than you deserved," he growled, ad-
ministering a playful shake.

". . . not to mention the agonies she suffered when she
discovered that he was consorting with a whole aviary of
'birds of paradise'?"

"Jess," he groaned, "I have explained all that."

Her voice dropped to a mere whisper. "And would a

sister go to her brother's bedchamber in the middle of the night, yes, and kiss him as I kissed you?"

The words of accusation were out before he could stop them. "Then why did you let me think that my conduct that night had given you a thorough disgust of me? Yes, and you needn't deny it, Jess. A word, a look from you the next morning, and I would have consigned Aunt Sophie and all her well-intentioned advice to perdition. But you could scarcely bear to look at me."

"I was so ashamed," she confessed, hanging her head. "I was sure, you see, that you must think the worst of *me*. And when you sent me away, my worst fears were confirmed. From that moment on, I resolved that no one should ever again have cause to reproach me for my . . . depravity, especially not Roger Moreton."

"Jess," he said, tipping her chin up, forcing her to look into his eyes. "I sent you away for your own good. If you had remained with me, I could not vouch for my good behavior, no, not even with a chaperone in residence."

"I know that *now*." She permitted herself a small, watery smile. "Oh Roger," and a sob broke from her, "all these years, I've been gammoning myself."

"Have you, Jess?" he asked softly.

She nodded. It took a moment before she could compose herself. With love shining from her eyes, she said, "Though I did not know it then, the last thing I wanted you to be was my brother."

"Truly, Jess?"

"Truly," she breathed.

"Don't stop now," he encouraged.

She inhaled sharply. "I don't want you for my brother. I don't want you for my friend. I want you for my . . . 1-lover."

He was fascinated by the color which stole across her cheekbones. "And how, may I ask, did you reach that conclusion? And not before time, let me tell you."

Her eyes slid away from his. "Because, when I am with you, I want to be b-beautiful, and elegant, and w-wickedly, wickedly feminine, and . . . quite simply . . . wicked."

Baffled, he exclaimed, "Then why did you run away last night after I kissed you? And the look on your face! I was sure that all my hopes had come to ruin."

"But so did I! If you had only seen the look you gave *me!*"

For a long moment, they gazed into each others eyes. "Jess," he said, "kiss me."

It was an impossible feat. Jessica's wickedly, wickedly feminine high-poke bonnet kept getting in the way, and she refused to remove the absurd object. *Nothing* daunted, Roger bent the damsel over his arm, and kissed her with gratifying ardor.

"Roger, if we don't make haste, we shall . . ." Aunt Sophie halted on the threshold and glared at the incorrigible couple locked in a passionate embrace. "This is the outside of enough," she declared.

No response.

"Jessica, you forget yourself!"

Jessica forced Roger to release her lips. "Aunt Sophie," she said, "what do you think? You had the right of it. Roger wants to be my lover."

"Roger!" appealed Aunt Sophie, her voice shrill with horror.

"Husband," he corrected. "I wish to be her husband," and he bent to his pleasurable occupation.

Aunt Sophie's look of horror slowly converted to one of extreme complacency. She glanced at the clock on the mantel. "You have two minutes, and not a second more," she told the couple, both of whom were quite oblivious to her presence.

Though she had meant, circumspectly, to turn her back on them, her eyes strayed to Jessica's bonnet and became riveted. She looked away, and looked again. It must have been her imagination, she decided. Stuffed birds could not possibly wink.

She sucked in her breath as it happened a second time. *It's only a trick of the light,* she told herself severely, *only a figment of an old woman's imagination.*

She felt in her reticule and removed a pair of spectacles, Roger's Christmas present to her, and she perched them on her nose. That was better. Everythmg came sharply into focus. Her old eyes had been playing tricks on her. It was only a stuffed bird after all.

Satisfied that she had plumbed the mystery of Jessica's bonnet, she gave the couple her back, and began to make plans. The betrothal would be announced over dinner. She must delay the musicians and caterers, if it were possible. The wedding, if she knew anything of her nephew, would be arranged as soon as may be, possibly before the New Year. She did not relish her role as chaperone until that day should arrive, and decided, grimly, that she had better be alert on all suits. Beginning now.

"Time's up," she exclaimed. "Come along, children. The vicar won't like it if he has to delay church services till we get there."

The couple slowly disengaged and smiled into each others eyes. With one arm around Jessica's shoulders, hugging her to him, Roger escorted her to the waiting carriage.

The church bells pealed on. A light sprinkling of

snow began to fall. Jessica stored away every sight and sound for future reference. One day, when she was asked to describe her most memorable Christmas, she would have a tale to tell. It would begin, she decided, with the moment she had set eyes on her Christmas bonnet in the milliner's shop window. *Sheer Sorcery,* she thought, and smiled.

Historical Romance from
Jo Ann Ferguson

__Christmas Bride	0-8217-6760-7	**$4.99US/$6.99CAN**
__His Lady Midnight	0-8217-6863-8	**$4.99US/$6.99CAN**
__A Guardian's Angel	0-8217-7174-4	**$4.99US/$6.99CAN**
__His Unexpected Bride	0-8217-7175-2	**$4.99US/$6.99CAN**
__A Sister's Quest	0-8217-6788-7	**$5.50US/$7.50CAN**
__Moonlight on Water	0-8217-7310-0	**$5.99US/$7.99CAN**

Available Wherever Books Are Sold!

Visit our website at **www.kensingtonbooks.com**.